Also by Warren Adler

Novels

OPTIONS
BANQUET BEFORE DAWN
THE HENDERSON EQUATION
TRANS-SIBERIAN EXPRESS
THE CASANOVA EMBRACE
BLOOD TIES
NATURAL ENEMIES

Short Stories

THE SUNSET GANG

"THE WAR OF THE ROSES"

FIC
CI

Warren Adler

WARNER BOOKS

A Warner Communications Company

Copyright © 1981 by Warren Adler
All rights reserved.
Warner Books, Inc., 75 Rockefeller Plaza, New York, N.Y. 10019

 A Warner Communications Company

Distributed in the United States by Random House, Inc.,
and in Canada by Random House of Canada, Ltd.
Printed in the United States of America
First Printing: April 1981
10 9 8 7 6 5 4 3 2 1

Library of Congress Cataloging in Publication Data

Adler, Warren.
  The war of the Roses.

  I. Title.
PS3551.D64W37   813'.54   80-23036
ISBN 0-446-51220-6

Book design by Helen Roberts

For Page and Clyde

ACKNOWLEDGMENTS

The author is grateful for the cooperation, kindness, and expertise of Barbara and Howard DeFranceaux, Victor Shargi, Viola Drath, Joseph Lyman, and Rose Bailor.

1

A cold rain whipped across the clapboard facade of the old house, spattering against the panes. Like everyone else in the bone-damp parlor set up theater style with folding wooden-slat seats, the auctioneer raised his gloomy eyes toward the windows, perhaps hoping the gusty rain would shoot out the glass and abort the abysmal performance.

Jonathan Rose sat on an aisle seat, a few rows back from the podium, his long legs stretched out on the battered wooden floor. The room was less than half full, no more than thirty people. Behind the auctioneer, strewn around like the aftermath of a bombing, lay the assorted possessions of the family Barker, the last of whom had lived long enough to make some of this junk valuable.

". . . it's a genuine Boston rocker," the auctioneer droned, his voice cracked and pleading as he pointed to a much abused Windsor-style rocking chair. "Made by Hitchcock, Alford and Company, one of the finest names in chairs." He looked lugubriously around the silent room, no longer expectant. "Damn," he snapped. "It's a genuine antique."

"Ten bucks," a lady's voice cackled. She was sitting in the first row, bundled in a dirty Irish sweater.

"Ten bucks?" the auctioneer protested. "Look at these tapered back spindles, the scrolled top rail, the shaped seat. . . ."

"All right, twelve-fifty," the lady huffed. She had been buying most of the furniture offered, and it seemed to Jonathan that the auction was being held for her benefit.

"The whole thing stinks," a voice hissed. It came from a veined Yankee face beside him. "The rain's mucked it all up. She's got the antique store in Provincetown. She'll get it all for a song and sell it off to the tourists for ten times as much."

Jonathan nodded, clicking his tongue in agreement, knowing that the rain was his ally as well. Most of the tourists who had crowded into Chatham on Thursday and Friday, hoping for a pleasant Memorial Day weekend at the beach, had left by midmorning. At the Breaking Wave, where Jonathan was a summer waiter, the dining room for the Sunday lunch looked and felt like an off-season resort, and his tips had matched the mood.

But the weather on Cape Cod, at best, was uncertain. He was used to it. All through Harvard undergraduate school, he had worked summers at the Breaking Wave, amusing himself at the antique auctions on those days he couldn't get to the beach. He was especially fond of those held at the old cottages after the owners had died off. Rarely could he afford to buy anything, although occasionally he picked up a Staffordshire figure for a song.

He had grown up being watched over by the four female figures of Staffordshire pearl ware representing the Four Seasons garbed in décolleté white robes. They peered out of his mother's dining-room china closet, emblems of his father's war service in England. Once,

he had broken Spring, which he had removed in a clandestine prepuberty compulsion to feel the little lady's
tits; the figure had slipped out of his hand, and was de-
capitated on the floor. Always good with his hands, he
had done a magnificent glue job and his mother was
never the wiser.

Now, as if out of guilt, he had acquired a modest
collection of his own, some common sleeping-child figures and a ubiquitous sailor and his wife and child. He
had done a bit of research on the subject as well and, although the figures were comparatively cheap, he suspected that, someday, they would increase in value.

The auctioneer reached for the boxing figure and
held it above his head. Then, putting on his glasses, he
read from the spec sheet.

"Staffordshire pearl ware. The pugilist Cribb. He
was the champion of England in 1809. . . ."

Jonathan stiffened. The idiot is breaking the pair,
he thought, appalled by the man's ignorance. Cribb was
white. There was a black figure as well, Molineaux, an
ex-slave who had fought Cribb twice, losing both times.
Both pugilists had been immortalized by caricature in
drawings, on pottery, and through figures like these.
They were always pictured together, facing each other,
fists raised.

"Fifteen bucks," the lady in the first row shouted.

The auctioneer looked at the figure and shrugged.
It wasn't, as Jonathan knew, a work of art. Merely a
souvenir, probably selling for tuppence when first
made by an anonymous back-street potter. The auctioneer glared contemptuously at the audience, obviously
wanting to hurry the sale.

"I have fifteen," he croaked. "Going at fifteen. Do
I hear sixteen?"

Jonathan raised his hand. The auctioneer smirked,
perhaps at Jonathan's youth.

"I have sixteen," the man said, showing a sliver of optimism.

The lady in the dirty Irish sweater turned in her chair. Her face looked like soggy dough; her red-tipped nose was runny.

"Seventeen," she cackled.

"I have seventeen," the auctioneer said, his eyes shifting back to Jonathan.

Jonathan raised eight fingers, clearing his throat as well. The heavy lady huffed and shifted in her chair. Reaching into his pocket, he nervously pulled out his money. He had thirty-seven dollars, representing his total weekend tip income. If he got Cribb, he wanted to have some left for Molineaux.

"Nineteen," the lady boomed out. A gust of rain spattered against the glass. The auctioneer ignored it, warming to his task. Jonathan's heart pounded. "Bitch," he muttered.

"Twenty," he shouted.

"Idiot," the woman rebuked, turning to fix on him her gaze of utter contempt.

"I have twenty. Twenty once." The auctioneer, a thin smile of satisfaction growing on his lips as he looked at the woman, raised the gavel. "Twenty twice." Jonathan held his breath. Down went the gavel. "Sold."

"Goddamn," Jonathan muttered, energized by the experience, savoring the flush of victory.

"Well, you beat the old cow," the Yankee beside him twanged.

The black figure came up a few moments later. Jonathan felt his guts tighten. It's a pair, he told himself, pumping his resolution. He peeled off what he had spent on Cribb and tucked the money safely in his pocket, clutching the remaining bills in a sweaty hand. There was only seventeen dollars left.

"This is another Staffordshire pugilist, the fighter. Molineaux, a former slave, who boxed in England in the early eighteen hundreds."

"Ten bucks," the lady in the dirty Irish sweater shouted. She did not turn to look behind her. Jonathan shouted out, "Eleven." Please, he begged in his mind, enjoying the excitement, sensing his surrender to his determination. At the same time, he rebuked himself. He had no business squandering his money.

"Twelve," a voice chirped from behind him. He turned quickly, startled by this new voice. Two rows behind him, a young girl with long chestnut hair hanging from under a sailor cap smiled primly, a flush on her apple-contoured cheekbones.

"Shit," Jonathan mumbled as the auctioneer responded.

"I have twelve."

"Twelve-fifty," the girl shouted without hesitation.

"Don't they know it's a pair?" he whispered to himself, as if their bids were, somehow, a form of vengeance. He held up his fist, in which he clutched the sweaty bills.

"I have thirteen," the auctioneer called, staring directly at the girl. She's hesitating, Jonathan thought.

"Do I hear thirteen-fifty? . . . I have fifty—thirteen-fifty," the auctioneer shouted. Jonathan was sure the auctioneer was playing games and scowled at him, then turned and rebuked the girl with his eyes.

"Fourteen," he growled. His throat was tightening. He felt the tension in his stomach. Damned bitch, he cried inside himself. It made no sense at all to break up the pair. The auctioneer looked toward the girl.

"I have fifteen," the auctioneer shouted, warming to his task, ignoring the whiplash of rain that pounded against the house. The audience grew restless.

"Sixteen," Jonathan croaked.

"Seventeen," the girl responded quickly, her voice carrying over the din.

"It's a damned pair," Jonathan shouted, shaking his head. He opened his palm and unrolled the bills, checking the denominations. Seventeen. That was it. Not even small change.

He turned again and looked at the girl. She was calm, almost serene. But there was no mistaking her determination.

"I have seventeen," the auctioneer said, staring at Jonathan, his glare offensive, intimidating.

"Eighteen," Jonathan shouted, his voice crackling. The room seemed to grow quieter. The sound of pounding rain faded. Knowing he hadn't the money, he felt sinister, manipulative. His breath came in short gasps.

"Nineteen," the girl responded.

"Twenty," he shot back.

The girl hesitated and a lump rose in his throat. He looked at the girl again. Their eyes met. There was no mistaking the fierceness of her determination.

"Twenty-one," she snapped.

All right, he decided, nodding, thankful for the reprieve. Tough little bitch, he thought.

"I have twenty-one once." The auctioneer paused, watching him. Jonathan felt his blood rise. So I'm a coward, he told himself, wallowing in his humiliation.

"Twice . . ." The auctioneer shrugged. Down went the gavel. "Sold."

Jonathan sat through the rest of the auction in a funk. Hell, he could have borrowed the money. But why? What was the point? By the end of the auction he had calmed down, and when he went to pay for and collect his figure he confronted her.

"It's a pair," he said. He must have been eyeing the

figure acquisitively because she seemed to draw it closer to her. "They go together."

"That's not the way they were sold," she said, flashing green eyes, widely set, in rebuke.

"He didn't know what he was doing."

"I liked it," she said as they walked out of the parlor, huddling in the crowded hall as the group opened umbrellas and prepared to walk into the gusty rain.

"All I had was seventeen bucks. I deliberately bid it up." He felt foolish and vindictive, telling her that.

"I got carried away," he added, hoping to blunt his pettiness.

"So did I," she admitted. "That's me."

"Too damned stubborn."

"My father says tenacious."

She smiled, showing white, even teeth. The smile warmed him and his antagonism faded.

"Suppose I'd bid it up to a hundred?"

"I was worried you would."

"You would have gone along?"

"I hate to think about it."

He returned her smile and moved with her to the doorway.

"Why did you want it?" he asked.

She hesitated, coy now. He sensed the give and take of flirtation.

"It's for one of the girls at the Chatham Arms. I'm a baking assistant for the summer. Her brother's in Golden Gloves. She's one of the maids. Takes a lot of crap. I thought it would be nice. Instead of a tip."

He was touched, feeling guilty suddenly.

"A shame to break up a pair. Even for a good cause."

She opened her umbrella and stepped into the rain. He ducked under it, although it didn't do either of them much good.

"Hope you don't mind."

"I'm a sportsmanlike winner."

"I'm a lousy loser."

The Chatham Arms was on the other side of town and they walked through the main street. His hand covered hers as they jointly clutched the umbrella against the wind. The rain came at them horizontally and they finally took refuge in the doorway of a closed toy store.

By then they had traded vital statistics. Her name was Barbara Knowles. She was a student at Boston University. She had wanted to spend the summer as a volunteer for Jack Kennedy to help him win against Nixon, she told him. But she couldn't afford that.

"Anyway, I like baking. It's fun. And the pay's good."

"Unless you spend it all." He pointed to the figure wrapped in soggy newspapers.

"You, too." She laughed and he noticed that her eyes were really hazel and had turned from green to brown in the late-afternoon light.

"I guess I just like old things. They'll be worth more than money someday. Like these figures."

"You can't eat them."

"Unfortunately not. Anyway, I'll have to avoid temptation. Better stay away from auctions," he told her. "Harvard Law is damned expensive. I start in the fall. My deal with my folks is that they pay tuition and I pay living expenses."

They were huddled together in the tiny storefront entrance. When she spoke, he felt her warm breath against his cheek. A current, he knew, was passing between them. Something wonderful and mysterious. He felt her response.

"Don't give him away," he said, sensing his note of pleading. It was, after all, a symbol of their meeting. "Not yet."

"It's mine." She pouted with mock sarcasm, holding it over his head like a club.

"One isn't much good without the other," he said. "It's a twosome."

"I beat you fair and square," she said.

"Well, the battle isn't over yet," Jonathan whispered, wondering if she had heard his voice above the beat of the rain.

"Not yet," she agreed, smiling. She *had* heard him.

2

Through the dormer window of her third-floor room, Ann saw him open the side door of the garage. Holding his toolbox, he moved over the flagstone walk toward· the house. A reddish spear of light from the slipping September sun bounced off the metal tools laid neatly in the box. Startled by the sudden glinting beam, she moved back out of the dormer's niche, her heart pounding.

Hoping that she was out of his field of vision, she watched him pause and reattach a string of English ivy that had fallen from the high cedar fence. The fence formed a backdrop for a line of still-maturing arborvitaes that separated the back garden from the neighbor's.

Seldom could she study him so minutely, free of her self-consciousness and clumsy shyness. Besides, she was certain that Jonathan Rose viewed her as a country bumpkin from Johnstown, Pennsylvania, that is, if he ever took the time to assess her seriously.

In his beige corduroys and blue plaid shirt, he looked oddly miscast as a man who worked with his hands most of his spare time. Even in his basement workroom—surrounded by his neatly hung power tools; his nuts, bolts, nails, and screws in little glass containers; his circular saw, lathe, and myriad mechanical gewgaws—he could not shed the image of his regular calling, a Washington lawyer. Or, as he characterized himself: "Just a plodding barrister."

The deepening orange light set off his wavy, prematurely salty gray hair, which he still wore long, despite the new convention. His lightly speckled thick mustache and jet-black eyebrows gave him the look of an anglicized Omar Sharif, a resemblance quickly dissipated when his wide smile flashed and his blue eyes caught the right light, giving away his Irish antecedents.

If Jonathan could have surmised the extent of her interest, he would have been flattered, of course, but appalled. Ann herself was appalled. The sensation had crept up on her, like the muggers who, she had been warned, prowled the Washington streets. Not here in the Kalorama section, of course, where there were almost as many embassies and legations as private residences and, therefore, fully protected by a vast army of special police. Her newly acquired neighborhood snobbery amused her as she recalled her sense of logic. She was afflicted, she decided, tearing her eyes from the dormer window, with an adolescent crush, an emotional aberration hardly worthy of a twenty-two-year-old woman. She was, after all, despite the warmth of her acceptance in the Roses' household, merely a glorified *au pair* girl. The label, she knew, was unfair to them. They tried so hard to make her part of the family, and the free room and board, traded for vaguely defined "services," gave her the wherewithal to pursue her history master's at Georgetown University.

Looking suddenly about her room, she could not

repress a joyful giggle as she recalled the flat offer of "room and board" that had tantalized her in the classified pages of *The Washington Post.*

Barbara had described each piece of furniture with the confident authority of a museum guide. Ann had no knowledge of antiques. Yet living among these pieces of tangible history piqued her interest and she would wonder how other past lives had fared among these objects.

In one corner of the room was a sleigh bed, circa 1840s; beside it an inlaid-mahogany Empire table on which stood an Art Nouveau Tiffany lamp guarded by a rustic Staffordshire porcelain milkmaid who had wandered in from the downstairs collection. On one wall was a chest-on-chest festooned with intricate ormolu and a French *bibliothèque* with glass doors. Near the dormer was an English folding desk on which rested a hurricane lamp.

"We get a knee-jerk reaction every time we get near an antique auction," Barbara explained. "We're like antique junkies. We even met at one. There's no more room to put things."

"It's fantastic," Ann had replied.

"We've been at it for years," Barbara told her. "But they say that people who collect never really stop. Maybe we're afraid to . . ." Her voice had trailed off as if she were wary of the sudden intimacy. "Anyway," she had chirped, recovering her lightness, "you can commune with all the ghosts of times past."

"With pleasure," Ann had said. "My major is history."

But if the "room" part was overwhelming, the "board" part staggered her. Ann remained endlessly fascinated with the Roses' kitchen.

It was a carpeted rectangle lined with French provincial walnut cabinetry and rough stucco walls, designed to resemble a French country kitchen. Built into the walls were two double sinks, two double ovens—one electric, one gas—a huge refrigerator with an outside ice-water tap, a matching freezer, and a dishwasher. Also built in were tiers of open shelving filled with cookbooks, bottles, spices, canned goods, pots, pans, plates, jugs, trays, and bowls of various shapes and sizes. Huge drawers containing silver and flatware were fitted below the counter tops. Shiny copper pots and pans hung on hooks in various corners and cubbies. And on the counter tops were a microwave oven, two blenders, a coffee maker, a toaster oven, a warming oven; an inventory that never failed to expand in Ann's eye with each inspection.

In the center of the kitchen was a large rectangular island over which hung a huge hood. Built into the island was another stainless-steel sink, two four-burner stoves—one electric, one gas—an army of utensils, colanders, ladles, spatulas, pans, and more pots hanging from the hood; a wooden box filled with upended knives in slots, a wide marble top built into the cutting-board counter, and an electric kitchen center designed to accommodate a variety of mixing bowls and whatnots.

Remembering her mother's broken-down, noisy refrigerator, the gas stove with a pilot light that never seemed to work, and the chipped and stained porcelain fixtures, Ann felt she had wandered into a fantasy land.

"I cook," Barbara had announced, the understatement obviously carefully honed from long use. Ann followed her into an alcove that served as a storage pantry and in which was a large, humming, temperature-controlled wine vault.

"We planned and built it together," Barbara explained to the baffled Ann. "Jonathan's a whiz at fixing and making things. And I've got a degree in plumbing from the school of hard knocks."

She was, Ann remembered, as eager to make a good impression as Barbara was to be ingratiating. Yes, there was a certain indelibility about their first meeting, despite the confusing, information-packed grand tour.

Barbara had given particularly detailed descriptions of every piece in the dining room.

"Duncan Phyfe," she said, rapping her knuckles on the shiny table. "Queen Anne chairs. And that rococo monstrosity is my favorite." She had pointed to an elaborate candelabrum with room for more than a dozen candles. "Decadent, don't you think?"

"I guess they knew things would outlive human beings," Ann replied, patting a marble-top credenza for emphasis.

At that first meeting, Barbara's curvaceous figure was encased in tight jeans and a T-shirt on which the word HAUSFRAU was stretched tautly over ample bosom, intimidating the statement. She possessed, as a miner's daughter like Ann would observe, Slavic good looks: deep-set hazel eyes, peering cautiously behind apple-contoured cheekbones, under a broad forehead. Her chestnut hair was cut to cascade, like a wild brook, down either side of her head, almost to her broad shoulders, which served as a sturdy crosspiece for her magnificent bosom.

"I'm going pro," Barbara had announced, as if it were necessary to explain the kitchen. She had flashed a wide, ingenuous smile, growing momentarily wistful. "Hell, I've got the talent and the facilities. That's for sure." Her attention had suddenly departed from Ann, as if there were someone else she had to convince. But when her attention came back to Ann again, she explained that she had just sold a batch of her special *cassoulet* to an embassy in the neighborhood and her *pâté* was becoming a staple at the French Market.

"It's just a humble beginning," she had said. "But

that's why I need a little help with the kids. Just a
watchful eye. A little tidying up. Perhaps some help for
me. Nothing heavy. A maid comes in to do the hard
stuff. Teenagers need a maternal surrogate when
Mom's busy in the kitchen." She laughed nervously,
which, by inference, put Ann at ease, as if illustrating
that she wasn't the only one with anxieties about the
new arrangement.

As she talked, Ann remembered, she had lifted
Mercedes, the spayed Siamese, from one of the upper
open shelves, wedged between a can of Crisco and a box
of brown sugar. The cat snuggled against her hair and
briefly shared an Eskimo kiss before jumping to the
floor, scurrying off to a sunny adjoining room that appeared to be filled with plants.

"There's an overgrown standard schnauzer, whose
bark is worse than his bite, that you'll meet shortly. He
spends the day servicing the local bitches. Mostly, he
obeys only Jonathan, who says that's because they both
share the same drives." She had flashed her smile again
and giggled a throaty, girlish laugh. The reference to
men's drives seemed to offer a female bond, and from
that moment, sisterly affection began to ferment. Ann's
confidence rose. The little exchange seemed to under-
line that first impression.

Barbara had mentioned in passing that the schnauzer's name was Benny, but it was Eve, their sixteen-
year-old daughter, who had explained to Ann the not-
so-subtle connection.

"Mercedes-Benz. Of course. I should have caught it
immediately." Ann had actually felt embarrassed.

"No reason to, Ann, really. It's just one of those
very inside family things. It was Dad's idea."

Reticence marked their first encounters. But Ann
thought that was understandable, since the assignment
of an *au pair* girl to watch over a sixteen-year-old

seemed an insult by definition. Eve's first move was to give Ann the shock treatment.

"I keep my stash of pot behind Louisa May Alcott," the girl explained as she introduced Ann to her room, the style of which was an obviously deliberate attempt on Eve's part to stem the tide of antiques that had engulfed the house. Every piece in it seemed ruffled with flowery prints except for the pink bookcases and Andy Gibb poster. The inside of the closet was a mess and schoolbooks were scattered under the bed.

"And I'm on the pill," she said, watching Ann's face for a reaction. Ann's features were calculatingly immobile. She herself wasn't on the pill for two reasons, health and infrequency. She wasn't shocked, although she had made a mental note as to how much lower the starting age was now.

As if to buttress her rebel image, Eve offered Ann a cigarette, then lit up and inhaled deeply.

"Screw cancer." She shrugged. To Ann, the bravado was a dead giveaway. Eve wasn't a brat at all. Just unsure, like most teenagers . . . and adults.

"I don't smoke," Ann had replied. "I chew."

Eve's giggle, like her mother's, seemed to break the tension.

"Really?" Eve had exclaimed, showing her age.

She was, Ann observed, vulnerable and gawky, still unfleshed and willowy, but with all the promise of inheriting her mother's Slavic sensuousness. With her father's blue eyes and rich, thick hair, she would soon be quite a beauty.

To make it with Eve, Ann knew instinctively, was to find some important way to illustrate her trust in the girl. She detested being so calculating as she searched for opportunities. But it meant a great deal to win Eve's favor, especially in practical terms. The job in the Roses' household was a stroke of luck. Banishment, for whatever reason, would be a personal and financial disaster.

The opportunity arose when Eve flunked math at Sidwell Friends School, a posh private school of Quaker origin for the children of the Washington elite. Eve, too frightened to tell her parents, confided the horror to Ann.

"I've disgraced them," she cried.

Calming her down, Ann agreed to act as go-between, a role not without its risks. Jonathan had been disappointed, but resigned. Barbara had been angry.

"Lack of preparation is a curse," she had snapped. "I know." Ann had learned by then that Barbara had married at nineteen and had dropped out of college.

"I promised them you'd go to summer school if there were no recriminations or bad words," Ann had announced proudly to Eve, who collapsed in shivery tears. In its way, it was a kind of victory and certainly represented a turning point between them.

"I'll make them proud," Eve promised, her lips pursing in determination. There was, Ann had discovered, an invisible, fiercely competitive standard loose in the household. She wondered if it was a good thing.

This standard was at its most obvious in twelve-year-old Josh. What he wanted most of all was to be a member of the Sidwell Friends junior-varsity basketball team. She heard his basketball rattling, with irritating punctuality, against the backboard that his father had made in the alley over the double garage.

Like his sister, he, too, was a well-made mixture of his parents' genes: hazel eyes, cheekbones like his mother's, and a space between nose and lip that would surely in late adolescence sprout his father's thick mustache. His hair, sadly, was his mother's chestnut, which meant that he might not grow his father's salty, waved hair. Like Eve, he wore braces and it was a family joke, one of many, that the Roses were an orthodontist's dream.

Ann's relationship with Josh started out vague and unpromising. She had barely any memories of prepubescent boys, having gone to a Catholic girls' school. To the stern sisters of that establishment, young boys, if they existed at all, were messengers of Satan. To her, Josh was, nevertheless, a challenge to be surmounted.

She found him one day hunched over his basketball on the third-floor landing outside her room. She had been studying and it was obvious when she saw him there, gloomy and distraught, that he had been waiting for her to come upon him "accidentally."

"You look like you just lost your best pal," she had said, standing over him. He was holding the basketball in a tight embrace. He looked up at her, dry-eyed, but with a visible trembling of his lower lip that threatened the total collapse of his pseudo-manly courage. She sat down beside him, noting that he had deliberately left room for her on the step.

"Damned coach," he said, telescoping the message that he hadn't made the team. It was enough of a signal to set her mind racing to find something reasonably reassuring to say. Providentially, the Johnstown house was on the edge of a school attended mostly by black children.

"Any black kids on the team?" she asked.

He held up one finger.

"Get a chance to play with any black kids?"

He shrugged, obviously having no idea where she was leading him.

"Go to the schoolyards where the black kids play. Couple months of that and you'll run rings around those lily-white honkies."

He took the advice, still sulking as he brushed aside her attempted caress of his shoulders. It was weeks later, when he suddenly broke out in black street talk, that she knew he had taken her advice. Pure chance, she had decided, but a definite icebreaker.

The sun was barely visible through the arborvitaes and would soon be hidden behind the cedar fence, leaving a soft hush in the air. From the kitchen two floors below, exotic, mouth-watering odors wafted upward. In the oven, Ann knew, was a crusting *cassoulet*, layers of simmering goose, pork, lamb, and sausage on a bed of flageolets, bubbling in an essence of garlic, thyme, bay leaves, and other glorious herbs and spices. Cooling on the marble of the kitchen island was, a deep sniff confirmed, a loaf of fluffy banana bread. Barbara was at that moment probably mixing a light salad of greens and mushrooms in the big wooden bowl inundated with the tart oils of a thousand previous concoctions. There would be sliced *pâté de campagne* as well and a chocolate *mousse* to sweeten the celebration.

God's in his heaven and all's right with the world, Ann thought, prompted by the smells and the delicious knowledge of her treasure chest of family secrets. The festivities were Barbara's original idea to celebrate Eve's summer-school victory, a B-minus in advanced algebra. Ann had spent half the summer sweating over that one with Eve, certain that her effort had lifted the grade by one whole letter jump.

And Jonathan had embroidered the victory with his own contribution. He had bought Eve a silver Honda, which, unbeknown to the victorious scholar, lay in wait in the garage next to his prized Ferrari, rarely used but fondled and caressed like a precious baby.

"You mustn't breathe a word," Jonathan had warned. "Not a word."

Barbara had come to her that morning with two secrets.

"Josh made the team. But don't tell Jonathan. It's a surprise. We'll spring it at dinner."

"You said two secrets."

"I just got a hell of an order. Chicken *galantine* for twenty-four. For the Paks. They're entertaining the French ambassador Tuesday night. Just don't tell Jonathan. Let it be my surprise." Barbara took Ann by the shoulders, looking deeply into her eyes as if they were a mirror. "You know, I'm going to make it big as a caterer someday. I mean big."

Eve came into her room sometime later with a further announcement and Ann literally had to turn away to hide her amusement.

"You might think this dinner is for my B-minus, but Dad's got a topper to that. The firm picked up one of those big Fortune Five Hundred clients in New York. But don't tell Mom. He's going to break out the Château Lafite-Rothschild '59. When he does that, we're into heavy duty."

Any more secrets and Ann was certain that she would burst wide open. Surprisingly, she didn't feel left out. She had her little secret, too, reminded of it again as she passed Jonathan on the back stairs. He had just come from the sauna that he had built in the basement, complete with adjoining shower. Sometimes the family gathered there. Nakedness was not a hang-up, although in deference to Ann they no longer went about the house without robes, another secret that Josh had confided.

Passing him on the stairs, she turned quickly away as her eyes caught a tantalizing picture. The damp had curled his hair and the terry-cloth V showed a profusion of jet-black body turf down to his navel. She could not bring herself to look below that but she could not ignore the piny scent that his skin exuded, embellishing the exciting aroma of his maleness. Passing him this close, with him in a state of semiundress, was dizzying.

"Soon," he said, winking as he passed her. "I'm going to give Eve the Honda keys at dinner."

In the kitchen, Barbara was wearing a long mauve velvet at-home dress with a single strand of matched pearls and even Eve had parted for once from her jeans and was wearing a more fitting, preppyish outfit of pleated skirt, blouse, and saddle shoes. As always, when it came to clothes, Ann felt inadequate, despite the fact that she wore one of Barbara's beige slack-suit hand-me-downs, a far cry from the J. C. Penney polyester she had worn that first day.

As if by silent consent, Ann picked up the cooling banana bread and joined the procession to the library, which doubled as a kind of family den. They moved through the marble-floored foyer, over which glistened a huge crystal chandelier, hanging three stories high in a brass-banistered stairwell. From the foyer's corner, a tall clock in an inlaid-mahogany case offered seven chimes to underscore the Roman hour on its dial.

Jonathan had built the walnut bookshelves in the library to hold their rows of leather-bound old books. Against a blank wall was a huge, carved nineteenth-century armoire, nine feet high, which he had fitted with shelves that now held an assortment of liquor. On the fireplace mantel was an array of Staffordshire figures. The Staffordshire collection was Jonathan's pride and there were more than fifty figures scattered around the house—milkmaids, sailors, Napoleons, Garibaldis, Little Red Riding Hoods, and crude, rosy-cheeked farm boys.

On a marble table in the foyer were displayed what had become the legendary Cribb and Molineaux, poised in their eternal pugilistic confrontation. The story of the Roses' first meeting had been repeated in the household ad infinitum.

Over the library fireplace hung a large English oil, a hunting scene, appropriate to the leather Chesterfield couch and matching chairs in front of it.

It was, Barbara admitted, a mishmash room, but perfect for squatting around a heavy, low oak "rent table," on a Sarouk blue-and-red Persian rug, to have Sunday dinners.

"It seems to be the only time we're all together," Barbara had told her, offering a mysterious, wistful look, disturbingly out of character.

By the time Jonathan arrived, with Josh trailing smugly behind, the platters of *cassoulet* and *pâté* and the big wooden salad bowl had been laid out. An unsuspecting Eve picked at the banana bread and dropped little morsels in her mouth, unaware of the impending surprise.

The family squatted around the table while Jonathan, with great ceremony, poured the Lafite-Rothschild '59 into crystal wineglasses. He looked about, offering a cryptic smile, winking at Barbara and lifting his glass.

"Before we dine on this magnificent repast," he said, savoring the arcane language, "we must toast this moment of triumph." He looked at Eve, who smiled broadly, two rougelike puffs of excitement on each apple cheekbone. "B-minus will not an A make, but it's a hell of a long way from F." Josh snickered. He always brought home straight A's and was not above teasing his sister on this score. "And a longer way from H."

"H?" Eve asked, squinting in bemusement.

"H for Honda," Jonathan said.

"Honda?" Eve looked at the faces around the table in confusion. Jonathan raised his glass higher and from

his pocket drew out a set of keys and his electronic remote-control garage opener.

"Just don't hit the Ferrari on your way out."

"Not if you value your life," Barbara joked.

Eve squealed with hysterical joy, grabbing her father around the neck, kissing him with passionate grate-
fulness. She repeated the ritual with Barbara, then with
Josh and Ann, finally picking up the keys and garage-
door opener and dashing out toward the rear of the
house.

"We're spoiling her rotten," Jonathan said when
she had gone, bringing the rim of the wineglass to his
lips. Everyone followed suit. "But it feels so damned
good."

"We didn't get our first car until three years after
we were married," Barbara said.

"Different times." Jonathan shrugged. "Why all
the hard work if not for this?" He moved his free arm
through the air, the gesture taking in all the visible surroundings, including the people.

"I made the team," Josh said suddenly, as if a bubble had suddenly burst inside him.

"Damn," Jonathan said, putting down his glass and
slapping hands in black-jock fashion. "Bad. Man." He
had picked up some of the jargon from Josh.

"I'll drink to that," Josh said, lifting his glass and
swilling down the expensive wine as if it were Coca-
Cola.

They heard the horn blasts of Eve's new Honda,
which she had driven around to the front of the house.
Gathering at the window, the family waved and Eve
sped off in a cloud of carbon monoxide.

"Lucky bitch," Josh said.

"Well, now it makes it obligatory for you when you
hit sixteen," Jonathan said. "You now have a standard.

That's what fatherhood means. Setting standards." He laughed at his own little joke, then the family regathered around the table.

"There are other family victories to announce," Barbara said quietly, her eyes smiling in their deep sockets, her full lips curling tremulously over her white teeth. She made her announcement in a flat, somewhat restrained tone, but with a determined flourish. There seemed a disturbing note of bravado in it as well, although Ann felt she was the only one who appeared to notice. Jonathan moved closer to Barbara and kissed her on the lips.

"Fantastic," he said as Ann quickly turned away, annoyed at her sudden burst of jealousy.

"I guess what I have to say is anticlimactic," Jonathan said just as Eve burst through the front door, flushed with joy.

"It runs like a dream. Like a dream," she cried, squatting beside Ann and squeezing her hand. "I'm so happy."

Ann lifted a finger to Eve, in mock rebuke, as Jonathan continued.

"Just a new client. More lucre for the family coffers. A huge retainer. My colleagues are quite pleased with my resourcefulness. I'm off to New York tomorrow to seal the deal."

They exchanged more kisses and soon everybody was digging into the feast, mumbling ecstatically, with full mouths, over Barbara's wonderful cookery, embellished, they all agreed, by the rich taste and bouquet of the '59 Lafite-Rothschild.

Watching them in what she could only characterize as their splendor, Ann could not escape the comparison with her own shabby family, locked in the prison of their tiny wood-frame house in Johnstown. More like Dogpatch, she thought, where the big treat was snaring

Polish sausages with a bent fork from a big jug and swilling down six-packs.

The rich *cassoulet* melted in her mouth as the movie in her mind froze into a single ghastly frame. In it, her mother's swollen body squirmed like jelly in a torn, flowered housecoat as she reclined on a sprung, worn couch in front of the television set, gun-muzzle curlers poised to shoot out Laverne and Shirley, while her father, his beer belly hanging over his belt like jelly mold, added cigar-ash dust to the frayed carpet from which sprouted his Archie Bunker chair.

Suddenly, as if to start the reel moving again, she tapped her wineglass with a silver spoon, the tinkling crystal forcing the silence.

"I can't tell you how much . . ." The words stuck in her throat and she had to clear it and begin again. "I can't tell you how much it has meant to me to be here with you. You cannot imagine . . ." She stumbled again, the images of her past life too vivid for the rush of words. Her gaze washed over each face, even Jonathan's, which, surprisingly, she viewed without the earlier shame. "It's been the most wonderful time of my life. The way you've taken me in and become, for me, my family." She swallowed hard to hold down a ball of phlegm. "Such a happy family . . ." She shook her head, too overcome to continue, then searched with her lips to find the rim of the glass, which she tipped, sipping the wine.

What a happy house, she thought, wondering how she had had the good luck to find them.

3

Jonathan felt the first stab of pain just as Mr. Larabee finished talking, a familiarization lecture, really, outlining the company's special problem with the Federal Trade Commission. He had been taking notes on a lined yellow legal pad and now the pencil made jiggling swirls as if it were writing independently. They were sitting around a conference table in the chairman's office in Manhattan and he'd already had more cups of coffee before lunch than was his custom.

At first he tried to dismiss the pain, but when he began to break into a cold sweat, a charge of panic gripped him and he put down his pencil and tried to cover up his discomfort with a cough. Then the chairman began to direct his remarks to Jonathan, and the words sounded muffled, incoherent, and far away. He tried to humor the pain away, hoping to extract a laugh from the abysmal predicament. It was everybody's dread to be struck down suddenly in the middle of some important event. Bladder and bowels would void. There would be vomiting and, worst of all, he would be inconveniencing everybody around him, all of whom couldn't care less. And there was the perennial joke about clean underwear just in case, but that usually applied to women.

"You feel all right, Rose?" the chairman asked.

Jonathan managed a nod but knew it was unconvincing. Someone poured him a glass of water from a silver pitcher, but he couldn't get it down.

"This is ridiculous," he whispered.

He was led to a leather couch, and he lay down and managed to open his collar and loosen his tie.

"I'm sure it will pass," he croaked. That, too, seemed unconvincing. The stabs of pain were becoming an onslaught behind his breastbone.

"His color stinks," someone said. He felt a hand on his forehead.

"Cold as ice."

He heard someone say "ambulance," and realized suddenly that his sensory powers were becoming numb. His heart seemed ready to break out of his rib cage. His mind raced back and forth in time and memory and he wondered if he was the proverbial drowning man watching his life pass across his mind like a film in quadruple time.

"This is stupid," he heard himself say, knowing that the words had not been spoken.

"You'll be fine," Larabee said unctuously. Jonathan had detested the man immediately and resented his concern.

I'm only forty, he thought as panic turned to pity, directed inward. He prayed he wouldn't soil his pants, remembering old admonitions from his childhood. There they were, the first signs. What galled him, too, was the lack of planning, and he wondered if he had paid all his insurance premiums. If you died at forty, your family would get a million, the insurance man had assured him, and Jonathan had snickered at that, choosing term instead of whole life.

How can I die? he thought. My parents are still living. My grandparents on both sides died in their eighties. Then he counted all the people he would be letting down and that only increased his panic and he wondered if he would soon lose consciousness.

He lost track of time as he lay there. Someone covered him with a blanket but he still felt icy.

"You'll be fine," the chairman said, his jowly face flushed with either concern or annoyance.

I've blown the first big interview with a new law client, Jonathan thought, imagining the reaction of his colleagues in the firm. Poor old Jonathan. Sorry son of a bitch. Two antiseptic-smelling, white-jacketed attendants lifted him to a wheeled stretcher, and he saw the oxygen mask coming quickly toward him. He also saw his own finger crooking in front of his eyes, beckoning. Larabee's face came closer.

"Call my wife," Jonathan croaked. The oxygen mask was clapped over his face, and he felt the motion of moving wheels, then the swirl of outdoor sounds and the ear-splitting siren as the ambulance shot forward. An icy stethoscope startled his suddenly bared chest.

"Who knows?" a voice said as the stethoscope was lifted.

"Am I going to die?" he whispered futilely into his mask. He burped and for a moment felt incredibly relieved until the pain started again. His mind had momentarily cleared, then he felt insular again as he pictured Barbara's tearstained face, and Eve's and Josh's, hovering over him, waiting for the exact moment of demise, a deathwatch. I've let them down, he rebuked himself.

A flood of letdowns careened down the spillway of his anxiety-ridden mind. Who would feed Benny? Who would turn the wine, care for the orchids, wind the tall mahogany clock? Who would repair the broken appliances, watch over the antiques, the paintings, the Staffordshire figures? And who would tune up the Ferrari? How dare they separate him from his chores, his possessions? The idea was almost as unbearable as the pain.

He felt a pinprick in his arm and soon the pain eased somewhat, and he was floating in space, like an astronaut in a space capsule. Some horrible nightmare nudged at his consciousness. But he couldn't remember it, only that it was horrible. Then he sensed the ground moving under him as the wheels bumped along a corridor. Above him, the ceiling was lined with fluorescent white lights. The glare hurt his eyes.

When they removed the oxygen mask, he whispered again.

"Call my wife. Call Barbara."

Vaguely, he could feel them hooking him up to something and, in the distance, he heard a rhythmical blipping and unfamiliar sounds. Nearby, he could make out whispered voices hovering somewhere in space. If they could get to Barbara in time, he knew that everything would be fine. His life depended on Barbara. He would not die if Barbara came.

4

When he remembered again, the room had darkened; he heard the steady *blip* and *ping* of odd sounds, as if he were inside some huge clock, perhaps in the tall mahogany case in his foyer, the pendulum banging in his ears, the complicated works clanking in his head. Memory came and faded. They were on their honeymoon at the Groton Inn, an old, rickety colonial leftover. The dining room always seemed set for tea.

It was too hot for June. The sun baked through the roof and making love was a gritty, unsatisfactory business. She hadn't turned on, not the way she had before they were married, but he had attributed that to the tensions of the wedding, which had been opposed by both sets of parents. He still had two years to go at Harvard Law and she was two years from a degree at Boston University.

"I'll work my way through," he had told his parents on that nasty spring day on which he had made the dreaded announcement. It wasn't that they were opposed specifically to Barbara, but they couldn't imagine him inhibiting his career by marrying a poor nineteen-year-old girl, saddling himself with responsibility.

"But I love her," he had protested with surety, as if the words were all that was needed to explain such a radical change in his life. He supposed it was their humdrum married life and their exaggerated dreams for him that prompted their opposition and he was gentle with them. A state employee's ambition for his only son was no fragile thing.

"I won't let you down," he had promised, knowing how hard the money for his education had come. "But I can't live a single minute more without her." It was 1961, before all the revolutions, and living together without benefit of legal marriage was still a few years away.

"You're crazy," his father had said. His mother had simply sat at the kitchen table, hands folded, head bent, and cried.

"And I don't expect you to pay my tuition," he told them. "I'm on my own now." He hesitated. "With Barbara."

"Between us, we can make it," Barbara had assured him.

It had struck her parents even harder, since they were both high-school teachers, and the prospect of her dropping her education appalled them.

"I love him," she had told them. It was still a time when those three little words were glorified as the highest of attainments. To be in love was all. They were, as the saying goes, moonstruck. All he wanted, he remembered, was to touch her, to smell her, to hear her voice.

"I love you more than anything else in the world," he told her, repetitively, holding her. He was always holding her.

"I would die for you, Jonathan," she had sworn.

Die? His mind cleared with an explosive start.

He could not understand why he was thinking about this, lying there in the darkened room, surprised suddenly by an erection that pressed against the tight cover sheet, showing its outline. Well, I'm not dead yet, he thought, discovering also that the pain was gone. The sedatives or whatever he had been given had made him headachy and drowsy and he hovered in a kind of half-sleep, hearing the voices of professionals exchanging bits of medical information, which, he assumed, were about his own mysterious carcass. At any moment he expected to hear Barbara's heels clicking down the corridor and to feel her cool, soothing touch.

For some reason he began thinking about the Louis XV vitrine cabinet of inlaid tulipwood with its original beveled glass and ornate mounts, signed by Linke, which he had been tempted to buy. It was Barbara who had restrained him and he had argued with her. All the logic was on her side.

"We haven't the room," she had protested, holding his arm, which twitched as the auctioneer watched his face.

"But it's gorgeous."

"The house is finished, Jonathan."

She was right, of course, and he remembered that the idea of that disturbed him for weeks. Finished? They had been fooling with it for more than ten years, ever since they fell in love with its somewhat seedy facade on its high vantage point overlooking Rock Creek Park, with a magnificent view of the tall, graceful arches of the Calvert Street Bridge. Besides, it was the best neighborhood in town, and in Washington a man was known by his neighborhood.

For years the house had, like quicksand, sucked up every spare sou as they redid its ramshackle interior, room by room.

He dozed fitfully, sensing a moving stretcher, and an endless line of fluorescent lights marching along the ceiling.

"We're going to X-ray," a black attendant explained. Jonathan heard him talking about a ball game in the elevator. Perhaps, he thought, visitors were deliberately being kept from him, and Barbara, nervous and tearstained, was sitting in some lounge, waiting for the results of tests. He wanted to ask, "Am I really dying?" Fearful of the answer, he didn't ask.

He started worrying about his cymbidium orchids, which he had proudly coaxed from their indoor pot beds with loving care and which were now on their way to maturity beside Barbara's hanging forest and clusters of potted African violets and Boston ferns in the sunroom. It had been a challenge to try his hand at such delicate plants.

He also began to worry about Benny, the schnauzer to which he was a deity, proving his obeisance with great delight. Neither Barbara nor the kids could handle him. The tools, too, required maintenance, and the garden. Then there was Barbara's kitchen. . . .

God, don't kill me off yet, he cried within himself.

He was lifted onto a cold, metal X-ray table and rotated like a chicken on a spit. A white-smocked technician poked at him in a businesslike way, and he heard an intermittent buzz, which, in his clearing mind, he assumed was the sound of the picture-taking process. Why don't I feel pain? he wondered, noting that a clock on the wall read twelve.

"What day is it?"

"Wednesday," the technician answered.

Later they brought him back to another room, where he was isolated by a screen. They did not hook him up to any mechanical devices, and he noted that his arms and buttocks tingled, apparently from needle pricks. He slept some more, then was awakened gently by the touch of a cool hand. Blinking his eyes open, he peered into a bespectacled pinkish face.

"You're a lucky bastard, Mr. Rose."

"I'm not dying?" he whispered.

"Hardly. It's your hiatus hernia. Quite common, really. We thought it was a heart attack and took all the precautionary measures. You had one hell of a gas pain. It sometimes simulates an attack."

He pushed himself up, feeling a sense of renewed life.

"So I'm born again," he snapped, feeling the residual aches of the medication and intravenous devices, and a lingering hurt in his chest.

"You never died."

"Yeah. A lot of people will be disappointed. I'll be the laughingstock of the firm." He swung his legs over the bed. "Tell my wife to come in and get me the hell out of here." He looked at the doctor. "No offense, but if all you can do is come up with a gas pain, you should close up shop."

The doctor laughed.

"I just talked to your wife and gave her the good news."

"She's not here?"

"It would have been for naught," the doctor said.

"I suppose . . ." Jonathan said, checking himself. He was entitled to feel insecure.

They brought him his clothes, wallet, keys, money, and briefcase, and he dressed, still feeling shaky. In the hospital lobby he went into a phone booth and called home.

"Oh, Jonathan. We're so happy." It was Ann's voice.

He formed a quick mental picture of her, wheatish hair, light freckles, round face, with a smile that set off deep dimples. He realized suddenly that she was always surreptitiously observing him. Why was she on the phone? he wondered. Where was Barbara?

"I wouldn't recommend it," he mumbled.

"Barbara's just left. She'll be back in a little while. She's been quite busy on the Pakistan Embassy order." She hesitated, as if she were debating something more. But nothing came. He was disappointed.

"I'm going to see my client here. But I'll definitely be home tonight. Are the kids okay?"

"Worried sick. I called them at school after the doctor called."

"Super." He was about to offer the closing amenities and hang up. "Ann," he said, "when did they call Barbara? The first time . . . I mean."

There was an extended pause.

"Monday morning. I remember I answered the phone. Barbara was very disturbed." He felt the stab of pain again, but it passed quickly, no longer worrying him.

"Well, then . . ." He seemed suddenly disoriented, troubled as if by a chess move that he could not dope out, knowing the answer was there. "Just tell her I'll be home for dinner."

After he hung up, he looked mutely at the phone box, still trying to understand the vague sense of loss. To put it out of his mind, he called Larabee.

"You gave us quite a scare," Larabee said. He remembered the unctuousness and the "just fine" admonitions. It annoyed him to know the man had been right all along.

"You called it," Jonathan said, irritated at his own attempt at ingratiation. But he could not shake the notion that his display of vulnerability, notwithstanding that it was beyond his control, had somehow spoiled his image. In a lawyer a show of weakness could be fatal. He felt the gorge of his own rhetoric rising, and, as if in counterpoint, a burp bubbled out of his chest and into the mouthpiece.

"Hello . . ." Larabee said.

"Must be a bad connection," Jonathan said, feeling better psychologically as well.

Later, he came away from the chairman's office with the feeling that he had restored some measure of confidence again, shutting off allusions to his indisposition with quick, almost impolite dispatch.

"Even the doctors felt stupid for making such a fuss," he lied, closing the subject once and for all.

But on the plane his ordeal reopened itself in his mind and he found himself making doodles on his yellow pad, watching the changing light of a sunset in an incredibly blue sky. What was nagging at him since being discharged was the lingering sense of utter desolation, of total aloneness. He also felt more fear now than when he was in the hospital. It was beyond logic. He had, after all, been grasped, at least figuratively, from the jaws of death. Then why the depression? Why the loneliness? What was wrong?

"Call my wife," he had whispered to someone. In his memory the words resurfaced as a plea, a drowning man shouting for help. His imagination reversed the roles and he saw himself panicked and hysterical as he dropped everything to fight his way toward Barbara. The images were jumbled. He saw himself swimming through choppy seas, slogging over shifting desert dunes, climbing upward over jagged rocks, a panorama of heroic acts, just to be near her. Then the fantasy exploded, leaving him empty, betrayed. How dare she not come to his deathbed?

5

Why had she not come? Barbara asked herself, smirking at her inadvertent double entendre. The boning knife, working in her hand by rote, carefully separated the chicken skin from the neck bone, a crucial step in achieving a perfect boning job. This was her fourth chicken-boning operation that afternoon and her mind had already begun to wander. It wandered into strange places, as if she had little control of her thoughts. She did not often think about sex and was surprised that the subject surfaced in her mind.

He made love to her tenderly, fervently, but lit no fires in her. She was always dutiful, enduring what had become for her a dreary process, barely remembering when such contortions and gymnastics had ever brought her pleasure. He was not, she knew, oblivious of this indifference despite her Academy Award performances.

"Even when it's not so good, it's pretty great," he told her often, usually after he had calmed from a panting, shivery episode of obvious and sometimes noisy personal pleasure.

"It's there to enjoy, my son," she had responded,

hiding her disappointment behind the light humor. Wisecracks were great truth-hiders. She hadn't really understood her sexual indifference, especially since she was once a firecracker as far as he was concerned. But that was long ago. Then, before their marriage, all she had to do was to touch him to feel all the pops begin inside her.

For years, when considering their marriage, she had toted up lists of pros and cons. Sex had become one of the cons, although she did not blame him wholly for her odd lack of response. Something had changed in their chemistry, she decided. After all, it took two to tango. Secretly she knew she was excitable and could occasionally summon up fantasies and with a little digital manipulation was able to coax out a reasonable response. But she detested even thinking about that.

The list of pros was formidable and, in her mind, she saw the items actually crawl off the page. He had become a fantastic money earner. Two hundred thousand a year. Not bad for a bureaucrat's son. She was damned proud of him for that.

And there was the house. It was to his credit that he had seen the possibilities instantly. The neighborhood, Kalorama, tucked behind famed Embassy Row, was, of course, spectacular. It was laced with lovely old trees in full maturity, surrounding homes built earlier in the century for the then elite of the capital. Foreign governments had grabbed up the largest homes for embassies and legations. But Kalorama Circle was the diadem of the neighborhood, especially on its Rock Creek side, a clifflike perch looking downward into what in summer and spring was a lush valley. From the front of the house was the unobstructed view of the lovely Calvert Street Bridge, with its graceful arches and fluted columns topped by heroic eagles. It was certainly a great pleasure to the eye, notwithstanding the fact that it was a favorite jumping point for despondent suicides.

At the time they bought it the house was extremely run down, but the outlines of its French-chateau architecture were in perfect scale, and a coat of white paint on the smooth stucco and the addition of shutters that actually closed and were painted black did wonders for the facade. The double front doors were stripped and finished with a matching black stain and fitted with gold knobs and knockers. The two rusted light sconces above the doors were replaced with elaborate crown-shaped ones topped with complicated embroidered fretwork.

With its high windows on the ground floor, the ornamental wrought iron below the sills of the second, and the dormers built into the rustic slate tile of the third—all windows were sixteen lights—the house exceeded even their own high expectations. They were so delighted with its looks they had a copperplate engraving made of it, which they sent out each Christmas. The house, after all, was them.

Collecting antiques was a joint passion and their weekends were taken up by sorties to auction houses or with combing the old Virginia and Maryland homesteads searching, with a canny eye, for a bargain. Most of their European vacations were devoted to this activity and sprinkled among the furnishings and accessories were memories of each trip, which, in time, became part of the mystique of their collection. Considering the way they had met, collecting antiques seemed a natural extension of their married life, as if they were acting out some youthful fantasy.

She had also always been interested in cooking. Her mother had been an excellent cook, and she had learned a great deal working for professional cooks and bakers on her summer vacations. As the kids demanded less of her time she began to harbor vaguely commerical ideas. There was, she knew, a sense of inadequacy fermenting inside her, although she consciously resisted seeing herself as the traditional woman, which, she thought, was a cruel label hung on some females by their more zealous sisters.

She had designed the kitchen with a commercial idea in mind. Jonathan was enormously supportive, although she was never quite sure whether he was merely patronizing her or really believed in her ability to make it as a caterer. Nevertheless, he threw himself into the idea with vigor, devoting his weekends to every aspect of the kitchen's construction. With his knowledge of electric circuitry and craftsmanship, he gave the contractors a fit. She, in self-defense, learned to decipher much of the background mysteries about how things worked and had even become quite proficient in changing washers, tightening faucets, cleaning grease traps, and repairing the garbage disposal. One Christmas he had even given her her own tool chest. For years he had taught her how to use them in his own basement workshop and she had helped him build the sauna and the adjoining shower, done without the help of a contractor. They had also restripped and finished some of their antique furniture together.

As an upwardly mobile lawyer building his law practice, he traveled frequently, but managed to keep his weekends reasonably sacrosanct. The house, they both knew, enclosed the real limits of their world and they sought out things connected with the house that they could do together. Like indoor gardening, although their interests splintered eventually as he began to cultivate orchids and she continued with her Boston ferns and African violets.

The pro side was, indeed, considerable. They had tried to get the children to share their interests but their lives, it seemed, were on another tack, although both parents believed that the exposure would stand them in good stead as adults.

There were other pros as well. He was intelligent, attractive, articulate, humorous, with a wide variety of intellectual, as well as material, interests. And she did bask in the joy of his colleagues' and clients' approval, despite the occasional jealous bitchiness of their wives.

So, then, she asked herself—or was the question directed to the chicken whose skin she now rolled away from the carcass as if it were a sweater?—why did I not come?

She detached the lower part of the main wing bone with shears so that the lower end of the bone would slide along with the skin. Then, carefully, she began to detach the fibers from the carcass. When the skin reached the middle part of the drumstick, she severed the bone and detached the skin, repeating the operation on the other drumstick. The tail came off with the whole skin and she snipped it free with the shears.

Satisfied with her handiwork, she flattened the skin on the cutting board and began to mend what had inadvertently become torn, then she banged it flat with the side of a cleaver.

"Because I didn't give a damn," she cried out to the chicken's denuded carcass. She felt a ball of anger growing inside her, swirling about for definition, detesting its inarticulateness. She searched her mind for reasons.

"I must have reasons," she whispered as the anger burst into the reality of the kitchen and she banged the pointy edge of the cleaver into the wooden cutting surface, scarring it irrevocably.

What she really wanted after she had received the

first call from the hospital was for him to die. That was the absolute truth of it. She wanted him to expire, to be eliminated from her life as painlessly as possible, extracted like a rotten tooth.

Jonathan dead? The idea frightened her and she shuddered. Surely the thought was an aberration. To wish him dead implied hatred. Hatred? Such a response seemed inhuman. She swallowed hard and her body shook. But she could not suppress the urgent clarity. She had, indeed, hoped he would die.

6

Jonathan barely remembered the cab journey over Memorial Bridge, the swing around Lincoln Memorial, past the State Department, around Washington Circle. All these landmarks passed in front of him like indistinct photographs. Ann had apparently been watching from a front window and opened the door before he inserted his key. The mahogany clock in the hallway read two minutes to six, he noted as he dropped his briefcase on the marble floor. Even in his semiconscious drugged state in the hospital, he remembered, he had heard the chimes in his mind like ancient echoes.

"Josh is at basketball practice. Eve is at her ballet class. Barbara is delivering an order of *pâté*." There was a note of apology in her tone and her face searched his, betraying anxiety.

"I'm fine," he said. "Perhaps I look a little pale."

"A little."

He walked back to the sun-room to see his orchids, which, like him, had miraculously survived. He felt the soil around the root, which was still damp.

"Not to worry. Daddy's home," he whispered to the flowers.

He went up to his bedroom, undressed, debated whether or not to use 'the sauna, then opted for a long hot shower instead. For some reason he felt the need to shock himself, hoping it might chase the depression. He turned off the hot water and turned on the cold. His skin tingled and for a moment he had to catch his breath, but the pain did not return, and he wondered if he missed it, like an old friend.

Barbara burst into the bathroom as he toweled himself, and kissed him on the lips. He drew her to him and enclosed her against his damp body.

"It scared the shit out of me," he whispered into her chestnut hair, stifling a sob. The warmth of her was reassuring.

"It must have been awful," she said, insinuating herself out of his embrace. His body was damp and it had wet her blouse, which she unbuttoned now. Watching her, he noted that she studied her face in the bathroom mirror, throwing back an errant strand of hair.

"I'm fine now," he said to her image in the mirror. Running the gold-plated taps, she dipped her face into scoops of lukewarm water. He studied the ridgeline of her spine, wanting to trace his fingers over its peaks and loops. Slipping into his velour robe, he moved back into the bedroom and sank into a bergère chaise, lifting his bare feet to caress the curled wood. From there he could not see her, but he could hear her moving about, then came the rush of water and the cascaded flush. She walked out, wrapped in a terry-cloth robe.

He wasn't, he realized, simply observing her as he did frequently. He was inspecting her, noting that the years had been kind to her willowy body. Her legs and thighs were still tight and youthful, and her large breasts still high, although their weight had begun to bring them lower than when he had first seen them. He felt the urge to touch her, and there was a brief hardening in his crotch, but she seemed self-absorbed, her mind elsewhere.

"You'd be proud of me, Jonathan. I sold the Ecuadorans a weekly package. Next week my chicken *galantine*. After that my *cassoulet*. And, of course, my *pâté de campagne*."

He was always supportive, and he was surprised that he could not concentrate on what she was telling him. She had moved to her Queen Anne dressing table and began brushing her hair. Still she seemed elusive, like a stranger.

"I thought I was checking out," he said, turning his eyes to their lacy bedspread with its battery of high pillows against the carved headboard. Dominating one wall was a high chest of drawers with an elaborately carved bonnet in the rococo manner, which they had both stripped and finished. The drapes were not drawn and through the floor-to-ceiling sixteen-light windows, he could see the moving lights of the rush-hour cars crossing the Calvert Street Bridge. Between the windows was a Capucius secrétaire, with its top open. Barbara used it as a working desk. On its surface was a picture of the four of them at the Grand Canyon, a color print with a blaze of orange painting the rear cliffs. On the walls were prints of slender Art Deco ladies, languorous and sensual. He looked at them, but they gave him no pleasure. Watching them, he felt the sense of emptiness begin again.

"I can't understand why you didn't come," he said, swallowing hard, talking to the pictures. So this was the elusive chess move, he discovered suddenly. He had cut to the heart of the matter. Although he did not see her, he knew she had turned toward him.

"I was in constant telephone touch," she said testily, with a hard edge to her voice.

"They had no definite diagnosis until this morning." He spat the words at her, still not looking at her face.

"They said your condition was stable."

"I was in pain. I thought I was dying."

"But you weren't."

"You could not have known that."

"Don't get prosecutorial, Jonathan."

He allowed himself a long pause, surprised that his chest was free of pain, although his stomach seemed to have tightened. He burped and his breath tasted sour. He looked at her now. This time it was she who turned away.

"If the situation were reversed, I'd be there as quick as I could." The display of his own vulnerability galled him.

"But it wasn't reversed," she said, getting up and going to their dressing room. She emerged quickly in a long robe. "I've got to see about dinner. The kids should be home soon."

"It's your attitude," he said. "I don't understand it." He deliberately moved so that he could see her face. It was composed. Her hazel eyes scrutinized him calmly. He detected no outward signs of insecurity or lack of self-confidence. There was no tension or anxiety. To him now, her persona seemed reconstructed, different.

"Maybe I'm suffering from the escape-in-the-nick-of-time blues." He sighed, acknowledging to himself this gesture of surrender, certain that it was a lie. "It's just that . . ." He began to grope for words, uncommon for him. "When you're on the edge of the abyss, you think everyone is writing you off. It's a nasty feeling."

"I think you're overreacting, Jonathan." She started to move, but his voice recalled her.

"I guess I just wanted reassurance." He sighed, deliberately posturing. He was surprised that he knew this. What he needed now was to be held, caressed. Perhaps like a baby at his mother's breast. God damn it, he screamed within himself. I need you to love me, Barbara.

"Believe me, Jonathan," she began. "If I'd thought it was something awful, I would have come. You know that." What disturbed him now was that he felt she was trying to convince herself. He forced himself to obliterate the suggestion, stood up, and drew her toward him again. She didn't glide, hesitating before she moved.

"You're fine," she whispered, embracing him without conviction. "That's the bottom line."

It was an expression she had picked up from somewhere. Perhaps from him. It signaled an unrecognizable inner voice, warning him. Something in his world was awry, misplaced, out of focus. He wasn't sure.

"I'm sorry, Barbara. I don't understand."

She watched him, shrugged, then smiled. That, too, seemed hollow. Perhaps, he thought, the drugs had interfered with his receiving apparatus and were working hell on the emotions as well. He was picking up indifference. *Indifference.* An invisible antenna seemed to crackle in his head, confirming reception.

"You'll feel better after dinner, Jonathan. I'm sure of that."

"Why should you feel so sure? And me, so unsure?"

She shook her head and turned away, and he could hear her padding down the steps, going away. Was it for long? he wondered.

7

She was alone in the kitchen. Ann and the children were studying in their rooms. In the distance she heard Benny's persistent, grating bark. It was sure to prompt a neighbor's complaint. Mercedes lay asleep on one of the top kitchen shelves. Forcing her concentration, Barbara put the chicken flesh, neck, gizzard, hearts, livers, and bones into the large enamel stock pot already in place on the gas burner. She added water and salt and lit the burner, hearing the pop as the flame from the pilot light ignited the hissing gas from the burner ring.

Wiping her hands on her apron, she wandered into the dining room, touching the cool marble of the serving credenza. She saw her image in the silver punch bowl, studying its distortion, considering whether the reflection were really her. Perhaps, she wondered, she was merely an ornament, as static as the silver candelabrum beside her with nothing behind the facade but history. She remembered her mother's words suddenly, their tone of disappointment and rebuke when she had announced that she was quitting college to devote herself to Jonathan. Ancient history, she thought with contempt.

"Loving someone doesn't mean you have to give up everything," her mother had warned.

"It's just until he gets out of law school," she had assured her.

"But you need something for yourself."

She had been surprised at that, since she believed that her mother had worked out of financial necessity.

"You have to understand what it means to love someone as much as I love Jonathan," she had responded, as if that were all that needed to be said. Why hadn't they warned her of the transience of such emotions? Nothing lasts except things. Her fingers traced the curled design of the elaborate candelabrum.

Yet she was less angry with her mother for not pressing the point harder than she was with herself, deriding her stupid, utterly ignorant nineteen-year-old self.

Love, she thought, remembering it now only as something that had tricked her. Love lies.

Her earlier emotion returned, stronger than before. It was not as if she had wished that a healthy Jonathan would die. Certainly not. That would be cruel, immoral, and unthinkable. But since, as the first call from the doctor had indicated, he was gravely ill anyway, the unthinkable became . . . well, thinkable.

With a thought like that, she asked, how could one live with oneself? And how could one live with Jonathan?

It was not the first time she had contemplated a life without her husband. The idea had been smoldering inside her for a long time. Perhaps from the beginning. She could not, of course, pinpoint the moment, since they were always so busy planning ahead, building, growing children or plants, collecting antiques. Their life together seemed divided into projects. Supporting him through law school. Playing good wife to upwardly mobile public servant. Being especially nice to his senior law partners—the quintessential traditional spouse. Chunks of time devoted to being ingratiating. Making him a cozy oasis of a home, a place to restoke the fires. They had gone from tiny apartment to split level in the far-out suburbs. Then came car pools and dancing classes and more car pools and orthodontists. All that culminating in this ... this giant, all-consuming, magnificent house project in which they had jointly poured every drop of their energy and fantasy. So what happens now that that is finished? she asked herself, walking into the library, where he was reading the paper. It was a question that demanded an answer. And she had it ready.

"I didn't come rushing to New York to visit you in the hospital, Jonathan, because I didn't care." It was not precisely the answer to the question as posed. Yet it said it all. He looked up from *The Washington Star*, squinting over his half lenses.

"Didn't care?"

He removed his glasses and balanced them on the Chesterfield's leather arm.

"I just didn't care," she said clearly.

"You mean it didn't matter if I lived or died?" His fingers tapped a crossed thigh and his eyes had narrowed.

"No, Jonathan."

"Are you serious?" He seemed genuinely confused, and she thought of the millions of other women somewhere who had suddenly imparted this same truth.

"Dead serious. Without doubt. I don't care. I haven't cared for a long time." She calmed herself, having determined that she must be both calm and cautious.

"Just like that." He snapped his fingers. "You dismiss a life. A relationship. A family." He snapped his fingers again. "Just like that."

"Just like that." She, too, snapped her fingers. No, she thought. It wasn't at all just like that.

She watched him grope for control. He stood up, opened the doors to the armoire, and poured himself a heavy scotch. He swallowed deep and hard.

"I can't believe this," he said after a long pause.

"Believe it."

She was sitting in the matching Chesterfield chair, her back stiff, her fingers digging into the hollows just behind her knees. The Staffordshire figures seemed a live audience. He rubbed his chin and shook his head.

"Is there someone else?"

His voice cracked and he cleared his throat. Apparently he had deliberately choked off a sob.

"No."

"Do you want someone else?" he asked quickly, and she sensed the trained lawyer's mind emerging.

"Maybe."

"Always be vague under cross-examination," he had told her once.

"Is it something I've done?" he asked gently, obviously grasping at some shred of hope.

"Not really."

"Then is it something I haven't done?"

She formed her reply carefully. "It has nothing to do with your conscious self," she said softly. She watched his face as it mirrored his growing anger.

"What the hell is that supposed to mean?" he exploded. His anger was, she knew, unavoidable. She hoped he wouldn't cry. She did not want to show him how unmoved she would be.

"It means," she responded calmly, "that you have no control over the situation and probably no blame. It's me." She paused, shrugged, and tightened the grip behind her knees. "I don't believe I can stand the idea of living with you for another moment. As I said, it's not your fault. . . ." He started to speak but she held up her hand. "And any injuries you might have afflicted on me were not done consciously."

"Injuries?" His voice shook. "I don't know what you're talking about."

"I know. I wish I was more articulate. But you see I've never had the training. . . ."

"So that's it," he said, finding sarcasm. "You gave up your life for me."

"A part of it."

"I made you quit school. Made you a slave."

"In a way."

"And you're—what is the cliché?—unfulfilled."

"That, too."

She sensed his rising contempt, steeling herself for what she knew was coming, had to come.

"And the kids? Don't they have a say?"

"The kids will be fine. I have no desire to abdicate my responsibilities in that quarter. And, no, they don't have a say."

"Jesus." He squinted into her eyes. "Is this you?"

"Yes. It's me."

"Not Barbara. Not the girl I married."

"Not her. I'm sorry, Jonathan. Really sorry. I wish I could do it so it wouldn't hurt."

There was a long pause as he paced the room. Stopping, he turned away and looked blankly at the titles of the leather-bound books, then circled the rent table and finally went back to the armoire and poured himself another drink. He gestured with the bottle, offering a drink. Obviously he had no idea of what was supposed to come next.

"No. Thank you," she said politely.

He shrugged and gulped down another drink, suddenly jabbing a finger below his breastbone.

"This is playing hell with my hiatus hernia."

"Take a Maalox."

He sighed, grimaced, and breathed deeply, staring at her.

"You're a cold-blooded bitch."

"I'm sorry if that's your perception." But the label made her uneasy. She was not cold-blooded, nor did she wish to be cruel.

"There is no easy way to do this, Jonathan. I'm sorry."

"Sorry?"

His lips trembled and she sensed that he was holding back more recriminations, making an effort to contain his anger.

"I guess it's an epidemic. All the girls of our generation with your checklist of unfulfilled dreams, lusts, and fantasies. We've busted our asses to make you content. Now you shit on us. We gave you too damned much. . . ." His voice faded. She had expected that, too. Had gone over all the potential arguments.

"So I guess you want a divorce?" he asked.

She nodded. "Yes."

"Not even a trial separation. *Fini?*"

"I told you how I feel, Jonathan. Why flagellate yourself?"

He shrugged, and a nerve began to palpitate in his jaw.

"I thought I was doing one hell of a job. I thought this was supposed to be success."

"It isn't."

"It's going to be a bother," he said.

"Life's a bother."

"Don't be so fucking philosophical, Barbara."

She stood up. What more was there to say? Through her own pain, she felt bells of freedom ring in her head. Save yourself, the rhythm urged. She supposed he'd move out in the morning.

8

He didn't move out in the morning. He was too disoriented. To avoid another confrontation, he got out of the house at six, before anyone had risen, and slipped into the surprisingly nippy morning. He always walked to the office.

He never took the Ferrari to work. Besides Barbara's Ford station wagon, they didn't own another car except, of course, for Eve's Honda. And whom could he trust with such a work of the automaker's craft? The Ferrari lay tucked in its cozy wrapper, in the garage, like a rare gem. As he walked to work, even on the coldest days, it gave him pleasure to know it was there, sweet-tuned and ready just in case. He took no pleasure in the knowledge today.

He hadn't slept. He wasn't used to the high, canopied Chippendale bed in the spare room across the hall from their bedroom. It had looked so inviting and comfortable when they bought it. It was too high and too hard. They had furnished the room strictly for guests, with a beautiful Hepplewhite secrétaire of figured satinwood decorated with marquetry, a mahogany dressing table, and a japanned commode. On the floor was a round Art Deco carpet and draperies that matched its beige field. The room, he decided, was too showy for comfort.

From his tossing and turning, the sheets had bunched and parted from the mattress, which added to his discomfort. Yet he refused to straighten them out, perhaps out of some masochistic desire to be punished for his marital shortcomings, whatever they were.

This phenomenon—it seemed the only way to label it—was not an uncommon experience among his acquaintances. "She just upped and said, 'No more marriage.' Like her whole persona had been transformed. Maybe it's something chemical that happens as forty gets closer." He had heard it said in a hundred different ways.

"It's endemic," he decided, heading down Connecticut Avenue, almost at a jog, until, breathless, he found himself leaning against the fountain rim at Du-Pont Circle. It was there that the realization hit him. He was on the verge of starting a whole new life for which he was totally unprepared. And in lousy physical shape to boot, he thought, noting his labored breathing. Perhaps he would have been better off with a heart attack.

Sometime near dawn he had run out of explanations, having traced his life with her from the moment he had first clapped eyes on her in the parlor of the rickety Barker house in Chatham. Cribb and Molineaux. They had finally joined the two on their wedding night.

"Let them do all our fighting for us," Barbara had told him then.

The story had worn well over the years, although in the darkness and his new circumstances, the punch line had lost its humor. Once, the auctioneer's error had come from providence. Now, once again, it seemed merely stupid. If the pair hadn't been broken, Jonathan might have been spared this.

He had, Jonathan told himself, been a good and loving husband. He had nearly offered "faithful" to complete the triad but that would have discounted his two episodes with hookers during conventions in San Francisco and Las Vegas when the children were small. My God, she has everything she could possibly want, he had railed into the night, sapped finally by the exhaustion of his disorientation.

What confused him most was that he had not been warned. Not a sign. He hated to be taken by surprise.

"You look a mess," one of his colleagues said to him cheerily as Jonathan passed his office in the corridor. A jogger, the man was always the first to arrive. Jonathan had not wanted to be observed, since he knew his demeanor told his whole story. He had seen it a number of times himself, the unshaven, abject figure in the rumpled suit and curled collar arriving before seven, another marital victim of the sisterhood's rage.

"Don't say another word," he had admonished the innocent colleague as he lunged for his own office and plopped helplessly into the swivel chair behind his desk. In a silver frame, Barbara stared back at him, offering a Mona Lisa smile. He flung the picture into the wastebasket. He could not remember how long he sat there, blank and empty, wanting to cry.

His secretary, Miss Harlow, a jolly, middle-aged lady, came in and almost immediately saw Barbara's picture in the wastebasket.

"I need lots of kindness this morning," he said.

"So I see."

"And a doughnut with my coffee from now on."

"Jelly or plain?"

"I'm not sure," he admitted, looking up to face her misty eyes. "And don't try to cheer me up."

Soon after she left, Harry Thurmont called. Jonathan had secretly hoped the call would be from Barbara,

contrite and apologetic. He knew Harry, a divorce lawyer, only casually. People called him the Bomber. His
heart sank.

"She's retained me, Rose," Thurmont said. His
voice had a gleeful note.

"I guess you're as good as any," Jonathan said
gloomily. He was annoyed that she had wasted no time
in getting herself legal counsel. He realized he would
have to do the same.

"I think if you're reasonable we can work things
out," Thurmont said.

"I'm really not ready to talk about it."

"I know. And I'm real sorry. Believe me, I tried to
talk her out of it. That's always the first step. That's
what they teach us at law school. I'm afraid she's adamant."

"No give at all?" he muttered into the mouthpiece,
instantly sorry for letting his anxiety show.

"None," Thurmont replied.

"I don't care. I haven't cared for a long time," she
had said. It was still impossible to believe.

"Suppose she changes her mind."

"She won't."

"What makes you so sure?" he asked testily.

"It's gonna be a nut cutter," Thurmont said
abruptly. "Better cover your ass."

"As bad as that?"

"Worse."

"I don't understand."

"You will."

"When?"

Thurmont ignored the question.

"You'd better get yourself your own man quick
time," he warned. His tone was ominous.

Jonathan nodded to the empty office. He knew the
cardinal rule of the legal profession. Only a fool acts as

his own lawyer, especially in a domestic case.

"Maybe if things cooled down a bit . . ." he began, being wishful again. Thurmont chuckled. It was the cackle of a predator and Jonathan hung up. He looked at the phone in its cradle for a long time, wondering if Barbara had told the children. With shaking fingers— he had to rub them to get them to do the job—he dialed his home number. Ann answered.

"She's gone to the French Market with a new batch of *pâté*."

"Well . . ." He started to say something. You're not part of it, he wanted to assure her.

"Is there anything you'd like me to tell her, Jonathan?"

"Lots," he answered. "Mostly bad."

"I'm sorry."

It wouldn't be long, he was certain, before his wife turned her against him. The children as well. But why? If only he had some real clue to his crime. Perhaps, then, the punishment would be acceptable.

He asked one of his recently divorced colleagues for the name of a good divorce lawyer. The man, Jim Richards, answered instantly.

"Harry Thurmont."

"That's hers."

"You poor bastard."

He shook his head and looked at Jonathan sadly. "Run for the hills. He'll take your eyeballs."

"I doubt that," Jonathan said. "I expect we'll be quite civilized about it."

"Civilized? Harry Thurmont isn't civilized. You're in the jungle now." He thumbed through his phone book. "Try Murray Goldstein. He's in the building. He's an ex-rabbi. You'll get lectures and lots of sympathy. You'll need it."

"All she wants is out," Jonathan muttered.

"That's what they all say."

He made an appointment for the same day—professional courtesy. But before he left the office he tried Barbara again, just to make sure he hadn't dreamed all this. She answered the phone.

"Still mad?" he asked gently. At what? he wondered. Hell, he thought, you don't just throw your life away. He was willing to forgive.

"I'm not mad, Jonathan."

"And you're still"—she was making him say it—"thinking about divorce."

"Didn't Thurmont call you?"

"Yes, he did."

"It's not a question of mad. We have a lot of practical details to iron out. The District has a no-fault provision."

The legalese angered him. So she was already getting educated.

"God damn it, Barbara," he began, feeling his chest heave. The memory of his hospital stay invaded his mind. "You just can't do this."

"Jonathan, we went over that last night." She sighed.

"Have you told the kids?"

"Yes. They had a right to know."

"You could have at least waited for me. I mean I don't think that's quite fair."

"I thought it was best they hear it directly from me, with all my reasons."

"What about *my* reasons?"

"I'm sure you'll offer your own explanations." She paused. "We're not going to have needless custody problems, Jonathan?" Her calm reasonableness irritated him. He felt burning begin again in his chest, a spear of pain. He spilled two Maalox tablets into his palm and chewed them quickly.

"I guess not," he said, confused.

"Why disrupt their lives? I told them that we were going to live apart, but that you'd still be easily accessible. I assumed that. You are their father. I hope I didn't overreach."

"I don't want them to suffer," Jonathan said lamely, feeling the palpitation subside. He swallowed repeatedly to get rid of the chalky taste in his mouth. She's torpedoing my life and making me a party to it, he told himself. He felt helpless. Utterly defeated.

"So that's it, then?" he asked. His ear had been groping for a single shred of contrition. He hadn't found a minute sign of it. Her response to his question was silence.

"If only I had been prepared. Seen a sign. Something. I feel like I've been shot between the eyes."

"Don't get melodramatic, Jonathan. It's been disintegrating for years."

"Then why didn't I ever see it?"

"Part of you probably did."

"Now you're a psychiatrist?" He had no urge to check his sarcasm. If she were in the room at that moment, he was certain he would have hit her. He wanted to smash her face, obliterate those innocent Slavic features, gouge out those hazel eyes, surely mocking him now.

"Bitch," he mumbled.

"I expect you'll be coming by for your things," she said calmly.

"I suppose. . . ." What more was there to say? He dropped the telephone into its cradle.

"*Fini,*" he whispered to the empty office, putting on his rumpled jacket and going out to keep his appointment with Goldstein.

Goldstein had a benign, Semitic face. He talked like a rabbi, an idea embellished by diplomas in Hebrew lettering hanging next to his law degree. He had a fringe of curly black hair, ringing a broad, shiny bald pate, and thick horn-rimmed glasses behind which droopy-lidded eyes offered lugubrious comments on the human condition. He wore a white-on-white shirt, Yemeni cuff links, and a striped Hermès tie. He lit up a large cigar as Jonathan settled into a soft chair at the side of the desk.

Goldstein was rotund, with puddles of chins, and his fingers were short and squat as they tugged daintily at the cigar. Staring out from the top of a low bookcase was a framed picture of what was undoubtedly the Goldstein ménage in younger days, three rotund children and an obese wife.

"I hate divorce," he said, shaking his head and directing his gaze to the family portrait. "Broken families. A *shanda*. I'm sorry. It means a 'shame' in Yiddish."

"I'm not too pleased with it myself."

"Whose idea?" Goldstein asked.

"Hers."

Goldstein shook his head and blew smoke clouds into the air. He looked contemplative, sympathetic, wise. Jonathan pictured him in a beard and skullcap, dispensing solace. A priest would have inhibited him with vague, unspoken guilt feelings. What he needed most was confession. Confess what? He felt his mind begin to empty in a long stream-of-consciousness narrative heavily larded with justifications, recriminations, and revelations, all of which seemed designed to give Goldstein a distorted, self-serving, self-pitying portrait of his eighteen-year marriage.

Goldstein listened patiently, puffing and nodding, his cigar dead center between his lips, his fat fingers cast in a delicate cathedral.

When he was finished, Jonathan popped a Maalox into his mouth. The ex-rabbi destroyed his cathedral and put his smoldering cigar into an ashtray. Nodding, he stood up, reached for a yellow legal pad, and began to shoot questions at Jonathan.

"Is there another man?"

"I don't think so."

"Whoever thinks so? And no other woman?"

"None."

"And joint property?"

"The house, of course, and all the antiques and other possessions in it. That's where we put everything we had. I'd say the house might fetch at least a half million, with probably another half—or more—in antiques. God, did we lavish love on that place." His eyes misted.

Goldstein nodded, as if he were a psychoanalyst listening to a patient unreel his life.

"What are you prepared to settle for, Mr. Rose?" Goldstein asked, the gentleness gone.

"I'm not really sure. I haven't had time to think about it. I really don't know. I don't think the kids will be a problem. I earn a good living. I want them to be comfortable. I'm prepared to offer reasonable support."

"And the house?" Goldstein asked.

"I don't know. Say half the value. After all, we did it together. Half of everything is okay with me."

"You want a good divorce settlement or do you want to be sentimental? If you want to be sentimental, then you shouldn't get a divorce. In fact, I would rather you didn't. I hate these situations where children go from pillar to post like punching bags. Children are supposed to be a *brucha*." He looked at Jonathan and shook his head. "A blessing."

"Look, Goldstein. It's not my idea." He felt the blood rise in his face.

"I understand." Goldstein flapped a pudgy hand.

"You must be calm. Don't excite yourself." Jonathan felt him taking charge.

"I know what that means," Jonathan huffed. "You want it short and sweet. No problems. No headaches. A nice fat fee."

"From your mouth to God's ears."

"I hope she feels the same way."

"Never be sure," Goldstein said. "It is the first rule of domestic law. Never be sure. Divorce makes people crazy."

"Well, it won't make me crazy," Jonathan muttered. "If it's meant to be, then let's get it over. You just proceed along the fastest track."

"There's a waiting period for a no-fault divorce in the District of Columbia. Six months if the parties don't contest. That's the quick way. If there's problems, there's a year wait. A divorce you get either way. But the property settlement is separate. It could go on and on. If it goes to court, there's more waiting. A judge decides." Goldstein bent over, blowing smoke. "All judges are *putzes*."

Jonathan nodded. It was going too fast. "It won't come to that."

"You hope."

"We're reasonable people."

"That was yesterday."

"I know lawyers. They can fuck things up. They call Thurmont the Bomber."

"Personally, I have mixed feelings. A court battle can help make me an even richer man. I have a loving, devoted family, Mr. Rose." He looked longingly at the picture of his rotund children and obese wife. "They are all going to college now. I have a very large house in Potomac and a maid that lives in, two Mercedes, and I go to Israel twice a year. Harry Thurmont has all these things and, in addition, an airplane and a house in Saint Thomas and he's always very tan, which means he gets away often."

"I don't need the lecture, Goldstein. I'm also a lawyer."

"The worst kind. You need the lecture more than a plumber. We can chop up your estate like scavengers and leave you nothing but the bare bones." Goldstein's cigar had gone out, and Jonathan caught a whiff of his bad breath.

"All right, you've scared the shit out of me, Goldstein. I already told you I want to settle this amicably. No hassle. I detest the idea of anyone getting rich from my misfortune."

Goldstein relit his cigar, puffed deeply, and exhaled smoke clouds into the atmosphere.

"I'll talk to Thurmont and get back to you," Goldstein said, getting up. "From here on in, we talk to your wife only through Thurmont."

"And I pay for both?"

"I don't make the rules."

"Just the money."

"I don't make the divorces, either."

"But it wasn't my fault," Jonathan protested.

"It was mine?"

Jonathan, sorry now he had engaged Goldstein, was more confused than ever.

"Have you moved out yet?" Goldstein asked as Jonathan rose.

"No. Perhaps tonight. I can't seem to manage it."

"Why not?"

"I'm not sure," Jonathan replied, wondering about his candor. "It's my nest. I can't seem to fly away. It's my place, Goldstein. My orchids. My wines. My workshop. My Staffordshire figures are there."

"Your what?"

"Little porcelainlike figures, beautifully painted. There's a cobalt blue—"

"I don't understand this, Rose," Goldstein interrupted.

"I don't, either. None of it." Never in his life had he been racked with such indecision. He searched Goldstein's eyes for direction. Through droopy lids, they stared back lugubriously. Their look depressed him.

"I need time," Jonathan said after a long pause.

"Time we got."

"Have we?" Jonathan asked. It seemed his first rational thought of the day. "I just threw out nearly twenty years." He felt too overcome to continue. "When you speak to Thurmont, call me," he muttered as he left the office, not certain of his destination.

9

can't believe it," Eve said. She had intruded on Ann, who was working on a bibliography for her thesis, "Jefferson as Secretary of State," just at that point when the number of books to read and sources to check seemed overwhelming. Ann was in no mood to be provoked by the perpetual crises of a teenage girl and had learned not to be panicked by Eve's propensity for dramatic overstatement.

But she looked up and saw in Eve's misty-eyed face an agitation that engaged her attention. Eve bent over her seated form and embraced her, putting her cheek against her own. Patting her head, Ann waited for Eve to unburden herself.

"They've split," she said, unable to hold back a chest-racking brace of sobs.

"Hey, what's this?" Ann said, turning and embracing the troubled girl. She waited until her caress soothed her.

"Mom and Dad. They've decided to go their separate ways," Eve said when she was able to speak.

Ann, of course, knew what had happened. But the idea hadn't quite sunk in. It was the unthinkable incarnate. She continued to deny it to herself. No one is prepared for a suddenly realized fantasy. She began to feel the full impact of her guilt.

"I'm sure it's temporary," Ann said quietly. Some secret, transient tension, she decided, not being privy to what really went on between them. "Married people are always having spats." She had never seen them raise their voices to each other.

"Not a spat, Ann," Eve said, finding her self-control. She seemed to be teetering on the edge of maturity. Such events, Ann knew, could be a catalyst, forcing adulthood. Eve sat on the edge of the sleigh bed and lit a cigarette, picking an errant tobacco crumb from her tongue.

"It was a declaration of independence, Ann," Eve said, clouds of smoke pouring out with her words. "I didn't know who she was, although I knew what she meant. She said it wouldn't affect my relationship with Dad, that it was all going to be very civilized and understanding. She was sure of that." Eve shook her head and sighed as Ann waited for her to continue. But what was the real reason? she wanted to ask. Eve seemed to read her mind.

"She said it was her idea. She said that I was a woman and would be sure to understand. What she wanted was to be free to fulfill her own aspirations and didn't want to be an appendage anymore. She said Dad was strong and time would heal his hurt." She looked up fiercely at Ann. "I didn't know what she meant, so I asked her and she explained." She paused and her face seemed bemused. "I never knew she was 'an appendage.' For me, the worst part was the thought that she wasn't happy with Dad."

"Maybe he wasn't happy as well," Ann blurted out, instantly sorry. In her heart she was fishing for another explanation.

"She didn't say."

"I'm sure there are reasons on both sides."

"After she told me, I felt like I was in a car accident. I'm still in shock. I mean everybody, all my friends, even me, believed they had the best relationship of any married couple anywhere. The way they did things together. Doing all the things with this house." Her voice rose and she mashed out her cigarette in a dish of paper clips. "She asked me to understand, to try to understand. I said I'd try. But I lied. I don't understand this at all. What does she want to be free from?"

Ann blew out a long gasp of air.

"Well . . ." She was groping for words of explanation. "Maybe it's too complex for us to understand."

"She has everything. Absolutely everything. And she's just started out on a great new business. Certainly we're no bother."

"Did she tell Josh?"

"He got it first. But you know Josh. When something hurts, he goes off into the corner like a whipped dog. Just like Benny when Dad yells at him. I saw him leaning against the tree in front of the house, just bouncing his basketball. I knew something was wrong. But this?"

"Have you discussed this with your father?"

"He was long gone. He slept in the guest room last night. No. I haven't discussed it with him. I'm afraid to. Considering what he's just been through. Thinking he was dying and all and none of us coming up to be near him."

It had confused Ann as well. She had watched Barbara's initial agitation when she first got the news. Then, with uncommon speed, it subsided. She hadn't, after all, heard the other end of the conversation and the way Barbara had gone about filling the casserole dishes with the *cassoulet* for the Paks one would have thought that Jonathan had only a mild indisposition. "He'll be fine," Barbara had said, and she was right. "It can't be a heart attack. He's too young. And the Roses have the genes of longevity."

"I can't blame him if he was upset," Eve said. "But I didn't expect her to be the one who . . ." She was obviously still confused by her mother's announcement.

"Maybe it will all come out in the wash," Ann said, disturbed by her own conflicting emotions. She was wondering, as well, how it would affect her own status in the house. Would they keep her on? Surely now Barbara would need her more than ever. But the thought of not being near Jonathan filled her with sudden anger, and she could not resist a vague, utterly illogical sense of betrayal. He will be leaving me, she thought, shocked at the depth of her feeling.

"She's already gone to see a lawyer. I'm afraid this is the end of the happy Rose family," Eve said with adolescent sarcasm.

"He hasn't moved out yet?" Ann asked, wondering if she had missed something.

"Not yet."

"He's a very resourceful man. He'll be fine."

"Will he?" The tears rolled over the lower lids of Eve's eyes, wetting her cheek. Her nose reddened. "Poor Daddy." She reached out and Ann was there to embrace her.

But who would soothe her? Ann wondered.

Sitting at her desk, she had been listening for his familiar step. Although she was growing drowsy and had difficulty keeping her eyes open, the sound of his key in the downstairs lock quickly restored her alertness and set her adrenaline charging. She heard Benny's bark and the click of his nails against the marble as they came into the house. Barbara would not let Benny in except when Jonathan came home. Did her disgust extend to the animal as well? Ann wondered. She waited to hear the sound of Jonathan's ascending step. None came. Then she moved through the doorway of her room to the head of the landing, peering into the darkness of the second floor, listening to the sounds of the sleeping house. She wondered if the others were listening as well, secretly observing with their senses what was, to all of them, a considerable household trauma.

She waited until she was certain that no one had stirred and, after a longer wait, walked soundlessly down to the second floor, listening first at Eve's door, then at Josh's, although she dared not move to the front of the house and Barbara's door. An alibi had already been concocted in her mind. She wanted a cup of tea, which she often made for herself when she studied late. Those previous occasions would make her story plausible. All she did was pop a tea bag into a cup and drown it with hot water from the Instant Hot tap.

In the kitchen, she deliberately placed the cup on the saucer with enough force to produce an audible tinkle. If anyone was listening, she wanted to dispel the impression that she was sneaking around. She had to see him, she decided. How could this have happened to such a man? How could Barbara possibly reject Jonathan?

She took another teacup off the shelf and dropped in a tea bag, filled the cup with hot water, and put both cups on a tray. Something was missing, she decided, looking around until she spotted a ceramic cookie jar in which Barbara placed her chocolate-chip cookies. She laid out some cookies on the tray and carried it to the library.

He was sprawled on the leather couch, looking haggard and unshaven, his hand shielding his eyes from the glare of the Tiffany lamp. Hearing her, he lifted his head, startled, revealing his disappointed reaction. Perhaps he was expecting Barbara.

"I was making myself a cup of tea and I thought you might . . ." Her hands shook, rattling the teacups on the tray. In the air was the sour odor of alcohol, and it struck her suddenly that he might be drunk. Beneath her quilted robe and pajamas, she felt her nakedness and a sudden stabbing sensation in her nipples. A nerve palpitated in her neck.

"No need, really, Ann," he said, his voice gravelly. But he had lifted himself on one elbow and was squinting at her, not quite sober but not quite drunk. She started to turn, but his voice stopped her.

"Might as well," he said, sitting up, running his fingers through his hair. She moved the tray toward him and he took the teacup, but left the cookies.

"Good," he said. "Nice and hot."

"I like it sometimes when I've been studying. Gives me a second wind."

He was, she imagined, forcing his politeness. He had never really noticed her. Certainly not as a woman. She put the tray down on the couch beside him and, still standing, began to sip her own tea.

"I suppose you know what's happened?" he said.

She nodded, but he did not look up, preferring instead to stare at the teacup.

"I started to come home for dinner. Then I thought, Jesus Christ, I can't come home for dinner. So I went to the Hilton and sat at the bar. Then I had dinner at the coffee shop. Did you ever realize how impersonal hotel living can be?" He looked up at her, then his eyes wandered.

She was thankful he was not waiting for an answer.

"It's beyond my comprehension, Ann."

He shook his head and looked around the library. "A man builds a fortress against the terrors of life." He looked at his hands. "I built a lot of things with these. I know some of the most intimate secrets of these objects. God, we worked like beavers on those shelves." He paused. "That rent table. We found the son of a bitch in a little antique barn outside Frederick. Something deliciously sinister about it. The tenant put the rent in one of those little cubbies and the landlord just revolved the top, scooped up the money, and put it in a drawer. Nice and neat. A kind of symbolic fortress. Did you know that, Ann?"

"Josh explained it once."

"Josh. Oh, shit."

"They're fine, Jonathan. I had a long talk with Eve."

He put his teacup back on the tray and surprised her suddenly by stretching out his hand to her. Since she was holding the teacup, she could not respond. She felt her knees shake.

"Dear Ann," he said. "You've been swell."

She could not resist. The palpitation in her body grew more forceful and her ears pounded. Putting down the teacup, she grasped his hand, continuing to stand but keeping her distance. God, how she longed to embrace him. His hand felt hot in hers.

"I don't know how the hell I'm going to explain it to them." He drew a deep breath between his teeth. "I feel so damned inadequate."

"Inadequate? You?"

He withdrew his hand and she let it drop. Let me love you, her mind screamed, frightening her. She watched his head droop into his hands.

"I've never been through this before. I don't know what to do. I can barely face anybody. Barely function. I haven't even got the will to move out. I'm, quite literally, paralyzed. Zombied into a state of shock. I was standing out there in front of the Hilton and I suddenly felt disoriented, alone. I panicked. I didn't know what to do. Maybe I even lost track of time. I don't know how I got home."

He lifted his head as if he wanted her to glimpse his anguish. Confide in me, she begged silently.

"I feel so helpless. I can't believe it's happening."

"Perhaps it will pass," she said. She seemed to hold her breath.

"Never. It's over, Ann."

She forced herself to hide her elation.

"I just want you to know . . ." She felt her face flush. "That I'm going to stick by the kids. I think they'll be fine. Just fine." She wondered about that. Eve was already smoking heavily. Josh had become withdrawn. Only Barbara seemed blithely content. "And if you need me for anything." She felt suddenly manipulative, sinister, hardly as innocent as she thought herself to be. A fantasy suddenly filled her mind. He was coming toward her, kissing her nipples, his fingers moving up her thighs. She felt her lips begin to swell. "Anything," she said. He closed his eyes and nodded. He reached out to her, and she took his hand again.

"I'm sorry," she said.

"Dear Ann," he whispered, more brotherly than she had wished. He released her hand, then lay back on the couch and closed his eyes. She watched him for a long time before departing.

10

Harry Thurmont was dapper in his pin-striped suit and high, oversized collar as he watched her from behind his free-form Plexiglas desk. Behind him, framed in a wide picture window, was the White House and, beyond, the Washington Monument. The senior partner in Jonathan's firm had a similar view, Barbara thought suddenly, remembering that Jonathan had once told her that such a view automatically doubled the fee.

"He hasn't moved out. I don't understand it," Barbara said. She sat in a deep easy chair, watching Thurmont's pink face. He had a reddish, bulbous nose and watery gray eyes. "A drinker" was her first thought until he announced that he was AA, insisting on the reformed drunk's obligatory précis of his life.

"My elbow is permanently bent," he told her. "But since I'm off the sauce, I'm mean as hell."

"I hope that side of you won't be necessary," she had told him at their first meeting two days ago. She wasn't so sure now.

"He's like some kind of animal. Almost invisible. He leaves early, before we get up, and comes home late, long after we've gone to bed. He doesn't take his meals at home. I know Eve called him at the office and they spoke for a long time. And he's been in touch with Josh. I think he met him yesterday after school. He's really a good man. Believe me, if there was another way . . ." Her voice trailed off.

"More or less typical," Thurmont said. "I'm in touch with Goldstein and we'll take it from there. The wisest thing is to let him phase out in his own time."

"Suppose he doesn't?"

"Well, then, are you prepared to move out?"

It had begun to confuse her. Not that she had thought through any of it. She was simply obeying her instincts, knowing that it was absolutely necessary to do what she had done. She felt, quite literally, free.

"Of course I'm not going to move out of my own house," she said flatly.

"It's also his," Thurmont said quietly, fastening his eyes on her face, inspecting her.

"It's unthinkable," she said. "You know that. I know that. He knows that." She stood up and walked to the window behind his desk, watching the sun glinting on the rump of Jackson's horse in the middle of La-fayette Park. He picked up a typed sheet, put on his half glasses, and studied the page.

"He's agreed to two thousand a month to run the house, the kids, the whole kebash. He'll pay the tuition at Sidwell Friends. That's for starters to get us going on the road to the final settlement. There's a whole proce-dure to be followed. Physical separation for six months. Things like that." He turned toward her, watching her, a canny smile on his face. The half glasses made him look shrewd. "In an uncontested situation, we'll just hammer out a plan. Goldstein's a pain in the ass. A tal-mudic Jew, always pinning arguments on great moral tenets. He runs up the rate. So far, your husband has been a pushover."

"He's very family oriented," she said.

He put down the paper and removed his glasses. "You're not home safe by any means." He reached over to a carved wooden humidor and drew out a short cigar, cermoniously sucking the wrapper before he lit it. "The major question in these events is how we divide the spoils. Possessions. It's the curse of the age. Next to child custody, which is wasteful and destructive. Property is different. It only looks simple. Here's mine. Here's yours. Like making a treaty in some ninth-century war between kingdoms. Your husband's accountant is doing an inventory and as soon as that's done we can cut into the carcass."

She hadn't been prepared for any of it. There's no school for divorce, her divorced friends had asserted. They hadn't gone into the substance of her material settlement, only the abstractions of what it meant to be on one's own, the joy and the pain. And, of course, the different men. Barbara had been mesmerized by that part of it. "Most of them are like children," one of her friends, Peggy Laughton, had pointed out. She had been a housewife, professional volunteer, and, as she characterized it, "an occasional Saturday-night fucker." She had been lighthearted, amusing, full of cute little dirty digs like "I didn't even know I was sexy. Now my blow jobs are getting great word of mouth." Remembering, Barbara grinned. She was eager to taste this aspect of her freedom.

"He's already offered you half the value of the house. But that's only the opening gambit. A bit of bullshit. It's you who probably have the handle on that one. Unless, as I said before, you intend to move out. The upkeep is going to be fairly steep."

"My business is starting to roll," she said. "With his payments and my extra income, that should do it."

He shook his head and smiled.

"You didn't understand the implication." She wondered suddenly why she hadn't consulted a woman attorney. Surely a woman would have been more understanding, more tactful. They are all in it together, she decided, gathering a cloak of caution around her, remembering Peggy's words: "It's that goddamned cock of theirs. All their brains are there. Never mind palm reading. Read the ridges of their cocks. You can really tell a man's character from that."

Suddenly the drawbridge over the moat went up. What she detested most was Thurmont's posturing and superiority, as if he were the possessor of some special knowledge.

"He offered you half the value of the house and its possessions. Not the house. Not what you have inside it. The value. Which means that an independent appraiser will look things over and determine what the real market value is. Then Jonathan will probably go out and borrow the money and make one big settlement. As near as I can figure without the inventory, you might walk away with, say, between four or five hundred thou after fees. It's a heavy wad. Should get you through the long, hard winter."

He stood up and walked toward her, leaving his cigar in the ashtray. She saw his shadow loom close and caught the whiff of his musky cologne. For a moment she felt herself bracing for a physical onslaught. For some reason, she was certain, he had decided to make a pass. He didn't, merely standing over her, looking down, underlining her helplessness.

"I don't think that's fair," she said.

"Fair?" He stopped abruptly and she wondered if

she had headed him off. She was annoyed that he had not made a pass. Maybe being fair game is what she really wanted, a real declaration of independence. With the exception of Josh and Jonathan, she had no idea of what other men really looked like, felt like. That, too, wasn't fair.

"Are you going to lecture me about 'fair'?" he said.

"I can't lecture you about something that doesn't exist." She enjoyed her jab at him. He offered a wry half smile, a broad hint of his arrogance. She was not intimidated.

"You think it's fair for me to have devoted nearly twenty years to his career, his needs, his wants, his desires, his security. I gave up my schooling for him. I had his children. And I devoted a hell of a lot more time to that house than he did. Besides, the house is all I have to show for it. I can't match his earning power. Hell, in a few years he'll be able to replace its value. I'll just have cash. Well, that's not good enough. I want the house. I want all of it. It's not only a house. It's a symbol of a life-style. And I intend to keep it that way. That's fair."

During the outburst his eyes had never wavered from her face and when she was through he offered her an unmistakably approving smile.

"Well," he said, "we have here a live one." He bent down and whispered in her ear, "Do you mean it? Or is it merely indignation talking? In the real world indignation collapses first."

"It's real as shit," she hissed, surprised at the extent of her firmness, wondering if it was really the way she felt inside. Was it possible that her resentment had been so deep? In the night, especially that first night, the guilt had come charging up at her, blocking out everything but her own imagined perfidy. She had called her mother in Boston and that hadn't helped one bit.

"I don't understand what you're saying," her mother had exclaimed after what Barbara knew was a long, garbled explanation. Hell, I don't need her approval, she had told herself. Of course they would think her mad. Everyone, including her children, might think her mad. In the cavern of her empty bed, she wasn't quite sure. All the resentment seemed to get screened through the lonely darkness and all that crawled into her mind was what one might call the good things. Jonathan had been so supportive of her desire to get out and do something. Anything. He had been the principal motivator behind the kitchen, urging her on to the pursuit of the commercial possibilities of what she once believed was merely her pedestrian housewife talent. So he must think that he has created a monster. He was always someone to lean on, to be protected by, steady and sure and knowing and handy and decent and loving. A good provider. A good father. A good son. So, then, why was she doing this to him? She had barely been able to get her doubts through the night. The next night she took a Valium and things were better. Last night it had been still better. She was beginning to agree with herself again.

"Up to now, Barbara," Thurmont said, intruding on her thoughts, "I would have thought you'd be the usual twenty-four-karat cliché. The I-just-want-out syndrome. The sad bleat of the unfulfilled woman. The beaches are strewn with their bloated corpses. They left home with empty purses, hot crotches, and high hopes. Fools. The lot of them. They didn't have to leave home empty-handed. They didn't even have to leave home."

"I don't know what you're talking about."

"It's possible, Barbara. We might be able to pull it off. But that will depend on you. He'll buck, of course. It'll be one hell of a mess. Dog eat dog."

"I won't move. I want it all."

"It will mean time. My time. Your time. Pain. Arguments. Anguish. Inconvenience. Is it worth the candle?"

"Damned straight."

Thurmont looked at her with satisfaction.

"You've got pluck, lady," he said happily, relighting his cigar.

In his words she read: I love messy divorces.

"It's my house. I worked my ass off for it," she said.

11

That morning he had started to pack, filling a suitcase in fits and starts. He went down to the library and fondly touched his Staffordshire figures, lifting a Little Red Riding Hood, a Garibaldi, a Napoleon, caressing them fondly as he replaced them on the mantel. Then his fingers lovingly slid over the intricate carving of the armoire. He remembered how happy he had been when it was delivered to the house.

In the foyer he opened the case of the face of the long clock, and as he had done every morning for more than five years, he cranked the winding key and, checking the time against his Piaget, moved the minute hand forward by two minutes. He loved the familiar click of the pendulum on its relentless journey through time and patted the smooth mahogany of the case.

Then he looked at the familiar figures of Cribb and Molineaux and, quickly, his eyes misted.

Not today, he decided. It hurts too much. Leaving his packed suitcase in the guest room, he walked swiftly to his office. Miss Harlow had his coffee and doughnut waiting. The first bite stuck in his throat.

How can I leave my own house? he asked himself,

feeling for the first time that justice, morality, decency, and fairness were on his side.

An hour later, Goldstein told him the news.

Jonathan looked at Goldstein in disbelief, but he saw no relief in the man's sad eyes, the hooded lids droopy with the weight of the world's sins.

"You're lying to me," Jonathan cried, his voice rising, the words reverberating in his mind as if it were a wind tunnel.

"You can't blame the bad news on the messenger."

"The dirty bitch."

Jonathan slapped Goldstein's desk, scattering papers with the rush of air his palm created.

"It's Thurmont. That bastard."

"It's natural. In a divorce action it's obligatory to hate the lawyers."

"Thank God I'm in a different kind of law."

"Do me a favor, Rose. Leave God out of it."

Jonathan slapped the desk again, overwhelmed by rage, the injustice of it. Was it possible he had invested almost half his life in this marriage? For this? For nothing?

"How fair can a man be?" Jonathan said after he had got his rage under control. "I've given her no trouble. No custody battles. I've agreed to a generous maintenance. Surely she can leave me with something."

"Why?"

"Because I earned it. It's mine."

"She says she earned it, too."

"Half. I'm willing to give half."

Again the anger ripped at his innards and he popped two Maaloxes in his mouth.

"I won't have it. I mean it's not fair. The house is ours. OURS. She takes the OU. I take the RS. I was going to give her the full value of one half its worth."

"She doesn't want the value. She wants the house,"

Goldstein said. "I probed all the possibilities. I offered half the house and told her she could continue to live in it with the kids."

"I didn't authorize that," Jonathan said, looking at Goldstein with daggers of hatred. "You had no right to offer that kind of deal. You never consulted me about that, Goldstein."

"I was probing. I wanted to find out how far they were willing to go. I wanted to at least show them we were reasonable. Who thought they would go this far?"

"Not me. That's for sure."

"It won't be nice," Goldstein said.

"Nothing is nice. Not anymore."

"Never mind nice. The subject is wealth. Yours. She wants to strip you of everything. What have you got besides the house?"

"My Ferrari," he said stupidly. "A three-oh-eight GTS. Red."

"They didn't include that. Not the wine, either. Or your tools."

"How generous."

"What else?" Goldstein snapped. Jonathan's mind clouded. "What about insurance?"

"I forgot about that. She's the principal beneficiary."

"Change it quick."

The idea curdled his guts. If he died now, she would receive a million. And get the house to boot. The recollection agitated him, but cleared his head.

"There's the phone." Goldstein pointed. "If you walked outside this building and got hit by a truck, you would be very unhappy . . . seeing that she would get all that money."

It took Jonathan a few moments to reach his insurance man, who happened to be in his office. He wanted to know details.

"Not now. Just change it to Eve and Josh. All right? Cut out Barbara." Jonathan hung up the phone without a word. It wasn't like him to be rude. But the call had made him feel better, although he still had to sign a form the agent was putting in the mail.

"I'll make arrangements to speed up the inventory," Goldstein said. "I want everything in that house on a piece of paper fast. Before she gets any bright ideas."

"She had better not take a damned thing. That would be stealing. I'll give up nothing. Not the house or anything in it. Never." His throat tightened and his voice cackled.

"Never say 'never.' "

"Fuck you, Goldstein."

Jonathan stood up, started to leave, then sat down again.

"I built my whole life around that house," Jonathan mumbled, his head in his hands, feeling a whirlpool of sentiment well up inside him.

"I have my workshop there. All my antiques. My collections. My paintings. It's a total thing. It can't be broken apart." He felt a terrible sense of persecution. All those years poking around antique auctions. "I have my wine. My Lafite-Rothschild '59's, my Château Margaux '64's, my Grand Vin de Château Latour '66's. My orchids. You don't understand. You haven't seen the place. It's a jewel. I lavished love on it. In ten years it'll double in value, maybe triple. And so will everything in it."

He caught his breath and sighed.

"You don't understand, Goldstein. I know every wire in that house, every fiber of wood and brick and slate. I know its pipes. Its innards. It is as much a part of me as my right hand."

"Spare me please, Rose."

"You have no sensitivity to that, Goldstein. It's not merely a possession." He shrugged. "People like you don't understand."

"Don't get anti-Semitic. It won't solve anything."

"Well, then, what the hell will?"

"The law. There is in the end always the law." Goldstein stood up to his full, squat, half-pint size and, marching over to a wall of books, patted them fondly.

" 'The law is an ass,' " Jonathan said, remembering Dickens's famous character.

"Not as big an ass as you think. There are still some arrows in our quiver." Jonathan grabbed the shred of hope like a drowning man grasps a piece of floating flotsam.

"Title 16-904, Section C," Goldstein said smugly, watching his face. "It allows a no-fault divorce even if a man and woman live under one roof. Separately, of course. No cohabitation. The waiting period is not affected."

"So I don't have to leave?"

"No. But . . ." Goldstein held up his hand. "Who gets the house and its contents is still up to the court. The judge could decide it's too contentious and order everything to be sold and the proceeds split. We could appeal. It could go on for years, considering the crowded dockets."

Jonathan felt a surge of hope.

"And my willingness to stay there. Fight for it. That will show my fervor. Maybe . . . my very presence will force her out."

"Don't get overly ambitious. There's still the kids to think about."

"Maybe she'll see the light. Hell, she's getting the kids. She can easily buy another place with the money I'm prepared to give her." He stood up and clapped his hands, then reality intruded again. "How in hell can I live in the same house with her? It'll be a nightmare. Who the hell thought up such a stupid idea?"

"The *schvartzes*," Goldstein said, getting up and starting to pace about the office. "Many of them couldn't afford to maintain two domiciles, so they made it easy on themselves and had a law passed."

"Maybe that's why there are so many domestic murders among the blacks," Jonathan said gloomily, his elation disintegrating.

"God damn it, Goldstein," he thundered suddenly. "I can't do it. I can't possibly do it. While she's there I can't possibly live in that house. The way I feel now I'll want to strangle her every time I see her."

"That," Goldstein said, pointing a chubby forefinger, like a threatening gun barrel, at his head, "is what loses cases." He paused and moved back to his desk. "Number one." He lifted a fat pinky. "Do you want to lose the house entirely?"

"Absolutely not."

"Then I strongly suggest 16-904, Section C," Goldstein said emphatically. A sudden thought seemed to intrude. "You could also make sure she doesn't sell anything . . . those collections."

"My Staffordshires."

"Or your wines. Then comes number two." Goldstein lifted the finger next to his pinky. It stood surprisingly straight, as if he had had much practice in exercising that particular joint. "You have to be willing to sacrifice. You mustn't give her a single cause for legal action. She will undoubtedly try to dislodge you."

"Like how?"

"By making you miserable."

"I can do the same."

Goldstein held up a hand, like a traffic cop.

"Don't interfere with the household. Be like a little mouse. No girlfriends in the house. Nothing she can hang a case on."

"No sex?"

"Not in the house. Better nothing. It's not long. A year."

"I thought you said six months."

"If one of the parties contests, it's a year. We're going to contest. The divorce will still get granted under no-fault. But why make it easy? Maybe the tension will break down her demands. This is a war, Rose. It's not Monopoly."

"You think we can win?"

"A judge is a *putz*." Goldstein smiled. "Also unpredictable. Who knows?"

"I have no choice, then."

"Of course you do. You can move out."

"That's no choice," Jonathan said firmly.

"All you have to do is live there. As innocuously as possible. Don't take your meals there. Leave her the kitchen. Let her run the house as always. Be just a squatter. The best tack is to be inconspicuous. As I said. Like a mouse."

"And the kids?"

"It doesn't look like the kids will be a problem. Be fatherly, but under no circumstances let them be made an issue. In terms of Mrs. Rose, try to be cool, polite, proper, and distant. If you think she's up to something fishy, tell me. Don't give her any cause for action. Don't do anything stupid. Don't take anything out of the house. If *she* does, tell me immediately."

"I've got to be a prisoner in my own house," he mumbled. Goldstein ignored him.

"Number three." The middle digit joined the others. "Be patient. Exercise. Go to the movies a lot. Play with yourself. Anything to keep your mind off your problems."

"Fat chance," he said. "And number four?"

"Number four," Goldstein said, shaking his head sadly and looking deep into Jonathan's face, "is not to be a *schmuck* and do something that you'll be sorry for. And number five"—Goldstein smiled, showing a line of spaced teeth like a picket fence—"is to pay my monthly retainer on time."

Jonathan sat in his office long after the others had gone. He had shooed away the cleaning woman, a portly Spanish-looking lady who looked at him knowingly. He was certain she had guessed that he was sitting there because he had no place to go.

Looking at his image in the darkened window, he seemed transparent. The eyes looked back out of hollowed pockets. The declivity of his cheeks had increased. The disregard for his usual fastidiousness showed everywhere. His tie was awry, the collar of his shirt rumpled. His beard seemed to have grown more rapidly than usual, and his mouth felt oddly smoky. He was sure he had caught Goldstein's halitosis and he blew into his palm to confirm it.

He could not stand the sight or smell of himself any longer. Leaving his office, he went into the street. He couldn't bear the thought of eating alone in a restaurant, waiting for service, choosing from the menu, feeling the butt of wandering eyes and their pity for his aloneness, speculating on his miserable existence, on his life of quiet desperation and terror. He continued to walk, unable to stop the jumble in his mind, bemoaning the tragedy of his life, once so promising. He had given up the possibility that he was dreaming. Indeed, losing Barbara had once been a consistent nightmare and always, upon awakening, he would reach out to her and cuddle his body full length against hers, proving her presence.

"I'll die if I ever lose you," he would whisper, wondering if she had heard. "I couldn't bear it."

It was a nightmare no longer confined to the darkness.

Without consciously making a decision, he walked into the Circle Theater, remembering Goldstein's suggestion.

They were playing a double feature—*The Lady Vanishes* and *The 39 Steps*—two early Hitchcocks. He bought the largest bucket of popcorn, drenched it in butter, and walked into the darkened theater. Both movies had been made before he was born, he noted, surely a less complicated time. Had people really been that simple and direct? The stories gripped him at times, took him away from his problems, but when his consciousness snapped back and revealed his isolation, he would feel a momentary wave of claustrophobia. What was he doing here, away from his family, away from his rightful place?

With sustained anger and not an iota of fear, he walked along the dark and crime-ridden streets, almost hoping that he might be attacked so that he could vent all his frustration on the antagonist. He tried to will himself to be a lure, slowing down when he heard footsteps approaching, disappointed finally when he discovered that he was in front of his house. As always, Benny was waiting, snuggling against his leg.

Through the front windows he could see the dull glow of the kitchen light and when he opened the front door the aroma of her cooking reached his nostrils. The meaty flavor of her *pâté* had once been overwhelmingly tempting. Now it filled him with nausea. Before he could reach the foot of the stairs, Barbara materialized, still dressed and aproned, her face flushed from activity. He turned his eyes away and felt his hands reach out for the coolness of the brass banister. The chandelier was unlit. In the dim light he could make out the tension in her face.

"I think we should talk," she said gently. His heart lurched as his mind leaped at the possibility of a reconciliation. It was too tempting to ignore. He wondered how he should play it. That depended on the degree of her contrition, he decided. Please, let God be magnanimous, Jonathan urged.

He followed her into the library. She turned on one of the Tiffany lamps and the soft glow enveloped her as she wiped her hands on her apron. Lady Macbeth. He smiled at the errant image. She sat down on the edge of one of the leather chairs, remarkably cool and businesslike. He wondered if it was an ominous sign, and was quickly rewarded for his curiosity.

"You can't stay here, Jonathan," she said crisply. "Not now." Her voice was soft but firm. He was ashamed of his hopefulness.

"It's a question of facing reality," she said, sighing. "I just feel it will be better for all parties. Including the kids."

"Leave them out of this," he snapped, recalling Goldstein.

She looked at him thoughtfully for a moment.

"Yes. I suppose you're right. But certainly it won't be a healthy situation." What troubled him most was her command of herself. Her firm assertion. You've come a long way, baby, he thought. Why are you doing this to me?

His gaze washed over the room that he had created, the rubbed-walnut shelves, the rows of leather-bound books, filled with so much now-useless wisdom.

"I thought I offered you a most reasonable solution," he said, trying to capture his usual lawyerlike demeanor when dealing with clients. But the tremor in his voice gave him away.

"Not to me," she said quietly.

"Reasonable? To take everything. Leave me with nothing. That's reasonable?" His voice started to rise, but he remembered Goldstein's caution.

"It's my payment for being your security blanket for nearly twenty years. I can't possibly earn in five years what you can earn in one. No matter how great my business goes. For me, that's reasonable."

He started to pace about the room, touching objects. He stuck a finger into one of the cubbies of the rent table and spun it around.

"I've invested so much of myself in this place. Surely as much as you." He was being deliberately calm, trying to hold in his temper. He looked down at her. She seemed cold, clear-eyed. Unbending. "I can't believe you're so ruthless about this, Barbara, considering all we shared for eighteen years."

"I'm not going to yield to any guilt trip, Jonathan. I've come to grips with that. The problem for you to understand is that I'm thinking only of myself for the first time in my life."

"And the kids?"

"Believe me, I intend to fully discharge my responsibilities." She frowned. "Now who's using the kids?"

"It's just not clear, Barbara. If I understood it, maybe I could be more tolerant."

"I know," Barbara said, with what seemed like a hint of compassion. She bit her lip, a normal gesture for her when she was troubled. "I'm changed, that's all. Not the old me. Any explanation sounds cruel. I don't want to be cruel."

" 'The lady doth protest too much, methinks.' "

"That's one of them. One of the things I detest so

much in you, Jonathan. All those literary allusions that forced me to ask for explanations, as if they were a proof of your superiority."

"Pardon me for having lived."

"Now you're getting hostile."

I need you, Goldstein, he shouted to himself, brushing his hands through the air as if that would dispel the conversation. Goldstein had warned him not to deal with her directly. But how could he avoid her, living under the same roof?

"Did you truly expect any other response?" he said quietly.

"It won't matter. I have to think of the long pull for myself." She stood up and again wiped her hands on her apron. "I'm sorry, Jonathan. I know it seems selfish. But I have to protect my future."

"You're inhuman," he snapped.

"I can't help your perception."

He turned to the library entrance and paused, emptying his mind of false hopes.

"I don't intend to leave this house. I don't intend to give it up. I do intend to fight you every foot of the way, regardless of expense in dollars or emotions. I want this house and everything in it. And I do not intend to lose."

"It's not going to be that simple," she said quietly. He marched up the stairs and into the guest room.

As he closed the door, snapping the thumb lock, he decided to put in a better lock, complete with key. From here on in, he told himself, reveling in his belligerence, this is company headquarters.

12

The house was staked out like a battlefield. Ann tried desperately to maintain a scrupulous neutrality lest it affect her own circumstances, although she did not know how long she could hold on in the midst of the unbearable tension.

Barbara and Jonathan had installed locks on their respective bedrooms. At first that seemed to Ann unnecessary until she began to observe the extent of their growing hostility. They had separate phones installed as well, leaving one of the original lines intact for the children. The kitchen was hers. He apparently had given up all rights to both the food and the facilities, although she saw a little carton of orange juice on the ledge of the side window of the guest room, conveying an utterly incongruous boardinghouse look. He never took his meals at home, and he maintained Benny from a stock of dry dog food he kept in his room. Benny spent the day poking about the neighborhood, continuing his endless service to the local bitches, and returning home by instinct so that he could spend the night sleeping at the foot of Jonathan's bed.

Jonathan also retained rights to the maintenance of

his orchids. And he continued to spend a great deal of time in his workroom. By silent consent, it was considered his domain. It was there that he generally met with the children and, at times, with Ann, who used the most transparent pretexts to visit. The Ferrari's special place in the garage was his domain, as well. Sometimes, when feeling very down, he would strip away the Ferrari's cover, remove its fiberglass top, and take it out for a brief spin, or he would spend hours tuning it and polishing its body. Allowing him such pursuits required no sacrifice on Barbara's part. Besides, she was literally working herself at double time to build her catering business. The house was constantly filled with the aroma of her cooking.

Ann was fully aware of her unrequited feelings for Jonathan, which prompted even more caution on her part. It was, she knew, downright dangerous to poke one's head above the shell holes of no-man's-land. Even the humor of it, the sheer illogic of the process, paled as the days wore on. By force of will, she maintained an observer's distance, while inside she seethed with a profound and exasperating curiosity.

Every movement in the house became a signpost, every unguarded look a nuance, every stray word a symbol of some impending action. At night she would go over what she had observed during the day, attributing motives, calculating advances or retreats.

She wondered if they observed her inspection and when she felt anxious about this, she retreated further into her pose of indifference. Even the children seemed to have given up. At first they had been slyly trying to effect a reconciliation, but that had quickly dissipated in the face of their parents' obvious unrelenting hostility and they assumed an air of grudging acceptance and, finally, tolerance.

"My parents have simply gone crazy," Eve told her

one night. The announcement seemed in the nature of an epiphany and Ann noted that Eve was spending more time with her friends, less time under her scrutiny. It was pointless, she decided, to attempt to maintain a more rigid discipline over the children at a time of such trial. Josh found solace in basketball and other sports and, since he had not lost contact with his father, he seemed to be maintaining a business-as-usual equilibrium.

Sometimes she felt uncomfortable about her inspector's role. It took effort and concentration. And, of course, she had to hide her own interest. Was it possible for Jonathan to see in her an alternative? The question gnawed at her and filled her with guilt.

"You're awfully quiet," Barbara remarked one day.

"I hadn't realized," Ann responded.

"I suppose I can't really blame you. The way things have altered around here."

It was her first real attempt at self-justification to Ann, who listened quietly, deliberately averting her eyes so they would not betray her. "Who can possibly understand but another woman who has undergone the same experiences? You can never really transfer your outrage. The house, in my opinion, is fair compensation. He can have another one just like it in a few short years. Maybe sooner. I can never have it again unless I marry. Then the whole cycle starts again."

Although she was working harder, she seemed more beautiful than ever, glowing, in fact, a quality totally incongruous, considering her "plight."

"I'm not competent to judge," Ann replied, remembering the undeclared war of her own parents' married life. She had rarely seen even the most primitive gestures of respect between them. They seemed to survive on a diet of mutual hate. "I'm not a good one to ask about married life. My background is very traditional," she lied.

"I know. The husband pulls down a paycheck and the wife cooks, cleans, and fucks." Ann had also detected that Barbara had gotten harder, more vocal and intransigent.

Between Jonathan and Barbara communication was, in the early days of the new arrangement, nonexistent. Sometimes it was unavoidable, and Ann would hear scraps of conversation that always disintegrated into a rising crescendo of vituperation.

"I'll pay all electric and gas bills that can be attributed to normal household operations. Not to your business activities. Those you pay for." He had confronted her in the kitchen late one evening. Ann, who was helping to baste a roasting goose while Barbara prepared a batch of baking dough, quickly faded from the scene, far enough to be out of their vision but close enough to hear.

"How can you calculate the difference?" Barbara asked sarcastically.

"I'm having a man come in from the electric and gas companies. If necessary, we'll put in separate meters."

"What about the power from your workroom and the sauna?"

"I take no profit from that."

"But I help pay for it."

"Would you like to charge me for the use of my room as well? The cost of my electric blanket?"

"If I could, I would."

"And I don't appreciate your fudging on the food bill. Thurmont agreed that you would keep those charges separate. There's no way the family can use six pounds of flour and three pounds of butter a week."

"And what about the orange juice? I know you filched a carton of orange juice the other day. It could only have been you." Barbara had asked the question so innocently of each of them, including the maid. Ann had wondered about the intense probing.

"I admit it. It was a damned mistake. I used it for screwdrivers. I ran out."

"I've been meaning to tell you. Those juice cartons on the ledge are ugly."

"It's my ledge."

"And I don't see why you have to lock up the liquor cabinet and the wine vault."

"What's Caesar's is Caesar's," he said facetiously, the logic deteriorating.

"And what's God's, God's. You bastard."

"I'm not kidding about the food, Barbara. I'm not counting the water."

"The water?"

"Water costs," he mumbled, but Ann could tell that his heart wasn't in the argument on that issue. "All I'm asking for is a reasonable estimate."

"You toss around that word 'reasonable' as if it were from the beatitudes."

"Now you're getting biblical. Are you going 'born again'?"

"Yes, as a matter of fact. You forced it on me."

"Well, you're not rid of me yet."

The matter, as Ann soon discovered, was resolved by an injunction. Barbara had charged harassment and violation of their maintenance agreement. Goldstein had gone to court and won, and an injunction forced Barbara to keep her business expenses separate.

"You've only run up our legal bills," Jonathan told her in still another confrontation.

"I don't care."

"You can't just run to the court every time we have

a dispute. It's bad enough we have to wait such a long time to resolve the main matter. But what's the point of these interim decisions?"

"I'm not going to let you harass me, that's all."

"I'm not harassing you."

For a long time after that they did not speak at all, and things appeared to settle down into an armed truce. Jonathan's routine was unvarying, and Ann noted that he had greatly curtailed his out-of-town travel, as if leaving the house meant giving Barbara a special advantage.

He would come home around midnight. After dinner at a restaurant he would go to the movies. Any movie. He carried around with him programs offered by the various repertory film theaters. He had shown them to her with all the dates checked off so that his secretary could record them in his calendar. For breakfast his secretary provided coffee and a doughnut, and a business lunch took care of his midday meal.

He had explained the routine to Ann on those evenings when, with Barbara out on a catering job, she mustered the courage to accost him on his way up to his room. For some reason, she had noted, he was nervous in her presence, a condition that she greeted with even greater curiosity.

"It's no life, Ann," he told her one evening as they stood in the foyer. "But the movies are a fantastic escape. Something about the darkened theater and all those strangers sitting beside you. Not like television. It's a damned lonely life."

In the privacy of her thoughts, she could be outrageously blatant in her efforts to seduce him, and, more than once, these fantasies had become quite aggressive. But, near him, she could not bring herself to make a single untoward move, although she watched him carefully for any sign of interest. It was a struggle to put those thoughts aside. Besides, she dared not hope. Her fear of rejection was gnawing at her, and its actuality might have sent her skulking into the street, never to return.

At times even their armed truce erupted into near-violent confrontations. Once, when Ann was out, he had broken into their old room to get a bottle of Maalox he had left on the shelf of their once jointly shared medicine chest.

The household was awakened by Barbara's frantic pounding on his door. The fury of her attack frightened the children and they huddled beside Ann on the third-floor landing, like spectators at a bullfight.

"You broke into my room, you bastard," she had screamed. She had been supervising a late buffet and had discovered the break-in when she returned. He had opened the door and confronted her, bleary-eyed with sleep.

"I needed a damned Maalox. I had a hiatus-hernia attack."

"You have no right to break into my room."

"All I took was the damned Maalox. It was too late—"

"There are all-night drugstores."

"I needed it immediately. I had no choice. I had run out. Really, Barbara, I was in pain."

"You had absolutely no right. That was a violation of our agreement. A legal violation."

"Bullshit."

"Breaking and entering. I have every intention of calling the police."

"There's the damned phone." He had pointed to the phone in his room and in her anger she stormed in and picked it up, dialing 911.

"I would like to report a robbery," she said. "Barbara Rose, sixty-eight Kalorama Circle." There was a long pause. "I'm not certain what else was stolen. But

I do know that a bottle of Maalox was taken. My husband broke into my bedroom. No. He did not rape me." She took the phone away from her ear and looked into its mouthpiece. "God damn it. We pay you to protect people. Not to ask silly questions." She banged the phone in its cradle. He had rarely seen her so agitated and he was amused.

"Feel better?" Jonathan had asked smugly. He leaned against the doorjamb, smiling.

"You had no right," she sputtered, storming across the corridor, slamming the door behind her.

"Don't talk to me about rights," he called to her through the door.

"This house has become a loony bin," Eve had whispered.

"It's like a television show," Josh said. "I wonder how it's going to come out."

Again Barbara took Jonathan to court, resulting in an injunction that Jonathan was forbidden to break into her room in the future.

"Will they put him in jail if he does?" Josh had asked his mother at the dinner table after she had announced the judge's decision.

"I'm afraid so," she had answered gently. But Josh was visibly shaken and had thrown his napkin on the table and run up to his room. Later, after she had comforted him, Barbara had knocked at Ann's door.

"May I come in?" She had already opened the door. Ann was reading.

"Of course."

Barbara wore a dressing gown; her face was cold-creamed, her hair pinned back. She looked considerably younger, more unsure and vulnerable.

"The worst part is having no one to talk with. At least Jonathan listened. But I always felt I was hiding something. It never seemed like the truth." She sat down on the bed and bit her lip. "This is one hell of a trial by fire, Ann. It isn't half as simple as I thought." She looked at Ann's face, pleading. There was no avoiding the confidences about to come, Ann knew.

"I suppose you think I'm an unfeeling rat."

Barbara waited for a reply, for which Ann was grateful.

"Actually"—Barbara thumped her chest with outstretched thumb—"I hate myself for what I know in my heart I must do. If I were religious, I would think of myself as a female Job." She bowed her head as her eyes filled with tears. They spilled down her cheeks. "I'm not superhuman. I don't like what all this is doing to the kids. Or even Jonathan. I just wish he would walk away and leave me alone. That's all I ask." She looked up at the ceiling, her lips trembling. "I suppose I could compromise. But I know I'll regret it for the rest of my life. I have to do what I have to do. Can you understand that, Ann?"

"Please, Barbara," Ann said gently, sitting beside her on the bed, holding her hand with sisterly affection. "Don't put me in a position where I have to make a choice of some sort. The whole thing is heartbreaking. I adore you all. I feel bad for all of you."

"I'm not a beast, Ann," Barbara whispered. "Really, I'm not. In my heart I know I'm right. Looking back . . ." She paused and sighed. "I felt persecuted. Helpless. We have only one life, Ann. Only one. I wasn't happy."

"I'm not here to judge," Ann responded. But she was judging. How could Barbara be unhappy with Jonathan? It was incomprehensible.

"If only he had left the house, like an ordinary rejected spouse."

"I'm sure it will all turn out for the best," Ann said stupidly, disgusted with her hypocrisy. She wished she could be truly honest. She could sense Barbara's pain.

She understood helplessness. But Jonathan was someone special, a prize. Hurting him seemed willful, ob-
scene. Still, she couldn't hate Barbara, whose anguish,
despite Ann's feelings for Jonathan, moved her. Suddenly Barbara embraced her. Ann felt the moist heat of
her cheeks, the sweet, womanly smell of her body. She
felt the fullness of her large breasts. In some oddly bizarre way, the closeness reminded her of Jonathan, and
she returned the embrace.

"Women understand," Barbara whispered.

After a while Barbara disengaged herself and stood
up, wiping her cheeks with her sleeve.

"You've been a real treasure, Ann. I want you to
know that. We all owe you a debt."

Ann felt unworthy of the gratitude.

It was Eve's idea to have a Christmas tree and she
and Josh and Ann dutifully set it up in the library.

"I don't care what's going on in this house. Christmas is still Christmas," Eve had announced, treating
Ann to a long litany of the joys of family Christmases
past—ski trips to Aspen, sunny days in the Virgin Is-
lands and Acapulco. When they stayed at home, they
would set up a Christmas tree in the library and both
sets of grandparents would come down from Boston
and there would be a fabulous Christmas dinner and a
big eggnog party for all the friends of the Roses', both
generations.

Actually, Ann hadn't intended to stay with the
Roses over the holidays, but they all seemed so forlorn
and depressed that she felt a sense of obligation.

On Christmas Eve both children were invited to
parties and Barbara was out, cooking and supervising a
large dinner. To keep busy Ann had welcomed the opportunity to assist Barbara in the making of pastry

loaves, a new recipe she had concocted, which she was preparing for a Greek Embassy buffet. Barbara had been specific in her instructions, which Ann had written down and followed to the letter. The ingredients were already prepared. All she had to do was mix them. She put the beef, onion, salt, and pepper into a large mixing bowl on the kitchen island, mixed in the bread, then added wine and broth to the batter. When it had been mixed to the right consistency, she made seven rectangles, wrapped them in tinfoil, and put them in the refrigerator, very satisfied with her effort. Barbara had been concerned that making the pastry loaves would interfere with Christmas Day. She was determined, she had told Ann, to spend the day with the kids.

Helping out was the least she could do, Ann thought self-righteously, not in the least perturbed about not spending Christmas with her parents, an exceedingly bleak prospect. Her parents invariably got blind drunk on Christmas Eve, and the day after consisted of nursing bad hangovers and coping with sometimes violent irritability.

When she had washed up, Ann filled a tumbler with wine and walked to the library, where the Christmas tree stood, decorated and sprinkled with tinsel. The gifts lay wrapped and scattered around its base. She noted that, true to form, Barbara and Jonathan planned not to exchange gifts. Yet she was pleased to see that both of them had gotten gifts for her. As she contemplated what Jonathan had bought her the lights, which switched on and off, suddenly flickered and lost their luster. She was about to pull the plug when she heard Jonathan's familiar step in the foyer. She hadn't seen him for a week, although Eve had reported that he would attend the gift-opening on Christmas morning.

Both apparently had agreed to be on good behavior for the sake of the children.

"It's a hell of a Christmas Eve," he said, walking to the armoire and pouring himself a heavy scotch.

"To better Christmases," he said, raising his glass. She raised her glass in response.

"Everybody's gone," she said, sensing her own deliberate mischief. He finished off the scotch and poured another.

"I saw two Italian pictures. *Down and Dirty* and *Bread and Chocolate*. The place was nearly empty. Just one or two other losers. I would have seen the pictures over again, but they cleared the theater. Christmas Eve. The projectionist, I suppose, wanted to be home with his family. Home with his family. Such simple joys." He sighed and poured himself another drink. He looked up suddenly as if acknowledging her presence for the first time.

"Why aren't you home with your family, Ann?"

It was a question she didn't really want to answer. "I guess I'm needed here," she whispered.

"Good for you, Ann. At least you're needed somewhere. I am apparently needed nowhere. Not even as an audience."

He finished his drink and squatted beside her. She had seated herself Indian style at the edge of the gifts, watching the fading, flickering lights.

"I'll fix those tonight. Wires need some soldering, I guess."

She stole a view of him in profile, then her eyes lingered. She watched his lips move.

"Christmas is only for the kids anyhow," he said. His lips began to tremble and he could not go on. She put her hand on his arm. Without turning, he put his hand on hers and pressed it.

"What a bore this must be for you, Ann." He turned to look at her. "I can't imagine why you put up with it. I don't know why I put up with it. None of it makes any sense, you know. Two jackasses rolling around in the mud."

"I'm not here to judge." She reflected suddenly that that was what she had said to Barbara.

"You should have been here last Christmas. It was a real old family time. My father made a toast. 'You're a lucky man,' he said. 'A truly lucky man.' He doesn't understand what's happened. He thinks I've got a mistress and Barbara's going through change of life. I tell him it's neither, but he's out of it. How do you explain this to anybody?"

"Don't try. It's nobody's business," she snapped, surprised at her assertiveness.

"I think it's coping with being alone that bugs me the most. The loss of companionship. I think that's what I miss the most."

"You'll find somebody," she said cautiously, her heart pounding. Notice me, she begged him in her heart.

"That's out for now. Goldstein says I should cool it. I never thought my life would one day be controlled by an ex-rabbi with halitosis." His arm played around to her shoulder.

"Dear Ann," he said. "You're like the only anchor in this damned, stormy sea. I don't know how we'd survive this without you being here. And the kids. What a godsend you've been to the kids. I'll bet you never bargained for this when you first came here. It was one of Barbara's better decisions, I guess."

The house was quiet. To Ann it seemed as if the earth had stopped rotating. She dared not move. His nearness was like an electric current pulsing through her. She felt his breath against her ear.

"I haven't had a single moment of solace," he said. "I can't seem to wake up from the nightmare."

For once she resisted caution, yielding to her body's responses. She turned to face his lips, her eyes probing his. His face moved closer and his lips reached for hers. She felt his tongue move inside her mouth, reach for hers, and, finding it, move and caress it. Her fingers reached for his hair. It had been a particular detail of her fantasy, her fingers entwining themselves in his beautiful, wavy salt-and-pepper hair.

She felt his urgency, the pressing hardness, as his hands groped upward along her thighs, knowing as she opened to him how deeply she wanted him to take her and enter her as she engulfed him. Just as she touched him she felt the shuddering response in herself, startling in its ferocity, like thousands of caressing fingers on every nerve.

His sudden disengagement surprised her, a wrenching movement, and a moment later she heard what had apparently startled him, the front door opening. She was on her knees immediately, straightening her clothes as she kneeled, fussing with the gifts, not turning when she sensed Barbara behind her. Her heart had leaped to her throat and Jonathan had moved into the shadows behind the armoire, just out of her vision.

"That you, Ann?" Barbara called. Ann turned briefly in response.

"Just rearranging the gifts."

She felt Barbara's eyes on her back. Please don't let her go any further, she begged, invoking God.

"I'm dead on my feet," Barbara said. "Did you finish the mix for the pastry meat loaves?"

"Yes."

"Kids not home yet?"

"Not yet."

"Well, tomorrow is Christmas. I dread it."

Ann could feel the tension in the room. She held her breath, frightened that Barbara might want to talk. She did not think she could bear it.

"Better get some sleep." Barbara yawned, backing away. With relief, Ann listened to Barbara's footsteps ascending the stairs. It was only after the bedroom door had closed that Jonathan stepped from the shadows.

"I'm sorry," he whispered.

Reaching out, Ann grabbed his hand and kissed the center of the palm. He quickly drew it away in what seemed like a gesture of rejection. Or rebuke. He tiptoed into the foyer, opening the front door, creating the impression that he had just come into the house. He hurried up the stairs. Straining to listen, she heard him turn the lock of his door.

She stayed in the library a long time, kneeling on the floor before the Christmas tree. Had Barbara seen them? She would not let such speculation intrude on her happiness.

Her eyes drifted upward toward the weak, flickering lights. It was only then that she realized that she had not reminded him to fix them.

13

The smell of burning had set off a reaction in his dreaming mind, suggesting fire and recalling a Boy Scout episode when a fire had gotten out of hand and burned down a country cabin. He was on his feet in a moment, bursting through the doorway, running down the steps in his bare feet.

The branches were smoldering and the flames were just beginning to sprout like orange needles among the green. He kept an extinguisher in a closet under the stairs. Grabbing it, he rushed back to the library, where the flames had already begun to eat away at the paper wrappings of the gifts.

Upending the extinguisher, he squirted the foam in large white arcs on the creeping flames.

"Daddy." It was Eve behind him, stifling a scream.

"Get back," he responded. The flames were quickly under control. But a foul, smoky smell permeated the room as he continued to pour out the contents of the extinguisher until the fire was out.

"The damned lights," he cried. "I should have fixed the lights."

"You've ruined everything." It was Barbara's voice, filled with anger.

"What was I supposed to do?" he shot back. "Let the whole house burn down?"

"You knew they weren't working right. You knew they were dangerous."

He dropped the extinguisher, banging it on the floor, and glared at her.

"I suppose I'm being accused of ruining everybody's Christmas."

Eve and Josh had begun to poke through the remains. Most of the gifts were charred or utterly destroyed. Jonathan had bought Josh a pair of binoculars, which the heat had bent out of shape.

"Well, it was a nice thought, Dad," Josh said, holding up the distorted object.

"I'll get you another pair," Jonathan said.

"What did you get me, Dad?" Eve asked quietly, wiping her soot-stained hands on her robe.

"According to your mother, a not-so-merry Christmas." He looked at Barbara, who turned away in contempt. I saved their lives, he thought, his eyes briefly flickering as they caught some sympathy in Ann's. She had just come into the room.

"Isn't it ghastly, Ann?" Eve said.

"Merry Christmas, one and all," Josh said, holding up his binoculars and smiling at the scorched tree. Orange shafts of the early sun had begun to filter through the windows.

"I guess there's nothing left to do but clean up," Barbara said, striding into the mess and beginning to sort out the remains. The Sarouk rug was sooty but not burned and the children rolled it away from the tree.

"I hope you didn't cancel our fire insurance as well," Barbara muttered as he stood around clumsily.

"Fuck Christmas," he said angrily, striding out of

the room. He detested her attempt to make him feel guilty.

In his room he lay on the bed and tried to ward off an oncoming massive depression. It was as if all his old values had been tortured into new shapes.

They had seen only the destruction, none of the fatherly concern. Remembering last night, he wavered suddenly, almost ready to accept blame. He had, indeed, forgotten to fix the lights, but hadn't Ann promised to remind him? *Ann.* The memory of desire stirred him, focusing his mind. His body responded and he caressed his erection. Any female who had found herself in his sights at that moment would have been fair game, he decided, dismissing the specter of any romantic involvement. That would be fatal, Goldstein had warned. "Don't get mixed up with another woman. Not just yet," he had intoned. "It's safer to court Madam Palm and her five sisters." He had been surprised at Goldstein's levity. Besides, Ann was too young. Yet he needed a woman. Any woman.

He remembered Ann's orgasmic reaction to his embrace. So I'm not completely sexless, he decided, like a prisoner in a dark black cell to whom any ray of light is a gift.

He watched his throbbing erection, tense and trembling, as if it had a mind of its own. Closing his eyes, he imagined Ann naked, thighs open, waiting, nipples erect. He was plunging his erection into her, plunging deeply, urgently. He reached for it, feeling the pleasure begin, then recede. Something was intruding on the mechanism of his fantasy. He tried to fight it away, but its momentum was relentless and his body reacted. The tide of blood ebbed. He saw Barbara's face, rebuking: "You knew they were dangerous," she had said about the lights. Had he really?

Leave me alone, he pleaded.

But he did not want to be left alone.

Not alone.

He stayed in bed most of Christmas Day, although both Eve and Josh came in to apologize or commiserate. He wasn't sure which. They had opened the windows to air out the house and he had said it was all right if they went out for Christmas dinner with Barbara and Ann. He knew it troubled them, not having him join them, but wisely they hadn't pressed the point. When they left, Benny jumped on his bed and burrowed his head into his chest. But he stank so badly of doggy odor that finally Jonathan had to swat him off. But the odor had given him some purposeful activity for the day.

Getting dressed, he went downstairs, first taking a peek at his orchids. To his dismay, they seemed to be browning along the petal edges, an ominous sign, surprising, since only yesterday they had been in mint condition.

"Don't mock me," he told them, proud of their beauty, especially compared with Barbara's more pedestrian plants. He watered them, offering whispered encouragement, then went down to his workroom, lifting a shaking Benny into the big cast-iron sink, which he filled with lukewarm water.

"You and me, kid. Merry Christmas," he told the frightened dog, whose brown eyes begged relief. As he scrubbed the stinking dog he remembered inexplicably their Gift of the Magi Christmas.

They had vowed to give each other something nonmaterial. He was a senior at Harvard Law then and they were tight for cash, barely able to survive on her job demonstrating kitchen gadgets at Macy's. By a stroke of providence—he used those terms then—he had gotten word about the job offer with the Federal Trade

Commission in Washington, providing, of course, that
he passed the bar exam. He kept the news from her for
nearly a week so that it would coincide with Christmas.
He had been curious, of course, about what she had gotten him, certain that, whatever she offered, his would
be the topper.

"I'm pregnant," she told him after he had made his
announcement.

It was, in a way, a total deception on her part. Fair
warning unheeded. He had hidden his confusion and
displeasure, wondering why she had complicated their
lives without consultation. The object is to control our
lives, not let our lives control us, he told her, and she
had agreed.

"But kids bring luck," she had said. "They're in-
centive."

She had sat on his lap, smothering his face with
kisses.

"I was worried sick you'd scold me. But here
you've come up with that fabulous job. Perfect timing."

"The Gift of the Magi," he had said, hugging her.
"A little love child."

The feeling of uncertainty quickly passed and he
remembered how by the end of that Christmas Day
they had become incredibly happy. Their future had begun.

He dried the dog and turned on the sauna. Leaving
Benny to dry in the workroom, he went upstairs for his
robe. The sauna relaxed him, sweated out his terrors,
and the dry heat and wet cold that the shower provided
left him mellow and relaxed. As he passed the sun-room
on the way back to the sauna he noted that the browning had increased on the orchids' petals and the stems
had begun to bend. Looking closely, he inspected the
plants, then dug his hands into the soil. The odor on his
fingertips was vaguely familiar, like the foam that had

spewed out of the fire extinguisher. It couldn't be. Another sniff confirmed his suspicion. Not Barbara, he thought. Hadn't she loved his orchids? Cimbidium was one of the few species that could be nourished indoors, and getting them to grow had been both a challenge and a chore. Not Barbara. Was she capable of that? Again he smelled his fingers. The odor was unmistakable. The confirmation removed his doubts. They were his orchids. *His.* For him to be the recipient of her wrath was one thing, but to vent one's frustration on a defenseless orchid was criminal. She's a murderess, he told himself. And a murderess must be punished.

He stormed about the house, thirsting for revenge, seeking a fitting punishment for this hideous crime. He went into the kitchen. Her domain. Opening cabinets, he looked over the myriad arrays of cooking equipment and foods, searching for something, although nothing specific had occurred to him.

Then he saw the neat silver bricks in the refrigerator. Removing one, he unwrapped it and sniffed at the meat. Of course, he thought with anticipatory pleasure. He contemplated the labels on the spice rack, removing containers of ginger, curry powder, and salt. Then he poured huge quantities over the loaf, kneaded them into the mix, and reshaped it to fit the tinfoil. He repeated the process with the other six bricks, using different spices, substituting sugar for salt, relishing the impending confusion as Barbara's customers argued among themselves what it was that had polluted the taste.

In the sauna he mourned the orchids, but the manner of his revenge had more than assuaged his sense of grief. He lay back on the redwood slats and felt the delicious heat sink into his flesh. For a moment the emptiness receded as he thought of the answer he had given to her message of death.

14

Harry Thurmont bore the brunt of her rage. Barbara had hurried over to his office after a most debilitating conversation with the Greek ambassador's wife.

"She said her guests were polite until two of them vomited, one directly on the table."

"That must have put a damper on things," Thurmont said, unsuccessfully trying to hide a smile.

"You're not taking this seriously, Harry. It's sabotage."

She was trying to control herself, to be cerebral rather than emotional. But her morning had been awful, absolutely awful. She had been summoned to the embassy at seven A.M. The ambassador and Mrs. Petrakis met her in the dining room, which smelled unmistakably of vomit. Without a word, they led her into the kitchen to view the evidence.

"Taste," the ambassador ordered. Their faces were dead white, their eyes bloodshot from lack of sleep. Barbara sniffed at the loaves, from which emanated peculiar odors.

"Taste." The ambassador repeated his order. From his wife's face Barbara could draw no pity, and she dutifully put a lump of meat in her mouth, spitting it out immediately.

"A caterer. You call yourself a caterer. You poisoned my guests."

She was too shocked to offer any explanation. Besides, her throat was paralyzed from humiliation.

"At first I thought the Turks had put you up to it."

"The Turks?"

"Then I decided I wouldn't dignify this sort of thing by putting it on the level of a diplomatic incident." His anger was accelerating. "It tastes like shit. *Shit*," he began to shout as his wife tried to calm him.

Barbara had run from the house in tears.

"I really believe we have an actionable issue here," she said calmly to Thurmont. "It's what we've been waiting for. He deliberately ruined the food." The memory made her stomach turn. "Not to mention the damage to my business. The loss of a client."

Thurmont stroked his chin.

"You have proof?"

"Who else could it be? I believe in Ann." She found herself strangely hesitant as the memory of Ann on Christmas Eve floated into her memory. Something barely detectable had surfaced and her mind fished for it. She had, she remembered, sensed the presence of Jonathan in the library, a fleeting sensation, just below the level of consciousness. She let the idea pass for the moment as Thurmont interrupted her thoughts.

"It won't hold up, Barbara. We could harass. But we won't win in a way that will satisfy you. It won't get him out of the house."

"He'll admit it. He'll have to admit it under oath."

"Barbara, do me a favor. Stop practicing law. Becoming an object of ridicule won't help your case."

She felt the provocation and her anger erupted.

"The orchids weren't a big deal. Not in comparison."

"The orchids?"

She hadn't intended to tell him, but now her words overflowed. She had told about the Christmas-tree fire but had left out the matter of the orchids.

"Christmas was ruined. I was throwing out buckets of foam. I saw the orchids and they made me angry. I'm afraid it wasn't very rational. Besides, I didn't know the stuff would kill them. That is, I wasn't sure. I wanted them injured. Not dead." He looked at her and shook his head in mock rebuke. She wondered when he would point a finger at her and say, Shame, shame.

"The name of the game is discipline, Barbara."

"It's easy for you to say."

"And I can't be available at every little crisis."

"*Little* crisis." She glared at him. "Harry, I can't lock up my food. I intend to make this business my livelihood. Why should he interfere with that? It's ... it's cruel, heartless."

"It's just that you need something more ... more damaging. More bizarre."

"You didn't do much with breaking and entering," Barbara huffed. But what he said had triggered the errant thought again of Ann and Christmas Eve.

"Something with moral turpitude," Thurmont continued. "You need a real hook."

"Like another woman?"

"Not necessarily." He looked at her shrewdly. "You need something that is damaging enough for a judge to say he'd better get out. It's a bad influence on the kids. A danger."

Jonathan was there. In the library on Christmas Eve. She was certain. She had sensed it, dismissed it. Little, innocent Ann.

"At least one good thing has come out of this," Thurmont said. "Jonathan can be provoked. If only the provocation wasn't so obvious. The thing you must avoid is the appearance of tit for tat. Judges don't appreciate that. It puts everything on a lower plane and the tendency is to compromise, which is exactly what we want to avoid."

"All right, Harry," she said smugly. "I won't be obvious."

What was obvious was that Harry Thurmont and the law could provide only the most limited of options. She was beginning to understand the process. He came around from his desk and stood before her.

"I have absolutely no objection to your driving him crazy, Barbara. But if he knows you're trying to drive him crazy, he won't go crazy. Do you understand that?"

"Perfectly." She smiled demurely, thinking about her new idea. He studied her in silence for a long moment.

"You look like the cat that swallowed the canary."

"Not swallowed, Harry. I've just discovered it chirping in its cage."

She had never really thought of the conception of Eve as an act of deceit. Loving, she had believed once, was more than just being together. Loving needed something tangible to validate it. And family wasn't real family without children. It was difficult now to reassess her state of mind at the time. It was too foreign to the present, to the end of love.

What she concluded was that her deliberate conception of Eve had not been out of love but out of fear. Perhaps it was merely intuitive at the time. Perhaps too, subconsciously, she had been frightened that her marriage was all there was or would ever be, a long, endless plateau of sameness. Jonathan, off to school each day.

Soon he would be off to a job, with meeting people, colleagues and clients. She loved those words, so exotic, full of promise and adventure. He, doing marvelous, exciting things. She, off to work at some dead-end job, doing silly things like demonstrating kitchen gadgets or selling ladies' underwear. Then, off to home, to prepare their dinner, to wait for her sun to rise. *Him.* The world was him. At the time, she must have thought it was the most wonderful way to live a life. Yet something, she must have sensed, was missing. *Something.* She was so sure then that it was a child. What was a woman's life without a child? Nature had decreed it to happen, hadn't it? It became her most pressing ambition. To have his child. *His.* That was why she had named the baby Eve. Joshua had come after that time had passed, merely because it seemed indecent to have an only child, and it was carefully planned that he would arrive just when Eve started nursery school. It was a time to be practical.

Looking at things in retrospect wasn't really fair, she decided, deriding the idea of "fair." Nothing was fair. Even the thought came to her in Harry Thurmont's voice, because he had said that to her and she had been immediately convinced.

"Fair is weather. Fair is not so good. Fair is a shindig. But fair is not life."

"Do you think he has any ladyfriends?" she had asked Ann one day. Her back was turned as she labored over a huge colander in one of the sinks, laying out leaves of romaine lettuce for a batch of *salade niçoise* she was making for a luncheon later that day. It was morning. The kids had just been sent off to school and Ann was lingering over a second cup of coffee.

Ann did not respond.

"Ladyfriends," Barbara repeated. "I mean it seems logical. What do you think he does every night? After all, a man is different from a woman."

When Ann still hadn't responded, Barbara turned toward her. "What do you think?" she pressed.

"I have no idea," Ann answered, avoiding Barbara's eyes. Clever bitch, Barbara thought.

"He's still a man."

"I haven't had much experience."

Barbara sensed Ann's discomfort and proceeded cautiously.

"Do you suppose he's seeing prostitutes?" she wondered aloud.

"I doubt that."

The response was whispered, almost furtive.

"You do? Why so?" Barbara turned again to watch her cope with her confusion, sure now that Ann was responding to the bait.

"He just doesn't seem like that kind of person," Ann said, her face flushing. Barbara pressed on.

"Men don't really care where they put it. They seem to have a very low threshold of pleasure compared to women. I never did understand it. That thing of his. Always saluting. How do they carry that around with them all the time? Like a popgun ready to go off."

She had gotten up and brought the cup and saucer to the dishwasher, sliding the rack out and placing them on it.

"I hope I'm not embarrassing you, Ann," Barbara said. "I suppose he's unhappy as hell. Probably thinks I put a detective on his trail. Not so. It doesn't really matter. He could even have an affair in this house and it wouldn't matter." She held her breath.

"It's none of my business," Ann protested, unable to hide her irritation.

"I know, Ann." She paused. "Actually, I wish it would happen. Another woman might solve things for us."

"What about another man? For you?"

Barbara laughed.

"I'm not going to fall into that trap so easily again."

"Trap?"

"It is a trap, Ann."

"And love?" Ann asked. The question seemed reckless, involuntary.

"Love? What's your opinion?" Barbara turned in time to see Ann blush scarlet. Good, she thought, remembering love.

"I have no opinion."

"Come now, Ann," Barbara snapped. "Surely you've had that I-can't-live-without-you feeling. That clutching of the heart, those palpitations of desire."

"I don't think about it," Ann replied nervously. "I'm too busy with my studies."

"Don't you?"

"It's not a priority. That's all."

Perhaps she had gone too far. Certainly she had stirred things up. She retreated quickly, sure now of this newly discovered weapon. Yet she was fond of Ann, and using this tactic made Barbara uncomfortable.

"I'm sorry, Ann," she said, half sincerely. "It's beginning to get to me. All this strain. Perhaps if I went away. Maybe up to Boston to visit my parents. And took the kids." She was being deliberately hypothetical, waiting for some reaction. But none came. Ann got up and started to move away.

"What do you think?" Barbara asked hurriedly.

"About what?" Ann asked.

"About me going away for a weekend with the kids."

"I don't know, Barbara."

You know exactly what to think, Ann, Barbara thought, laying the anchovies on the salad mound.

15

The children's excitement at going to Boston masked Ann's own. She helped them pack and wrote down a great list of instructions that Barbara had given her, mostly about shopping and defrosting, so that Barbara would be able to meet her commitments when she came back Monday morning. Ann had also promised to feed Mercedes.

"I'll miss you all," she cried, embracing each of them at the door, waving as they ran down the walk to the waiting taxi. She stood in the doorway for a long time, hoping they would see her lone figure.

But when they had gone, she wanted to shout for joy. Alone with Jonathan. It was all she had thought about. She hoped she had successfully kept Barbara's suspicions at bay. But that was merely a detail now. All's fair in love and war, she thought gleefully. Not that he had ever given her the slightest encouragement, especially after his apology for the incident in the library on Christmas Eve.

"I'm sorry," he had said, revealing both his vulnerability and his guilt.

She took a long, lingering bubble bath, perfumed and powdered herself, and put on a flimsy peignoir. She knew she was no physical match for Barbara. Ann's figure was spare but well proportioned, her breasts and buttocks small. Serviceable, she told herself, reflecting on her meager experience. Nothing had moved her as much as that brief moment with Jonathan. Nothing.

She hadn't told Jonathan of her conversation with Barbara, which had agitated her. At the same time, it made her feel safer. Jonathan, she was certain, believed that he was being watched and conducted himself accordingly. Perhaps now, possessed of the knowledge that Barbara had given her, she could allay his fears.

Nothing would have made her happier than to be the chatelaine of this lovely house. Was it a stroke of fate that Barbara had decided to divorce him so soon after she had arrived in the house? It was incomprehensible that Barbara could reject such a good and loving man. *Impossible.*

Ann had lit a fire in the library, selected a book from the shelves, and, while the words swam before her, concentrated on picking out his familiar step on the sidewalk and Benny's heralding bark. To calm herself, she opened the armoire and poured some vodka.

She hadn't long to wait. He appeared surprised when he saw her sitting in the library.

"I hadn't realized," he began. "I thought you might have gone away as well."

"Here I am."

He went to the armoire and poured himself a scotch, turning to look at her. He shook his head and smiled gently.

"You drop a spark on dry kindling and you get fire," he said, lifting his glass.

"Nature's way," she said, smiling.

"You're taking advantage of a peculiar situation," he warned with mock sarcasm.

"I know."

"It won't do either of us any good. Certainly not yourself, Ann."

"So I've been forewarned." She was surprised at her boldness. He walked to the window and, parting the drapes, looked into the street. Then he turned to face her.

"I feel uncomfortable," he confessed. "That last episode nearly unnerved me." He swallowed hard and his eyes roamed over the Staffordshire pieces on the mantelpiece. "It took years to collect those pieces."

"I know," she said.

His hand swept the air. "All those beautiful things. This house. I'm not going to let her have it, Ann. She doesn't deserve it." His belligerence was tangible, aggressive.

He sat down opposite her. "There's a lot of pain in this process. Some people might think it's self-inflicted. I could walk away. Say good-bye. Kiss it off. And start all over again." He looked up at her suddenly. "I'll bet that's what you think. Walk away and start all over again." She was shocked at the accusatory tone.

"No," she said cautiously. "I'm also a fighter for the things I want." But he ignored her, still focusing on the cause of his animosity.

"She's just being ornery. A bitch," he said. "Maybe it was there all the time. This meanness. But I was too stupid to see it." He shook his head. "I can't get rid of the anger. It's like a perpetual flame. Every time I think about it I get mad. Mad at myself. Mad at Goldstein, as if it were his fault that he's putting me through this. Mad at Thurmont because I know the bastard is advising her. Mad at my kids for not taking my side." He looked at her.

"Mostly I'm mad at myself for not having been what I thought I was."

"You're too hard on yourself, Jonathan."

"My ego died a few months ago." He turned away, and she saw the mist in his eyes. She moved toward him and embraced his head, kissing his hair. She felt motherly, incestuous. Opening her robe, she moved her breasts to his mouth.

"Let me love you," she begged, knowing he was beyond resisting, aching for comfort.

Her cheeks felt hot and the alcohol had rushed to her head. His body shook with sobs.

"Cry, darling," she urged, caressing him. She felt the power of her womanhood as she reached for his organ, caressing it, undressing him.

"You're beautiful," she said. He stood up and the joy of seeing him made her shiver with pleasure. Kneeling before him, she kissed him there. His response was immediate.

"I'm sorry," he whispered.

She drew him down to the couch and snuggled beside him. They lay together, hardly moving. She listened to the rhythm of his heartbeat.

"Thank you," he said when he stirred again.

He opened the armoire and grabbed a vodka bottle by the neck. Then, taking her hand, he led her up the stairs to his room. She had never been inside it since he had moved into it.

The room was dusty and had a foul, musky odor. It was in complete disarray, with files and papers strewn over all available surfaces. She saw a hot plate on the open desk of the Hepplewhite secrétaire and unwashed dishes on the japanned commode. Liquor bottles, some half filled, lay about the room. He caught her expression of distaste.

"What did you expect?"

She embraced him, hoping to soothe him. But he broke away and picked up a Staffordshire figure that stood next to the dirty dishes.

"Queen Victoria," he said, pointing to the figure. "Like my life, I guess. A forgery. We got stung in Atlantic City. I keep it around to remind me of my stupidity."

His tone was ominous and she wondered if she had contributed to his mood. She watched his eyes sweep the room.

"Look what's become of my life," he snapped.

"It'll pass, Jonathan," she said lamely. But he was not to be placated.

"I have to hide all my personal records in here. I don't want her to overvalue the house. I've had to research all the receipts and insurance estimates. What a waste of time and energy."

He brought two tumblers in from the bathroom, poured some vodka, then opened the window and brought in a carton of orange juice. He poured some into the tumblers.

He had spent long hours locked in this room. She had been curious about what he did there, and once she had listened at the door. There was no television set. Few books. It struck her as more of an animal's lair than a man's room. Among the odors she picked out was Benny's doggy smell, noting that he had somehow followed them into the room and now lay sprawled on an Art Deco rug beside the bed. Its beige background was stained, dirty.

She went to the bathroom, complete with bidet, which she used, mirrored walls, marble floors, and gold-plated plumbing fixtures. This room, too, was a mess.

"I'm not much of a housekeeper," he said when Ann came out. "I haven't had much practice. My generation depended too much on women."

"What about the maid?"

"I won't even let her in here. Barbara's ally." He looked at her strangely. "You think I'm paranoid?"

The question seemed aggressive and she ignored it, sitting on the high bed.

"So what are you going to do with your life, Ann?" he asked suddenly, as if dismissing his own gloomy thoughts.

"Jefferson is my life for the present," she mumbled. I'd like to be included in yours, she told him silently.

He looked at her kindly and touched her bare shoulder.

"You're a gift, Ann. A gift to the children. A special gift to me."

Barbara had offered gratitude as well and it pained her now. She felt a sense of her inferiority, but dared not ask him for comparisons.

"I'm not just giving, Jonathan. I'm taking, also."

He stopped caressing her. "Now you sound like her."

She felt a wave of panic. She had acquired a sense of independence and a posture of equality. It did not seem queer to voice her affection in those terms. She saw the gap now. He was of a different generation, with a different way of looking at women. So that's it, she decided, feeling odd waves of insight, as well as a sense of alliance with Barbara.

"Nobody wants to be dependent anymore," he said gloomily. "Whatever happened to man the hunter, man the protector?"

"Some people just don't accept the idea of males being lord and master anymore."

"I wasn't, really. We were a team. I was supportive of all her attempts at independence. How could I have known that the bitch was lying to me all those years? It was an act." His features became rigid. "Maybe this is an act as well." He pouted.

"It's no act," she said, determined to overlook his anger.

"I'm a little wary of the sincerity of women." He sighed.

"Now you're generalizing," she replied sensibly, scolding, yet trying to keep an air of lightness between them.

"Maybe so," he agreed. "I haven't known too many women. And the one woman I thought I knew I didn't know at all. That's what bugs me the most, the imprecision of my understanding of her, of what she was feeling and thinking all those years." He looked at Ann, then gave a sigh of resignation. "I don't think I'll ever again be able to believe what a woman tells me, or shows me."

"I can understand that," Ann said. "We're a clandestine gender. Lots of dirty little secrets that we've been conditioned to suppress."

"So have men," he replied quickly.

"Well, then, now that we understand each other . . ." She reached out to him and drew him to her. They made love slowly, tenderly, with less greed and transience than before. This time he did not preempt the act. Finally, he rolled over and lay beside her, their fingers locked together. Turning toward him, she watched his eyelids flutter.

"There is one thing," she whispered. "Why the house? Why? Considering that the family has already been split apart. It's only a thing. And all the possessions inside it are things. Why all the pain over the house?"

His eyelids fluttered open.

"A thing? You don't understand. It's the whole

world. Why should I let her take the whole world with her?"

"But it's also part of her world," Ann said gently.

"It can't be shared any longer. Not like this."

"Then why don't you simply sell it and split the value?"

"I'm willing to give her half the value. I paid for it. My brains. My sweat. *Christ.*"

He was frowning and she had the impression he was talking by rote, like an actor going over his lines in rehearsal. Suddenly he stopped talking and was staring at something on top of the bed canopy.

"What is it, Jonathan?" she asked. He moved leisurely from the bed and crossed the room. Slowly, with quiet deliberation, he moved a chair to a corner of the room and stood on it. He was naked and the act seemed odd and incongruous. She lifted herself on one elbow to observe him, but before she could speak he shook his head and put a finger to his lips. Stretching, he peered over the canopy's side, then stepped down again. He took a robe from the closet.

With a finger still on his lips, he quietly opened the door and went into the corridor. By then she was too curious to stay and she followed him into Eve's room, which was next to his. Ignoring her, he kneeled and began to feel along the baseboard. Then, finding a wire, he traced it along the side of one of Eve's bookcases. It snaked through a tiny hole near the floor.

"Bastards," he muttered, crawling, following the wire. It led from Eve's room, along the baseboard of the corridor, then upward again, to the window overlooking the garden. He bounded down the back stairs. She followed quickly behind him. He was lost in concentration. She watched him select a big knife from the wooden box on the kitchen island. Curiosity gave way to fright. She hung back in the shadows while he passed in front of her again and slowly opened the door to the garden.

When it was fully opened, he sprang out and, crouching, ran across the yard to the garage, flinging open the back door. She heard noises, groans, then silence. A light was switched on, bathing the quiet garden in a yellowish haze.

Disregarding the cold, she padded along the moist grass to the garage window. What she saw choked a scream in her throat. Jonathan had a knife to a man's throat. He was a little man in glasses, pale and frightened. She could see the indentation where the knife point pinched the skin.

He drew the man alongside a beige van, with an open side door, through which she could see lighted television screens and tape-recording equipment. Barbara had taken her station wagon and the van was parked in its place. Next to it was Eve's Honda and beside that, encased in its cover, Jonathan's Ferrari.

She saw the two men disappear into the van through the side door.

Then she saw the tape reels come crashing out of the van, unraveling on the cement garage floor. The man was screeching in protest. When they emerged again, Jonathan held the man in a hammerlock, the knife still pressed to his throat.

". . . just doing my job," she heard the man cackle in fear. Jonathan said nothing. A vein palpitated in his forehead. She had never seen him in this state.

Squinting into the glare of the naked garage bulb, viewing this scene of repressed rage and violence, she saw everything in isolation, without connection to herself. Jonathan removed the knife point from the man's neck and looked into the cab of the van. From its seat he grabbed an object, which Ann recognized as Barbara's electronic door opener. He looked at it for a moment, shrugged, then pointed it toward the heavy door, which opened with a rumble. Then he ordered the man into the driver's seat. The motor of the van caught and accelerated. A cloud of exhaust filled the air as it backed out of the garage. Reversing quickly, it headed full speed down the alley.

But as it moved, tires squealing on the asphalt, a shattering scream rent the air, a sound of deep pain. The van did not stop, but the sound had shocked Ann into movement and she ran along the gravel path around the garage, ignoring the sharp pain on her bare feet. Jonathan was standing over something, a still, black shape.

"The son of a bitch has run over Mercedes," Jonathan said, and knelt beside the dead animal.

The events were jumbled in her mind. She was frightened and the distorted, broken animal made her suddenly nauseated and she had a spasm of dry heaves.

"Serves the bitch right," Jonathan muttered. She could not recognize his voice. He stabbed his knife into the air and, winding up like a baseball pitcher, flung it into the darkness.

16

He sent Ann up to her own room and spent the next few hours dismantling the television equipment and removing the wire. Then he smashed the camera with a sledgehammer and threw the pieces into the kitchen garbage compactor. When everything was sufficiently flattened, he carted the refuse out to the trash cans in the alley.

He had worked in a sustained rage, unthinking, not conscious of his actions. As the heat of anger abated he felt himself unstiffen. His mind began to clear and his reason returned.

Stripping the cover off his Ferrari and removing the fiberglass top, he climbed in, felt the cool leather, and breathed deeply, savoring its aroma. Opening the glove compartment, he removed the key, placed it in the ignition, and flicked it. The eight cylinders caught almost immediately and the engine purred, soothing him.

It was a toy, really, but it gave him pleasure and he mothered it like a baby, changing its plugs, keeping it shined and covered. It was three years old, a work of art, and he knew its value was appreciating rapidly. Fifty thousand dollars' worth of car.

Perhaps, he thought, he should take this one acknowledged personal possession and ride off into the night, a lone cowboy, in search of new adventures, a new life, leaving the old behind. Me and my little red Ferrari, he thought, feeling the wheel, the close, warm security of the tight driver's seat. He stepped on the accelerator, listening to the satisfying whisper of the 205-horsepower engine. A 3,200-pound magic carpet.

Finally, reality intruded. He remembered Mercedes. Surely Barbara was responsible for its death. He climbed out of the Ferrari and shoved the cat into a plastic bag. Putting the crushed body into the seat beside him, he carefully backed the car out and sped over the darkened streets. The wind felt good, relaxing him. Momentarily forgetting the incident, he let himself merge with the Ferrari's power, savoring the sense of freedom. An escape. When he reached Memorial Bridge, he stopped, grabbed the neck of the plastic bag, and flung it into the Potomac River.

By disposing of Mercedes, he assured himself, he would spare the children any embarrassment over their mother's wanton act. She had used their child's room for her filthy spying. That was a crime worse than the spying itself, a disgusting act. It was no wonder that Mercedes had been killed. It was retribution. Let them think the cat was lost.

When he returned, he tucked in the Ferrari. Then he gathered up the tapes and burned them in the library fireplace. Nixon should have done this, he thought, watching the plastic curl and turn quickly to ashes. He wished it were Barbara.

At seven in the morning he called Goldstein and told him what had happened.

"Meet me at the delicatessen on Grubb Road,"

Goldstein said, responding to Jonathan's agitation. "We'll put some Jewish soul food in you. It will calm you down."

Goldstein was waiting in a booth, smearing globs of cream cheese on a dark brown bagel, on which he then placed two strips of Nova Scotia lox. His mouth was full and he pointed to a platter on the other side of the table.

"I want to take her to court. Invasion of privacy. Something. Anything."

Goldstein continued to chew without pause.

"Well, what you intend to do about it?"

"I'm thinking."

"You're eating."

"You think it's impossible to eat and think at the same time?"

"Nothing's impossible."

Goldstein quickly finished all the food on his plate and lit a cigar.

"Now I'm finished thinking," he said, blowing smoke toward the ceiling. Goldstein puffed again and began to speak.

"The strategy was as follows. Remember the objective. The house. The whole house. To make their case better, they want you out. Anyhow, any way. They catch you red-handed with the governess—"

"Not really a governess. Sort of an *au pair* girl." Jonathan was surprised at his odd defensiveness, as if he wanted to raise her in his own esteem.

"But involved with the children."

"You might say that."

"I did say that. They go to the judge and say you have been *shtupping* their child's governess. You are an unfit father, a moral threat to the children. *Shtupping* her under their noses, so to speak. Such an immoral action is dangerous to the children's welfare, et cetera, et cetera. They get an injunction. You go. The governess goes. You're finally out of the house."

"It's ruthless. She's an innocent."

"Sounds to me she's not so innocent."

"I don't mean that. She's only a bystander. She doesn't have to be hit with a bag of shit."

"Anybody within spitting distance of a divorce gets slopped with it. It can't be helped. Don't be such a dummy. Your lovely wife set you up. Leaving you alone in the house with a young, attractive girl. Am I right?"

"Yes."

"You are a sexually deprived man, right?"

Jonathan pointed a finger directly at Goldstein's chest. "That's entrapment. I want her in court."

"You want to have the gumshoe testify. Then what's-her-name. And the press comes. Before you know it, it's the plot for a pornographic movie. You want to subject your kids to that?"

Jonathan looked down at his plate of lox, cream cheese, and bagels. His stomach turned. He reached into his pocket for a Maalox and popped one into his mouth.

"Anyway, you destroyed the evidence. So they have nothing to go on. It was their move and they blew it." Goldstein looked covetously at Jonathan's plate. He pointed with the cigar. "You gonna have that?" Jonathan pushed the plate toward him and Goldstein began to eat.

"The inhumanity of human beings depresses me. And when I get depressed, I eat." Goldstein sighed through a full mouth, raising his shoulders to fill his lungs with air. Jonathan waited for him to swallow. The process seemed interminable.

"It is a kind of theater of the absurd." Jonathan sighed. "They do it with technology. Gadgets. Divorce is now show business. Nothing is sacred anymore."

"Only marriage is sacred. Not divorce."

Goldstein's philosophical homilies tried his patience. He is practicing his ex-profession on me, Jonathan thought, realizing that Goldstein's self-image was a far cry from the stubby little man with drooping eyelids, heavy jowls, and a paunch like an inflated balloon under his pants. He wore his pants high, a black leather belt strapped around what seemed to be his chest. Naked, Jonathan speculated, he must look like an overstuffed cherub.

"When you talk like that, I have to look behind you to see if you sprouted wings," Jonathan said. He knew Goldstein was winding up for a sermon.

"You can destroy the legal basis for the family," he began. "But the biological basis lives on. Thurmont has no regard for the human equation. *Ess iss nisht gut fur der kinder.* It is not good for the children. A *shanda.* A shame." Goldstein shook his head; his bald pate glistened beneath the overhead lights. "My advice now is as follows." He paused, drew in his breath. He saw himself, Jonathan was certain, as Moses the lawgiver coming down from Mount Sinai with the tablets clutched to his breast. "Ignore it. It never happened. They tried. They lost. If she doesn't bring it up, you don't bring it up. I'll talk to Thurmont. If someone brings it up, the children get involved. If the children get involved, they'll try to show you're a bad influence, which is what they tried to do in the first place."

"How can I ignore it? And there's Ann to consider. I don't know if it can be handled." He shook his head. "Barbara won't keep her mouth shut. She'll make Ann's life hell."

"If only you were a student of the Talmud, Rose. With such a biblical name like Jonathan. A *shanda.* Listen to me. Think of me not as a Murray, but as a David. David and Jonathan. Friends. Biblically speaking, Barbara will not jeopardize her own reputation as 'good mother.' You said yourself she is a good mother. You even thought she was a good wife. So why tempt guilt? Custody of the children for you won't do them any good. You have a practice. You travel. Think of me also as your spiritual advisor. Guilt won't do you any good. We Jews know about guilt." He paused, searching internally for the relief of a belch, which came in a loud, cascading rumble. "Sometimes a good *greps* gets rid of the cobwebs of the mind. A confrontation now is not smart. Don't upset the children. Tell Ann to stay."

"Suppose she won't."

"You said she loves you. For love, women do many stupid things."

"Like getting married," Jonathan said, suddenly assailed by a flash of memory of a younger Barbara.

"Love should never be the basis of marriage. It's a business proposition from the beginning. Read the Talmud, Rose. It will make you a *mensh.*"

Goldstein stubbed the remains of his half-smoked cigar into the greasy plate.

"The whole idea is repugnant," Jonathan said. "As a matter of fact, I'm getting tired of the way I'm living. If only she was reasonable. What's wrong with half?"

"Remember King Solomon and the baby?"

"What the hell has that got to do with it?"

"Our case rests with Solomon. We will have to prove we are the real mother of the house."

"But the real mother was willing to give up the child rather than see it destroyed." Jonathan was proud of his insight, but Goldstein looked at him sadly, his droopy lids fluttering.

"So who got the child?"

"I don't understand any of this," Jonathan said, getting up. Goldstein pulled him down again.

"The real mother."

He hurried away from the delicatessen in panic, more confused than when he had arrived. He found Ann in her room, packing.

"I'm going," she said. Her eyes were puffy from crying.

"Where?"

"I don't know. I only know I can't stay here. I'd rather make the break before she forces me to." Her suitcase was battered and one clasp was broken. He felt as if he had deliberately thrown her out on the street.

"Goldstein says you don't have to go."

"Then let Goldstein come here and stay." She turned toward him. "It can't work. She will know that we've had a . . . relationship. The detective will tell her. You're still her husband. Legally."

"But we're supposed to be leading separate lives—"

"And I can't see myself facing the children." She looked up at him and touched his cheek gently. "I hate seeing this happen to this family, Jonathan. I feel as if somehow I wished it to happen."

"Tell it to Goldstein. He's an expert on guilt."

She moved her face against his chest and he embraced her, feeling the heat of her cheek against him.

"I know I love you, Jonathan. I can't stand the idea of it under these circumstances. I've never had this kind of experience before and I don't know how to cope with it."

"Frankly, Ann, I haven't either." He remembered Goldstein again.

"Then, Ann . . ." He hesitated, doubting his sincerity, although he had admitted to himself he was moved by her. "If you love me." He paused.

"Please, Jonathan. Don't do that to me."

He was angry at himself. He disengaged and

turned toward the dormer window. It was a cloudy, gloomy day.

"Then let me ask you as a friend. If that's possible. I don't even want us to think of ourselves as lovers. I don't want to use you. All I want you to do is to stay a while longer. Goldstein says Barbara might not bring it up, for the children's sake. And I really believe that they'll be heartbroken if you leave now. And they'll suspect something that they don't really need to know about. Just for a little while."

She shook her head.

"I don't think I can, Jonathan. I haven't got that kind of pluck."

"Well, then, be selfish. Think of your own financial needs."

"There is too much selfishness around here as it is." She seemed instantly apologetic and her eyes began to fill with tears.

"For crying out loud, Ann"—Jonathan felt himself erupting—"we're not evil people."

"It's only a house, Jonathan. You can get another one. And these"—she waved her arms in the air—"are only things."

"She has no right to all of them." He turned away, his eyes now vague and inert.

"It's an obsession and it's making you and her do crazy things. I saw you out there last night with that knife. Nothing else mattered. I can't imagine why you didn't stick it into that man's neck. I felt certain you were going to do it. That's another thing, Jonathan. I don't like to see you people disintegrate. Even what Barbara did to me. I just don't see it as the real Barbara. If only you both could see what you're becoming." The long speech seemed to make her winded and she sat down on the sleigh bed. "I didn't like being a spectator to this. And I don't like being a participant."

He moved back toward her and sat down on the bed, touching the curled edges of the wood. He seemed mentally adrift, searching for a piece of flotsam.

"We found the damned thing in Middleburg," he said, speaking slowly. At first she was confused by the sudden change of subject. "It's part of the French phase of the early Federal period, built around 1810. We had it refinished. You know, when you refinish an antique, you hurt its value. Crazy, isn't it? We liked the idea of it. What marvelous fantasies those people had. A bed like a sleigh. Closing your eyes and going off to a peaceful slumber in a sleigh."

"They're still only things, Jonathan."

"I used to think that myself. But they're more than that. They're dreams, as if you're stepping into someone else's life. You begin to wonder how many others slept in this bed, what they thought about, how they looked at life." His eyes swept the room. "They're more than objects. Just thinking about them prolongs their life. Maybe life is a dream."

"I know they're beautiful. I understand your feelings about them. But they're still not flesh and blood. They don't feel. People are what count."

She turned toward him, and he embraced her. She felt his breath in her ear. "And I love the kids," she said. "I'm really attached to them. There's nothing I won't do for them. I think they've been fantastic soldiers through all this. They've gone beyond the call of children's duty to their parents."

"I know," he whispered. The mention of the children seemed to snap him back to alertness and he backed away. "And I don't want to see them hurt any more than they have to be. As a matter of fact, I've decided to send them to camp for the summer. They're better off away from here while all this is going on."

Actually, the idea had just occurred to him. Ann

could leave when they left. He hoped she would reach this conclusion on her own. Then another dilemma intruded. He and Barbara would be alone in the house for two whole months. *Alone.* He shuddered, wondering again how he had slipped into this purgatory. There was something happening to him, he acknowledged. Perhaps he was losing his self-esteem, his sense of manhood. Certainly he had lost control of events. He turned toward her again, seeking validation, searching for lost power. He embraced her, feeling aroused instantly.

"Save me, Ann," he begged.

"All right, Jonathan," she whispered as he began to undress her.

"I'm sorry," he mumbled. "Damn you, Goldstein."

"Goldstein?"

"He said women in love invariably do stupid things."

"He was right," she said. He grasped her, as a drowning man reaches for a lifeline.

17

Josh and his grandfather had shot the rabbits and she had packed them in ice, still unskinned, and driven them home. Earlier, she had eviscerated fifteen of the two dozen at her father's, bringing home the useful innards in plastic bags. The rest hung on pothooks, like punished criminals, above the kitchen island. She took them down one at a time, slit each lengthwise down its belly, and peeled away the fur. Then she slit open the rib cage, removed the entrails, sliced away at the meat, and put the strips in a large bowl.

Rabbit *pâté* had struck her as a novel idea and she had persuaded the French Market to try it. She was thankful that the work temporarily diverted her attention from the weekend's disaster. She had gotten Thurmont's call on Sunday. Everything had gone wrong. The detective was upset and threatening. He had demanded payment immediately, alleging that Jonathan had stolen some of his equipment, the remains of which she had already seen in the trash cans.

She hadn't been at all comfortable in what she had done. But, she told herself, she'd had no choice. If only he would understand and move out once and for all. She was surprised, too, that the episode had given her a twinge of jealousy. She considered the perils of male celibacy and knew that, under the right circumstances, Jonathan would react. Often when he came home after a long trip, he had fallen on her like a horny beast. She had dutifully submitted, of course, less out of sexual enjoyment than of validating her role as wife again. It was all part of the programming and gave her more reason to detest her former self.

In a way, she felt relieved that she would not have to confront the detective's evidence. But that softness in herself angered her and she hacked away at the rabbits as if they were tangible enemies. Who was the real enemy? Herself? Jonathan? Ann? She wanted to apologize to Ann. She was not being her true self. Her behavior was merely a device, a tactic. In war, people did things out of character, suspended compassion, kindness, consideration.

Thurmont had forbidden any discussion of the subject.

"Leave it alone. We blew it," he had barked into the phone, forestalling any protests on her part by hanging up abruptly.

The evidence in the trash cans testified to Jonathan's wrath. That, too, seemed completely out of character. Jonathan had always been cerebral, nonviolent, and rarely had he lost his temper. He was never out of control. It was another trait that she had grown to despise, his cool-headedness.

"Show me an emotion out of control and I'll show you certain defeat." He had burned that lesson into her and she was trying her best to follow his advice.

She had, she thought, pulled off her first meeting with Ann that morning with expert acting prowess. Not that they had exchanged any more than the most prosaic words about the weather, the weekend. She had begun a long, one-sided account of their trip, as if nothing had occurred between them. Ann had been remarkably cool, although little lip tremors and nervously shifting eyes revealed the tension between them. It was only when Ann went off to school that Barbara's real anger surfaced. The little bitch fucked Jonathan under my roof, in the room next to my daughter's bed. She ran up a full steam of rancor, which somehow increased the speed with which she hacked apart the rabbits.

The unusual circumstances had interfered with her morning routine and it wasn't until she put the rabbit livers and the other meat in the grinder that she realized that she hadn't seen or fed Mercedes. Barbara searched in the usual bunks around the kitchen, then poked around the cat's favorite haunts in the garden and the rafters of the garage.

"Mercedes," she called, offering familiar signals. She gave up in frustration and went back into the kitchen. Perhaps Ann had forgotten about Mercedes, considering how busy the girl had been, Barbara thought with a smirk.

After she had ground the rabbit meat, along with veal and pork, and added the onion and garlic to the mix, she called the animal pound, carefully describing the cat to the attendant.

"Call animal removal. She may have been run over."

Getting through to them was a bureaucratic nightmare, and when she did finally, it was futile. She was thankful that no dead animals had been reported. But it wasn't like Mercedes to disappear. She had raised her from a kitten; she had rarely strayed in the daytime, sometimes making a pest of herself as she clawed her way about the kitchen shelves. She would have to ask Ann when she returned. After all, Mercedes had been entrusted to her care. The irony disturbed Barbara. She felt more compassion for the missing Mercedes than for Jonathan. If only he had disappeared.

She mixed wine, cognac, salt, pepper, thyme, parsley, and oil in a small bowl, then added the mixture to the meat bowl, covered it, and put it in the refrigerator. Cold took the gaminess out of the meat. Before she closed the door, her eyes lingered a moment on the mixture and she thought again of the incident with the meat pastry on Christmas Day. *"Bastard,"* she cried.

Opening the garden door, she again called for Mercedes. Jonathan had never really liked the cat, and Barbara had always felt he had gotten Benny out of spite. Nor did he understand how it was possible for a woman to have a relationship with a female cat. She was sure Mercedes was the only one of the family who really understood her and it was to Mercedes that she had poured out her secret thoughts. Mercedes was wise and true, more perceptive and sensitive than the others. She could always be counted on for affection.

Once she had jumped on Jonathan's bare buttocks while he and Barbara were having sex, drawing blood and pain. He had insisted the cat be declawed, but since Barbara had already yielded on spaying, she refused.

"You can't take away her claws," she had rebuked. "She wouldn't have anything to fight back with."

"Or to attack me with," Jonathan had protested. The irony hit home now. Men just don't understand the female animal, she thought.

But she had suffered with Benny sleeping in their room for years, barking at every rustle or creak of the house, sometimes humping her leg with that ugly, distended red thing. The children showed little interest in caring for either animal and they became his and hers by default.

"Hasn't she come home?" Ann's response to Barbara's inquiry was neither convincing nor encouraging.

"Why else would I have asked?" Barbara said politely, avoiding a confrontation. Besides, Ann had quickly turned away.

Barbara was not, of course, reassured and Mercedes did not come back. Unable to sleep that night, she dressed early and went down to the kitchen to finish her rabbit *pâté*. Again remembering the meat pastry, she tasted the mixture to be sure no one had tampered with it. The memory inflamed her and she beat the eggs with uncommon zeal, mixing them into the flour to make a smooth paste. Cooking was surely her therapy, but it did not calm her now. Sometimes, making a dish could absorb her entire concentration. Now she found it difficult to focus her attention. It was a struggle to line the loaf pan with bacon slices, pack in the meat, press down the corners to avoid air holes. She even forgot to top the loaf off with bacon slices, bay leaves, and parsley stems, and had to remove the pan from the oven to finish the chore.

When it was back in the oven, she went out into the streets, searching for Mercedes, sensing it was futile. Was it possible that Jonathan had destroyed the innocent Mercedes in retaliation? It was difficult to get herself to believe that he was capable of destroying her helpless pet. Brooding over that possibility unnerved her. Still, she couldn't find Mercedes. She had also lost track of time. It was four hours later when she returned and she could tell by the odor of singed meat that she had forgotten to set the oven and had ruined the *pâté*. That only increased her irritability.

She called Thurmont.

"I think he's destroyed Mercedes," she blurted into the phone.

"Your car?"

"My cat."

"Are you sure?"

"I'm getting there. She hasn't come back in two days. That's never happened before. Ann is an anointed martyr and is being noncommittal. But Mercedes was an innocent animal. I can't believe he was capable of doing something so monstrous." She felt a sob begin in her chest.

"It's only a cat, for crying out loud."

"You men don't understand what a cat means. There's some strange chemistry, a different kind of love . . ."

"Have you got any proof?"

"Well, Mercedes is gone. That's proof enough. I put her in Ann's care. I figure that Jonathan's anger pushed him to it. Look what he did with that man's equipment, for crying out loud." Her lips began to tremble and she could not find her voice.

"Just don't do anything stupid," Thurmont said. But she could not respond and hung up. Unable to control her sobbing, she went upstairs, took a Valium, and fell into a dead sleep.

She awoke to the big clock in the foyer chiming eleven, which confused her, but helped bring back her sense of time and with it the depression inspired by Mercedes' disappearance. She heard Benny's bark and Jonathan's tread as he came up the stairs. She dashed out to the hall to meet him.

"You did something to Mercedes," she cried. She could hear Eve's stereo playing in the background.

"That's quite an accusation," Jonathan responded. He looked rumpled and unusually tired.

"I demand an explanation," she said, feeling the hatred rise. Her entire nervous system seemed to vibrate. "I didn't think you were capable of that."

"So you've already tried and convicted me."

"She was an innocent. She was all mine. That's why you did it."

He looked up and down the corridor.

"All right. Come down to the workroom so the kids can't hear."

Her knees shook as she followed him, watching the back of his head. His hair seemed grayer now. She remembered how upset he had been when the first speckle of salt appeared among the jet-black strands. He was twenty-eight, and she had teased him about it. "My old man," she had called him. "As long as you grow old with me. The best is yet to be," she had said. A lump rose in her throat and she wiped the memory from her mind. She would not let sentiment destroy her resolve.

He paused for a moment to switch on the sauna, then he moved to a corner of the workroom and leaned against a workbench, fiddling with the handle of a vise. She hung back, fearful of going near any of the tools or machinery. Once she had worked side by side with him, learning how to use everything. He had been patient, teaching her the intricacies. Now the equipment frightened her. He took off his jacket and removed his tie.

"Your little pussy has met his maker."

The words, coming so unexpectedly, shocked her and she bit her lip to stop its trembling.

"You had to set up this great production number," he continued. "In my own house. Using my daughter's room. It was disgusting. Uncivilized. Bestial." For a moment his voice rose, then he quieted his tone, his gaze rising to the ceiling. "I would be ashamed to mention such a thing to my children. Throwing Ann at me like a piece of meat."

"But Mercedes . . ." she began. "She was just an innocent."

"So was Ann."

"Ann isn't dead."

"Well, Mercedes wouldn't be dead, either, if it wasn't for your absurd caper." He looked at her and shook his head. "I didn't kill her. I don't kill animals. Your detective crushed her when he rushed down the alley in his van."

She tried to quiet her inner turmoil.

"You are responsible," she said, unable to hold back the panic. "Maybe indirectly. But responsible. And I suppose you're glad. You always hated Mercedes anyway."

"I never liked cats in general, especially females," he muttered, starting to unbutton his shirt.

"I'll never forgive you for this, Jonathan. Never." Her heart pounded and she felt inadequate to her anger, leaving most of it unexpressed.

"Forgive me? Here you've messed up our lives and you talk about forgiveness. I wouldn't even dignify the word." He shook his finger in her face. "You've become an unreasonable bitch. This thing you're putting us all through—it makes no sense. Take the money and run. But to want the whole thing, as if I hadn't existed, hadn't worked my tail off to pay for any of it. That's irrational."

"Don't talk to me about rationality. Was ruining my meat pastries rational?"

"And my orchids? I suppose that was an act of reasonableness." He continued to unbutton his shirt, then drew it out of his pants. She remembered how once she had coveted his body. "My beautiful god." The memory echoed and reechoed, as if it were lost with her irrevocably in an abandoned cave.

"I'm never going to give in, Jonathan. Never."

"The court will decide."

"I'll appeal. It'll go on forever."

"Nothing is forever." He turned away from her and removed his pants and underwear, flaunting his nakedness. She watched as he moved toward the sauna. Before he opened the door, he bent over.

"You can kiss my ass."

He went into the sauna and closed the door. She stood rooted there, beyond anger, oddly calm, feeling only hatred. Her eyes roamed his workshop. She was surprised how clearly her mind was functioning now. She saw a brace of chisels neatly lined up against a wall. Selecting one, she removed a wooden mallet hanging nearby and moved toward the sauna. Placing the cutting edge of the chisel in the crack of the heavy redwood sauna door, she swung the mallet against the wooden handle of the chisel, wedging it firmly in the crack.

"Make him well done," she muttered as she ran up the stairs.

18

He had heard the bang, but paid little attention to it. He had, of course, understood her anguish about Mercedes. The confrontation had been inevitable and he was glad that it was over, at least for the moment. To think that he was capable of killing Mercedes was a misperception. How could she possibly believe he was capable of such an act?

He had been confused by her hatred of him from the beginning, but it was only now that he realized the full extent of it. He was not at all the rejected spouse with whom she had shared what he thought were good and productive years; he was the mortal enemy. Maybe she was unhinged. In need of psychological help.

He hadn't really discussed such a tack with Goldstein. How could they prove she needed help? She would never submit to psychological testing. But raising the point might influence the judge. Perhaps she was crazy, had gone off her rocker. He had made her a reasonable offer. Surely Solomon would have ruled in his favor. The optimism mollified him. He was sure that, in the end, he would win.

The problem was that he was giving in to extraneous matters. He must guard against emotions going out of control. He would simply have to weather the waiting period, summon the patience to hold his line. She, on the other hand, had a tougher row to hoe. She was trying to prove that she had been damaged careerwise and, therefore, that her sacrifice had a value equal to the house and all its contents. A judge would have to be mad to grant such a depraved request.

The heat rose in the sauna and he felt his pores open and his body ooze into delicious liquefaction. Nothing was better than a sauna to relieve tension. He felt pain and anxiety slip out of his body.

He had set the sauna to its maximum heat, determined to cook himself into oblivion, so that the cold water of the shower, which completed the process, would shock him into luxurious relaxation. He would return, repeat the procedure three times, then drag himself up to bed and the dead sleep of physical depletion. There hadn't been any new movies to see and he had stayed in the office doing legal research, more to fill up time than out of necessity. He had bought himself a pizza, which had lodged itself somewhere halfway between his mouth and his stomach. She had chosen a poor time for a confrontation.

The wall thermometer indicated a temperature of 200 degrees, but he continued to lay supine on the redwood slats, feeling the sensation of melting, knowing how quickly the icy water would restore him, prod his adrenaline; then he would recede into sweet exhaustion. In the morning he would wake up fresh, able to meet the rigors of the new day.

The sauna, he had always found, chased his depression, renewed him. He watched the little bubbles of sweat ooze out of his pores and he reached out and smoothed the oily moisture over his body. The sauna isolated him in the little redwood room and, in his mind, it became a womb, warm and comfortable. Anguish was not allowed in the sauna.

By the time the temperature reached the red danger point of 220 degrees, he began to play a game with himself. He wanted to reach the furthest point of body heat, then quickly jump out into the shower. The change of temperature would shoot the adrenaline through him, recharge him, obliterate all terrors and anxieties. His body heat rose and he sat up and let the juices that had squeezed out of his body run down his chest and back. The oily liquid oozed out of his buttocks and he slid gently, enjoying the smoothness of the wood against his skin. He knew he was testing himself, pushing his endurance in the heat, if for no other reason than to prove the hardness of his will.

Finally, he was satisfied that he had fulfilled this promise to himself, and he eased himself off the high bench and pushed at the door. It did not open. He pushed again. Still no movement. He braced his shoulder against it and heard a brief creak, but the door would not budge. Making hammers out of his fists, he beat against the door. He began to scream. The sound echoed in the room.

He listened but heard no response. Weakening, he dropped to his knees and put his cheek against the wood slats of the floor, where the air was coolest. He rolled onto his back, with waning strength, and banged the door with the soles of his feet. He felt himself growing faint. He realized then that he had not shut off the sauna. Rising, feeling his weakness, gasping for each breath, feeling the heat singe his lungs, he reached up and switched the temperature dial to OFF.

Stretching out on the floor again, he tried to collect his senses. The heat, he knew, would drop very slowly. He had deliberately made the sauna tight. The redwood from which it was constructed was the best available and he had carefully fitted the joints. Lying on his back, he tried to shout.

"Please help me," he cried, but his strength was ebbing and he felt a numbing weakness. It was futile to cry out, he realized, even in his panic. They were two floors above him. He remembered the thump he had heard earlier—one stroke. He had thought it was her fist, a brief act of rage. Now he was certain that she had wedged something into the door crack. He no longer had the strength to move and his chest hurt. Looking upward, he saw that the temperature had begun to drop, slowly. It already registered below the red mark and was heading toward 200 degrees.

Closing his eyes, he waited. Physical danger had never been a part of his reality. Aside from the time of his false heart attack, he had never felt on the edge of impending death. He couldn't get himself to believe that he could escape twice, nor could his mind grasp the idea that Barbara was capable of such an act. Something had, indeed, changed inside her. Snapped. If he survived this, he decided, he would move out. Run as far away from her as possible. The temperature continued to drop and his panic slowly subsided. His strength was still spent. He rose to his knees, then fell back again, but the evaporation process had begun to cool him. Then his mind went blank and a profound drowsiness came over him.

When he awoke, he was cool and strong enough to stand. He tapped the door with the heel of his hand. The sounding showed him where she had placed the wedge. He saw his earlier mistake. He had put the pressure of his body on the center of the door. Bracing himself, his hands gripped the two-by-fours that held the bench overhang, and he smashed with his heels just below the point where she had obviously placed the wedge.

He felt the door give with a squeak. A few repeated blows pushed open the door and he heard the chisel drop to the floor. Still shaky, he staggered to the shower and turned on the cold water.

By the time he had toweled himself off he felt somewhat better physically, although his lungs still hurt. His first reaction was to bound up the stairs, break down her door, and pummel her with his fists. Worse— he wanted to kill her. He craved her destruction with a force so compelling that he feared to go upstairs.

His mind was not functioning clearly. Naked, he moved up the stairs, holding the chisel as a dagger. He proceeded stealthily, like a stalking killer. He was sure he needed something to kill, if not her, something of hers. Hers alone. Passing the sun-room, now bathed in the light of a full moon, he breathed in the aroma of the plants—her African violets, her Boston ferns—and the memory of his murdered orchids crystallized his sense of mission.

With the cutting edge of the chisel, he slit the stems, pulling them out of the pots and then putting them in a neat pile on a nearby throw rug. Still, he did not feel his urge placated. He carried them in his arms, as if they were dead bodies, into the kitchen and lay them beside the sink. He took the largest stock pot he could find and stuffed them into it, then filled it with water and put in on the stove over a low flame. Death by stabbing; death by drowning; death by boiling. The act was, he knew, pointless. Mad. But he felt better for it. He went upstairs to bed and fell asleep instantly.

"She tried to kill me, Goldstein. Pure and simple." He was still weak and when he breathed too deeply his lungs hurt. He had not the strength to take his usual walk to the office and had flagged down a cab on Connecticut Avenue.

"It sounds like an Agatha Christie method. How did she get so clever?" Goldstein had turned pale at the revelation puffing up thick clouds of cigar smoke.

"I'll admit that she's clever—and pretty handy too. I taught her an awful lot about mechanical things. She had put the wedge in just right." Despite himself, he felt an odd sense of admiration. He had created a monster.

"But you did get out. She must have known that you wouldn't have let yourself fry." He brushed away the smoke with his stubby hands, as if the gesture also cleared his mind. "I'm not condoning it. But to ascribe to her a deliberate intention to murder you sounds bizarre."

"It was bizarre, Goldstein." Jonathan clenched both fists and banged on Goldstein's desk. "This whole thing is bizarre." The violence of his act startled Goldstein, who resumed his usual all-knowing pose.

"You mustn't give in to it, Rose. You want me to press an attempted-murder charge. You need some proof that isn't circumstantial. You bring the police in on domestic matters, they laugh."

"It's not funny."

"To you it's not funny. To me it's not funny. To the police it becomes funny. And funny becomes ludicrous. And ludicrous becomes ridiculous. Besides, I'm not a criminal lawyer."

Jonathan stood up and paced about the office, then, feeling the pressure in his lungs again, he sat down.

"I know she wanted to murder me. Nothing you say, Goldstein, will convince me otherwise. She has simply reached a new threshold of hatred."

"And you?" Goldstein said shrewdly.

"If only you weren't so . . . so rabbinical, so superior, like you know all the secrets of the human heart."

"You didn't answer my question," Goldstein said, as if he were debating with God.

"Yes. I also wanted to murder her. It was a clear option and I very nearly took it. Fortunately I was way-laid by her plants and I murdered the plants instead. In retrospect it may sound odd, but she will get the message. On my part, I would say that the plants saved her life." He had spoken the words slowly, deliberately. Goldstein seemed to be chilled by this assertion and clasped his hands as if in supplication.

"What you felt is perfectly natural . . ." Goldstein began.

"So you're also a psychiatrist, Goldstein?"

"If I were a psychiatrist, I would add another fee to the bill. I'm giving you only wisdom. No charge. Everybody has a killer in him. The feeling passes. If it doesn't, we have troubles."

"That's wisdom?"

"There's more. If I were you, I would stay clear of her. Just live like you're in a vacuum."

"It's not easy."

"Who said it was easy?"

"Sometimes, Goldstein," Jonathan said, "I want to chuck it all. Get out of this city. Start all over again. If only I weren't a boiler-plate lawyer, locked into the FTC. It's too cushy. Too lucrative." He felt a huge wave of despair crash over him. "How easily we get corrupted by material things." It galled him to hear himself mouthing the cliché.

"They got a new word. Life-style. She doesn't want to give up her life-style. And let's face it—you don't want to give up yours. After all, what does a house represent? Shelter? Shelter shmelter. It's a symbol of prestige. A house, Rose, is not just a home."

"You and your fucking wisdom."

Goldstein sighed, looked at him again, and shook his head.

"A few more months. Then the judge will decide. They're all *putzes*, so either we or they are going to appeal."

"I won't let her have it all. I won't. Twice I escaped death for this. At least figuratively. I've stuck it out seven months, I'll stick it out the other five."

"Ignore her. What's so hard?"

"I'll try." He looked at Goldstein. "Mr. Wise Man, if you ignore the Angel of Death, does it go away?"

"I don't need the creeps so early in the day."

19

Ann sat beside him as the car moved slowly over the mountain road above the Shenandoah. The windows were open and she could smell the aroma of the awakening earth. The buds on the trees were newly opened and the leaves were still the light green color of early spring.

Quietly sitting beside him, she hadn't said much on the ride down from Washington. They had stopped on the way for a bucket of fried chicken and some Jarlsberg cheese, and he had taken two bottles of Château Latour '66 from the wine vault.

It was, of course, a violation of her pledge to him. But the seriousness of Eve's request had, she told herself, made it mandatory. She liked the word, almost as if she had invented it, and she had repeated it to him when she had called him at the office.

"It's really mandatory, Jonathan. It's not about you or Barbara or me. It's all about Eve."

"That's a movie," he had responded, but it had helped lighten his reaction and he had consented.

They had seen little of each other in recent weeks. He left earlier for the office and came home later, long after they had all gone to sleep. On weekends, too, he had made himself scarce, spending Saturdays at the office and nights at the movies. On Sundays he made half-hearted attempts at being with the children, but they always had other things to do. Dutifully, he had gone to all of Josh's basketball games.

Eve had come into her room one night. She had been secretive and inert of late, which seemed to be the operative mood of the Roses' household. Whatever the strategies for pretense, the hostility between Barbara and Jonathan permeated everything.

"I'm not going to camp, Ann," Eve began in a tone of belligerence that reminded Ann of their first meeting. But the announcement left no room for rebuttal. "I won't be happy there. And I know they're sending us away to get us out of this atmosphere."

"What's wrong with that?"

"You think I don't know what's going on here?"

"You'd have to be deaf and blind for that."

"The fact is, Ann, I'm afraid to leave them alone. That's the real reason, although I can only tell that to you and you've got to promise to keep that secret."

"Of course." Like Barbara and Jonathan, Eve had composed her own little lie, a facade for the others. She was giving Ann, for the first time, a real glimpse behind it.

"You'll be gone, Ann. And with Josh and me away, there's no telling what might happen. I'm afraid, Ann. Really afraid. I wish . . ." She hesitated and Ann noted that she had already expended enough tears on the subject. "I wish they would either make up or that Dad would move out. Or that Mom and us would move." She opened up a new pack of Virginia Slims and lit one. "I don't understand any of it. I try to. Really, Ann. But you can't talk to either of them anymore. It's like our family didn't really exist, except that we all live in one

house. I wish they would sell it, get it over with. What's
the point?"

"I wonder if they remember the point," Ann had
said. She watched as Eve slowly let the smoke meander
out of her nostrils.

"I want you to talk to Dad, Ann," Eve had pleaded.
"Please. I don't care what you tell him. Only please
don't let him send us to camp."

"How can I tell him that? What can I say?"

"Anything. Tell him things that make fathers worry about daughters. That I'm in with a bad crowd,
smoking dope, that I need strong parental supervision.
You know what to say. Don't tell him I'm afraid for
them." She paused and looked out the dormer window,
her eyes glazed and frightened. "I really believe that if
it wasn't for Josh and me, they would tear each other
apart." She shook her head. "Ann, how can love turn to
hate?"

"I'm not an expert in these things."

"But Dad will listen to you." The young girl had
looked at her shrewdly. "There are some things I sense,
Ann." Ann was thankful that Eve did not elaborate.

"I forgot such beautiful things existed," he said
suddenly. He had stopped the car at an overlook and
they could see the spectacular view of the valley below.
"Makes you feel clean and fresh." She looked up at him.
In the bright sunlight his eyes were cobalt blue, like the
paint on his collection of Staffordshire figures. The
thought agitated her and she turned away.

"Last spring I would never have dreamed that my
life would change so drastically. Last spring I felt so
safe. Imagine that. My principal summation of eighteen
years of marriage is safety."

"Does that mean that you don't feel safe anymore?"
she said, wondering why he hadn't said "secure."

"No. As a matter of fact, no." His voice rose. "I don't feel safe, either mentally or physically. And sometimes I don't feel anything at all." She reached out and patted his hand, her sisterly feeling disappearing abruptly. "The worst thing of all is that I don't like myself much anymore. Do you like yourself, Ann?"

This was not what she wanted to talk about, although she felt compelled to answer in the negative.

"Being with you is like a form of masochism," she whispered, removing her hand. Confronting her frustrations was not pleasant, she decided, dismissing her rising self-pity. "I came to talk about Eve. She doesn't want to go to camp." Ann hesitated, forgetting the scenario she had constructed in her mind. "She probably would be better off staying home."

"Home," Jonathan said. "She's better off getting away from us."

"Jonathan, she really doesn't want to go."

He got out of the car and lingered against the protective rail of the overlook, peering into the valley. Although the sun shone, the air had a slight chill. He looked upward, shielding his eyes.

"There's a trail," he said, observing a sign. The food and wine were in a canvas shopping bag, which he swung over his shoulder as they moved up the trail. Halfway up the slope, they reached a stone promontory, where they sat down and she began to unwrap the chicken.

"I don't really want to send them away, Ann," Jonathan said. Obviously he had turned the matter over in his mind. "But the atmosphere stinks. No sense their having to live through it."

"I think you're making a mistake," Ann said.

Jonathan picked up a small, flat rock and sent it sailing into the valley below.

"I'm really not in the mood to be manipulated by

women anymore," he began, picking up a handful of pebbles and flinging them into space.

"Now you're becoming a misogynist."

"Can you blame me?"

She was silent for a while.

"Well, then, don't think of her as a woman. She's your daughter and I know you love her."

"Of course I love her," he snapped. "And I'm doing what I think is best for both my children, getting them the fuck away from us. Like you're going to do."

It would go badly, she decided, knowing he was adamant, beyond advice. She handed him a piece of chicken and he bit into it without relish.

"Eve says you're not the same person you were a few months ago. You and Barbara."

"She's probably right." He became thoughtful. "Then why does she want to stay home when she can get away?"

"Because she loves you both." That was as far as she was able to go. She uncorked the wine. The cork came out with surprising ease. Then she poured the wine into plastic glasses, which she stood on the flat rock.

"You're all so wise and understanding, you women. Always thinking of yourselves. Your fulfillments and your pain and your anguish. Always thinking that we guys have done you in. Always conspiring, manipulating us with your goddamned pussy."

"I didn't come here for dirty melodrama, Jonathan. Please don't include me. And don't talk of manipulation. Which is the reason I'm still living in that house—"

"I'm sorry, Ann. I apologize for past and future wrongs."

"You haven't wronged me, Jonathan. I only went where my feelings took me."

"Then you are a masochist."

She had come to talk about Eve, but had been way-laid. A bubbling sob began to rise in her chest and she turned away.

"Shit," he said. "Let's have some wine." He lifted his glass and she followed. He was the first to spit the wine out on the ground.

"That lousy little bitch. Somehow she managed to get into the wine vault." He threw the glass over the cliff and smelled the mouth of the bottle. "She's gone and poured vinegar in it. Vinegar in Château Latour '66. A '66. Can you believe it?" He took the other bottle, uncorked it, and sniffed. "Oh, what a bitch," he cried, flinging the bottle into space. It crashed below. "She's probably scuttled all of it. Every good bottle. The Margaux, the Chassagne Montrachet '73, the Château Beycheville '64 and '66. If she touched the Rothschild, I'll murder her." He looked down at Ann, who was frightened now. She struggled up and moved away from the edge.

"It's only wine," she said lamely.

"Only wine," he shouted. He kicked the remaining bottle over the cliff, sending the food after it. "Lafite-Rothschild isn't only wine. Not a '59." His face flushed a deep red. "I don't understand you, Ann. If you loved me, you'd understand."

She started running down the path, confused, hoping his anger would abate by the time he returned to the car. She sat there a long time, waiting, wondering what all this had to do with love.

20

You should have left the wine alone, Barbara," Thurmont lectured. "The wine, we all agreed, was his. Not in dispute. What you did only complicates things."

"It was only a half case of the Latour. That's all I touched. I could have really been a rat and pulled the plug. That stuff has to be between fifty-four and fifty-seven degrees. I could have pulled the plug and ruined all hundred and ten bottles. That's if I was really a rat." She was determined to remain calm.

"Goldstein is threatening to take us to court for violating the separation agreement."

"Well, invasion of privacy was a violation and where did that get us?"

"He was restrained. That helps the case when we get down to the real arena."

"I think he's done it again." She was smug now, proud that she had learned to be unflappable. They were not going to grind her down. She was more determined than ever.

Thurmont had looked up at her over his half glasses. She smiled sarcastically, enjoying the situation. They all think women are dumb, she huffed to herself.

"I'm positive he's picked the lock and been inside my room. I'm absolutely positive."

"Are you hallucinating now, Barbara? The court doesn't deal in that kind of information."

"I know he's been there."

"That's not enough."

She left Thurmont's office unusually buoyed. He had been discouraging, especially when she had explained that she had ruined the wine because he had destroyed her plants. If he was such a smart lawyer, he would have included the plants in the agreement. She wondered again if it wouldn't have been a better idea to find a woman lawyer. A woman lawyer would understand. But then again, most judges were men and it would be like playing Russian roulette. She was certain that they all worked hand in glove, conspiring together to keep women in their place.

Whatever the consequences, the fact that he had actually discovered the ruined wine under the most-hoped-for circumstances elated her. So he was having trysts with Ann, she thought gleefully, little country outings. And she had spoiled one by ruining their wine. Even Eve's intrusion had not diminished her joy.

"I put her up to it, Mom. I just don't want to go to camp. I really don't know who to go to if I have grievances." Eve had confessed, revealing how efficient the household communication system operated. Jonathan to Ann to Eve to her. Goldstein to Thurmont. A round robin. She didn't care, reveling in her assertiveness and success. The French Market was demanding more and more *pâté*, and her chicken *galantine* had made a big hit at any number of big parties. She was making it. She was unstoppable. A winner. And she was certain she would win her case, although Thurmont had warned her not to become too successful until the divorce action came to court.

"Why didn't you come to me?" she had complained to Eve, but in her heart she knew this was a rote response, the expected one.

"Because you've got other things on your mind at the moment. Things are bad enough. I didn't want to complicate your life."

She embraced her daughter and kissed her on the cheek.

"What the hell are mothers for?"

"I just didn't want to go to camp—that's all. Frankly, I'm afraid to leave you two alone in the house."

Barbara laughed at herself, at her old image as dependent woman, fearful and unassertive.

"No man pushes your old mom around, baby." She did a mock Humphrey Bogart.

"He's Daddy."

"I know, precious. He's your daddy. Not mine." She laughed again.

"It's no tragedy. Just a plain old ugly divorce action. I think I'm right. He thinks he's right. The judge will decide. So it'll be a little ugly. So what? Why be afraid?" She waved her finger in front of Eve's nose. "It's a new world out there, honey. And don't you be a dummy when it comes to men. Equal strokes for equal folks. Don't give up what you want for them. That's the lesson for your life. You have a living example before you." She raised her arms and stood on tiptoe. "I feel a hundred feet tall," she said. "High as a kite. High on life."

"I've never seen you like this, Mom. So damned content."

"So, you see? Nothing to worry about. Go to camp. Enjoy."

In her heart, she forgave Ann. Forgave everything. Show the bastards no mercy, she told herself, thinking of Jonathan and all the rest of those cock heads.

As if to celebrate her newly perceived freedom, she bought herself a vibrator. It had a penis shape and wide ridges like corduroy along its shaft. The idea of it was almost as delicious as its effect on her private parts, which proved a revelation of pleasure as waves of orgasmic crescendos invaded her senses. Sometime in the middle of the day, she would announce to herself, Time for happy hour, and would go up to her room and proceed to use her cock toy, as she called it. It was better than Jonathan had ever been.

"You beautiful little technological miracle," she would whisper to it when it had done particularly yeoman service. Who needs them?

The high was accelerated by the deepening of spring. The trees along the circle were in full bloom and the view of the park and the Calvert Street Bridge in their spring wardrobe was magnificent. As for Jonathan, he was hardly a bother. More like a rodent who was never seen, although the evidence of him could not be missed. Sometimes at night she heard him puttering in his workroom, and if she awakened early, she heard him leave the house. As far as she was concerned, he was no longer a part of her life.

But she could not shake the idea that somehow his presence had intruded itself in her room. She had learned recently to trust her instincts, to act according to a deep, unrealized, and unarticulated intelligence. It wasn't anything she could pin down with surety. She had carefully inspected the room and her closets, looked under the beds, even into her shoes. At night, when she could not sleep, she reviewed in her mind this feeling, even tried to dismiss it. But it lingered, pervasive and intuitive.

During the day, dutifully, in addition to running her business, she went about the chores of preparing the children for camp. Eve was to be a counselor in training, which mollified her somewhat, in that it represented a euphemism for privileged camper. This meant greater freedom.

"Just be careful, Eve. We don't need any problems with you. Not now."

"I'm cool," Eve replied. Mother and daughter understood each other. Josh gave her little trouble. His life revolved around basketball and school. She wondered how she could be so negative toward males and still love her son.

But success bred its own problems and Barbara discovered the meaning of cash flow. She had agreed in the separation agreement not to use any household money for her business. It hadn't made much sense, but she did get her suppliers, the various food markets and wholesalers, to bill her with separate invoices, as Thurmont had instructed.

She wasn't the best bookkeeper in the world, but she reassured herself that all she had to do was add up the invoices for the purchases, then add up the bills to her customers, and the difference would be, she hoped, profit. She made simultaneous shocking discoveries. Her customers paid her very slowly and since she was so anxious for the business, she did not press them. But her suppliers demanded payment at shorter intervals. To keep herself afloat, she had borrowed from the household money.

"Nobody taught me anything about business, Thurmont," she protested when he rebuked her.

"Tell that to the man you buy your meat from."

"I did."

"And?"

"He cut me off." The memory fueled her indignation. "If I hadn't been a woman, things would have

been different. He had no confidence. I showed him my
bills to customers. He sneered at me. 'That's your problem, lady,' he said. It was the 'lady' that galled me and
I threw a handful of chopped meat at him."

"That was good business."

"It gets worse." She felt the anger solidify into a
hard ball in her stomach. "He told me that women
shouldn't be in business. They're too emotional. Then
he nearly struck me with his cleaver." She hesitated. "I
don't quite mean that. He swung his cleaver hard into
the wooden counter. But I knew what he meant. He
wished it were me. The bastard."

"You went too fast," Thurmont told her. "Your
business isn't really relevant to the case. In fact, your
success hurts the case."

"I'm sorry." She was sarcastic.

"What about the other household bills?" he asked.

"I'm behind on the gas bill, the electric bill, and the
telephone bill. Two months each. They're getting a little persnickety, but they apparently haven't talked to
Jonathan yet." She looked at him and frowned. "Why
don't you lend me a few thousand? You'll get it back in
spades."

"He's already behind three months with me."

"I've seen your bills, Thurmont. He sends me notes
with Xerox copies attached."

"I sell time, Barbara. Every time you come up here
for one of your sessions, it costs. Two hundred an hour.
It works by a clock. You knew that from the beginning.
I keep telling you not to keep running up here every
time you've got a problem."

"You're supposed to keep me out of trouble."

"I'm a divorce lawyer, not a business consultant. I
keep telling you to get payment on delivery."

"That doesn't help me now."

She went to a bank to borrow money. The loan officer was a woman and that made Barbara immediately hopeful.

"All I need is five thousand. No big deal." She explained her business problems and her current domestic difficulties.

"What sort of collateral have you?" the loan officer asked pleasantly. She was an intense woman who chain-smoked.

"Collateral?" She had only a vague idea of what the term meant.

"Like stocks, bonds. Your house."

"My house? We own it jointly. That's why we're having difficulties. You see I'm asking for—" She interrupted herself, feeling foolish. She seemed to be deliberately looking for allies. But she could see from the woman's indifferent expression that she had not been able to transfer her outrage.

"It's the litigation that scares us," the loan officer explained.

"I thought they had changed the laws to give women a break."

"They have . . . but you see—"

"That's bullshit," she said, getting up and walking out. She wondered if the loan officer also felt she was too emotional. Jonathan, that bastard, she thought, has crippled me. The idea only made her more determined and she tried two other banks. One loan officer, a man, offered to take her out for a drink.

"You mean if you fuck me, I'll get the money," she said, raising her voice so that others within earshot might hear her. She returned home shaking, mortified. Then she called up her customers and pleaded for the money. Her heart was in her mouth and her voice ragged and tremulous.

"We get paid slowly, too," the Thai ambassador's wife told her indignantly. "It takes a long time from overseas. You must understand that, dear."

She swallowed hard and tamped down her anger to avoid a confrontation. It wasn't at all like what she'd thought it would be. She worked so hard to make her products perfect, artistic creations, something of which she could be proud. She hadn't expected such indifference when it came to payment.

At night, she had imaginary conversations with Jonathan.

"I told you it was a jungle out there," Jonathan confirmed in her imagination. "Dog eat dog. I tried to protect you from that."

"You should have tried to teach me how to protect myself."

"That wouldn't have been manly. You agreed to love, honor, and obey. That meant to oblige me sexually, take my advice, and give me none of your lip." His voice seemed to come from a wind tunnel.

"But it's wrong to keep someone locked up."

She had deliberately avoided taking Valium for months. High on life, she had told herself, but the business problems began to crowd in on her. Soon the kids would be off to camp, she reasoned, and she might be able to scrimp and get back on her feet financially without Jonathan's finding out. If only he would get the hell out of the house. His presence galled her. It was unfair. Wrong. She admitted to herself that she would have been perfectly content had he been boiled alive in the sauna. She wouldn't have given it a second thought.

Then Thurmont called her.

"He's found out about the overdue utility bills. He's fuming. Goldstein was leering through the phone."

"Then we've simply got to ask Jonathan for more. It's simply not enough. I never had trouble before this."

"He cheerfully paid everything, Barbara. Remember, this is a divorce action. And there's a written agreement. The case doesn't come up for a few more months. If you get yourself more into the hole, you may be forced to compromise."

"Never," she said. She paused, then looked into the mouthpiece of the phone. "Are you charging me for this call?"

"Of course."

"Then bug off."

She spent a great deal of time now holed up in her room. It began to get warm, and she opened the windows. Before, she would not have thought twice about turning on the air conditioner. Now she resisted, concerned about the utility bills. Mostly she brooded about her former self, that stupid little doll baby willing to sacrifice herself, everything, for some silly, girlish romantic notion.

"For you, Jonathan," she had said, "I'll do anything. Anything." He had offered her the same assurance, but it didn't mean the same thing. She remembered how his every utterance was pregnant with wisdom. She had idolized him, worshiped him, remembering how she would watch his sleeping face in the quickening light of morning, kiss his fluttering eyelids, his puffed sweet lips, and when he held her in his arms, she knew that the world had really stopped just for her, just for that moment. In her mind, she heard bells now, warning bells, fire bells, ominous clanging, banging bells pealing for her lost innocence. They toll for you, Barbara, you dumb little snit, falling for that line. She blamed her parents. She blamed her friends. She blamed the movies, the songs of eternal love, the romantic lies. Sentimental bondage. Love lies.

One night she could not resist and took two Valium, expecting oblivion and relief from her racing thoughts. It didn't happen. She twisted and turned. She took a hot shower. Then an icy shower. Nothing helped. She felt agitated beyond her ability to control herself. Her heart pounded. She sweated alternately hot and cold. The drug's reaction confused her.

Terrors magnified in her mind. She felt she was drowning, choking. She could not sit in one place. She went downstairs and sat in the library. The Staffordshire figures seemed to come to life, moving, dancing, mocking her with their cobalt eyes. Like Jonathan's. Her hands shook and she opened the armoire and took a long, burning swallow from the bottle. It made her worse.

She went upstairs and changed into her jeans, then went outside. It was late May and warm and she walked through the quiet Kalorama streets, turned left on Connecticut Avenue, then walked as fast as she could. Sometimes she jogged for a few blocks. She could not stop herself. Once a policeman stopped his squad car and called out to her.

"It's too late for jogging, lady."

"Bug off. It's a free country."

"It's your ass," she heard him say.

The sweat poured out of her body and she was surprised to see that she had reached Chevy Chase Circle. She sat on a bench in the middle of the circle, watching occasional cars speed around it. The circling images triggered a thought. Then another. And another. Finally, a revelation. She crossed the circle and ran to a public phone and dialed Thurmont's number, hearing his sleep-fogged, panicked voice.

"He did something to the Valium," she shouted into the phone. "I know he did something. That dirty bastard."

Thurmont seemed confused, but her mind was clearing.

"He substituted something else for the Valium. It created the opposite effect. I was all strung out. I'm getting better."

"Where are you?"

"Near Chevy Chase Circle."

"Don't do anything stupid, Barbara."

"Don't worry," she said. "I will never do anything stupid again."

21

Jonathan didn't tell Goldstein about the mold he had made of the lock to Barbara's room and the key he had made from the mold. He could predict Goldstein's insufferable comments. How could that supercilious asshole know what it was like to walk in his, Jonathan's, moccasins? Nor could he tell Goldstein about the Dexedrine he had put into the Valium capsules he'd emptied.

With whom could he argue his justification? The acts, to any reasonable observer, would seem irrational, certainly provocative. But how could the observer react to what she had done to him? The sauna. The wine. The detective. This was no ordinary situation. He had to be alert, always. Watchful. And how could any reasonable person explain her actions. Like suddenly deciding out of the blue that it was time to break up the family. It was as if an alarm clock had rung in her head. "All right, Jonathan. Time's up."

"Patience," Goldstein had implored through a fog of cigar smoke. That was exactly the course he would take. Patience. The angels were on his side.

On the question of finances, Goldstein approached him cautiously.

"She's overextended businesswise. Be patient. Sooner or later, they'll come to us with a proposition."

"What about the utility bills? They'll shut us off."

"Close to the vest now, Rose. I've seen it a thousand times. Business always looks easy on the outside. She'll have to come to us. She has no other source of income."

"Two thou a month. Just to run the house, the bare minimum. My God, it's a fortune."

"Not if you're financing a business. She'll come to us. You'll see."

As Goldstein said, he was to be patient. Meanwhile, the utility companies called him repeatedly, threatening.

"My wife pays them," he had assured the various spokesmen.

"No, she doesn't."

The day the children left for camp, both he and Barbara showed up at the parking lot of the Sidwell Friends School. Driving the Ferrari, he had followed Barbara's station wagon, into which she had piled the kids and their luggage. Eve's eyes were still puffy after an emotional farewell to Ann. She had gone off to live at the YWCA on Seventeenth Street, informing him with a note she had slipped under his door.

"And if you ever need me," she wrote, "I'm ready." It was unsigned. Reading it, he had felt a pang of guilt. He had treated her badly, he decided, but he had not caused her to love him. Love. What a contemptible word. It should be abolished, especially since it did not accurately describe an enduring emotion. He had loved Barbara. Once he had told her, long ago, that love was just God's way of randomly splitting two people and letting them find themselves. When they did, they were one. That was love. That was, he thought now, unmitigated bullshit. No, he corrected himself, that gave it too much dignity. Love was a fart.

It was awkward saying good-bye to the children, who looked at them from the bus window with anxious eyes.

"I sure wish you two would either make up or make peace," Josh had whispered to him, and Jonathan assumed he had whispered the same thing to his mother. He hugged the boy, not without some additional pang of regret. What he regretted was that Josh had been created out of her genes as well. Part her. Somehow it diminished his love of the boy. Josh had his mother's deep-set Slavic eyes. He could not bear the guilt of such an unworthy feeling. He had the same feeling about Eve. It's wrong, he decided. Against nature. And seeing Barbara hug and caress the children before they stepped into the bus, he had to turn away. The sight disturbed him.

The parents watched the bus pull away, waving long after it was out of sight. A hush of mutual loss fell over the group and soon they got into their cars and drove off. He started to get into his car. Her voice stopped him.

"I know about the Valium," she said. "I don't know how you did it. Just don't think you're going to get away with it. Not ever." He had turned to look at her face, noting with pleasure the new nest of wrinkles around her eyes. He looked at her, said nothing, then jumped into the Ferrari and drove off.

He would have to be careful now. And prepared. He could see the hatred in her eyes, the thirst for retaliation. A nerve in his cheek twitched. He looked at his watch. It was too early for the movies to be open. He dreaded the idea of being alone. The loss of the children, he discovered, did move him, putting a lie to the ugly thoughts he had had just a few moments before.

Driving around in the Ferrari gave him no pleasure. A heavy blanket of gloom descended on him. Separation hadn't given him self-reliance. He was, under all
the bitterness and antagonism that had built up inside
him, a family man. House, wife, kids, dog. Just like on
television. He thought of his father, who had never really been what the sociologists call a role model. He was
just a white-collar bureaucrat. But when he came home
and shut the door in his clapboard house in Framingham, he was home safe. Home free. He had his chair,
his pipe, his plaid bathrobe, his sense of family. House.
Wife. Children. Dog. He was always his mother's 'man.'
She would even say it exactly that way. "My man likes
his eggs four minutes. My man hates rice pudding. My
man likes egg-salad sandwiches for his lunch and a Delicious apple. Not McIntosh." She was specific about all
his father's needs, highly detailed. Everything was done
to enhance the old man's life. The lucky bastard. He
was king of the universe. Like prunes for breakfast.
Good for the bowels. Or the Jell-O for dinner. Good for
the prostate. Or the fish on Fridays. Good for God and
the brain. They were Catholics by birth and inclination,
but didn't care much for the priests, although he knew
that his mother secretly prayed for their salvation. For
her husband and kids. Rarely for herself.

It was that kind of woman he had wanted Barbara
to be, had imagined she was. His mother's large bosom
was the world's umbrella. It was safe under there.
Warm. Wonderful. Next to her big, generous heart.
The tears mattered when they were shed under that
umbrella. It chased pain. It made home sweet, sweeter
than sweet.

"She is a good woman," his father had confided.
And she was that. How he envied him now. Sleeping
next to that big pillow of strength and love and safety

all those years. What was the jungle compared to that? His mind skipped backward in time and when he looked at his reflection in the car's side window, he had grown up. He hadn't lived at home for twenty years and although they were, he was thankful, still living, their lives were lost somewhere back there in the Framingham of twenty years ago.

He stopped the car and went into a Peoples' drugstore and called his family. His father answered.

"Hey, Dad." It meant flogging himself to be cheerful.

"Son." Jonathan could hear him yell, "Molly, it's Jonnie." And in a moment his mother had picked up the receiver.

"Jonnie?"

"Mom." He paused, swallowing the hard ball of phlegm that had lodged in his throat. "I just put the kids on a bus to camp."

"They're all right?" She was always suspicious when he called. Outside her home, life was uncertain and dangerous. They exchanged the usual amenities. How is Josh? How is Eve? How is your practice? How is your health? How is it going? That meant the divorce. His parents hadn't been down to see them since the breakup, although they had seen the children during Barbara's trip to Boston. Barbara hadn't come. Deliberately, his mother avoided any mention of Barbara.

"There's no way you can make it up?" his mother asked.

"No way."

There was a long pause in which he could read her mind and see her face. Such things didn't, couldn't happen in her world. Please, no tears, he begged silently, and after more innocuous words, they hung up swiftly, never having gotten used to long-distance calls. Nevertheless, he walked away comforted, wondering which was truth and which was fiction. Their life. Or his.

He hadn't intended to go back to the house, but his mind had lost all sense of space and time and before he realized it he had driven the car into the alley. When he saw where he was, he expected Benny to come running and that image brought with it the desire to go for a ride, maybe down to Hains' Point, where Benny could run around and catch a Frisbee, one of the few tricks Jonathan had taught him.

He went into the garden and whistled loudly, two fingers in his mouth. Usually this was enough to disrupt Benny's perpetual sniffing after bitches. He whistled again. No answer. Then he got in the car and roamed around the neighborhood, offering periodic whistling clarions. Benny slept at the foot of his bed, and although he snored and sometimes forgot that he wasn't outside, Benny was, as Jonathan acknowledged to himself, better than no one. A lot better.

Paradoxically, the irony cheered him. To think that the only loving member of his family in town was nothing but a mangy schnauzer amused him. At least Benny was sympathetic to his troubles, and on many an occasion during the past trying months Jonathan had poured out his heart to him. Some things simply had to be said out loud. And Benny had looked at him thoughtfully, big brown eyes smoldering with alertness, head cocked, ears standing up rigidly.

"You cute, horny bastard," he said when Benny looked at him that way, offering the mutt a hug, which required a special tolerance for Benny's usual gamy aroma.

It cheered him to think that he still had Benny and even his disappointment at not finding him couldn't dispel the sudden sense of optimism. Searching for him killed enough time for the movies to open and he sat through two Woody Allens at the Biograph, surprised that he could still laugh after having seen them for the fourth or fifth time.

He ate two roast-beef sandwiches and fries at a Roy Rogers and headed home, keeping the terror of his loneliness at bay as he listened for Benny's familiar greeting. Benny usually waited for him, stretched supine under one of the bushes along the perimeter of the house, springing up to cuddle his master's leg. Jonathan's coming in by car always confused Benny, since he had to run around to the rear and couldn't get into the garage. He would stand on his hind legs at the door, waiting for Jonathan to open it, then lunge playfully, invariably muddying up Jonathan's suit.

Benny still wasn't there. But still it wasn't time to panic. Often Benny would straggle home late at night or early in the morning. Sometimes Jonathan would leave the back door ajar and Benny would push his way in and scratch at the door to Jonathan's room. Still asleep, he would get up, open the door, and let the dog in.

Lying there in the large, canopied bed, alone, Jonathan listened to the sounds of the house, a rhythm he knew as well as his own heartbeat. The absence of the children and Ann was tangible and he could sense the emptiness around him. Somehow their presence in the house gave him some sense of belonging, of cohesiveness. And the house itself, its very familiarity, offered some comfort. His womb, he thought, wondering if Barbara, too, felt this same sensation. He sensed her lurking in what was once their bed across the hall. "Lurking" was the word that had come to mind. And he saw her curled in the embryo position, listening, as he was now, to the sounds of the house.

Unable to sleep, he got out of bed and searched the room for a vodka bottle. Finding one, he poured some into a tumbler, then opened the window and brought in a small carton of orange juice from the ledge. There wasn't much left and he emptied it into the glass and drank it hurriedly.

Then he went back to bed and quickly began to slip into drowsiness. Before he could get to sleep, he heard a scratching on the door.

Benny.

Without opening his eyes, he got up, opened the door, and heard Benny pad to his accustomed spot on the Art Deco rug. Jonathan got back into bed, feeling better, relieved.

It began as an abstraction. First came the loss of time. Then a burst of colors exploded in his brain and he opened his eyes. The room had become a toy kaleidoscope, with the patterns constantly changing.

He sat up, startled, rubbed his eyes, but the patterns merely changed. They did not go away. The Hepplewhite secrétaire grew bloated as he looked at it and the file cabinets seemd to be floating in midair. Reaching out, he tried to touch one. It seemed to evaporate.

But when he looked up at the canopy and saw it descending on him, as in the famous horror story, he heard a scream. It did not sound like his voice at all— a whiny cackle, like that of a rooster being strangled at sunrise. Jumping off the bed, he felt his knees buckle and he lay on the floor, panting, searching for some shred of reason.

My mind, a faint trickle of logic told him. My *mind*. He touched his head, which seemed larger, but soft, like a sponge. He sensed something moving near him, something luminous and large, glowing, like a large ball of white fire. It was alive and its breath stank. Something warm and moist covered his face. Sitting up, he watched the apparition. It was monstrous, hideous, moving. He hit it with his fist and heard a strange sound, amplified, bursting in his ears.

His eyes would not focus and he moved back, sliding along the floor, overturning bottles. Some of them crunched under his weight and he felt a stab of pain in his buttocks. He watched the apparition move, then he turned away in horror. He had never felt more terror, as if he had suddenly descended into a special kind of hell.

"Forgive me," he cried, but he could not hear his voice. Crawling on his hands and knees, he groped his way over objects. Looking back, he saw the apparition following. Colors continued to explode in his mind. Every object in the room seemed distorted, out of sync. His body bumped against something cool and hard and some brief trace of logic returned. He was in the bathroom, climbing into the tub. Still the apparition pursued him.

Clutching a fiery, golden metallic object, he felt it give and he was suddenly in a cold rainstorm. He lay back, letting the water run over him. Colored drops invaded the space above him, crawling over him like insects. The rain reminded him of something, something long ago. He heard pounding on the windowpanes and the muffled drone of a croaking voice. "Going once. Twice."

"Sold," the voice screamed. His body lurched, grew still. He was certain that it was his tears coming down as rain.

Logic returned in fits, like blips on a computer screen, first as random patterns, then as connections. The colors faded, disappeared. He could see a spear of sunlight through the water rushing above him and finally he was observing himself lying in the bathtub being sprinkled by a gush of water from the shower head.

Testing his reflexes before he made an effort to rise, he felt pain in his buttocks, and as he rose slowly his head spun and ached. Stepping cautiously out of the tub, he held on to the sink and turned off the water. There was blood on the bathroom tile and on his fingers where he had touched the cuts. His eyes focused clearly now, and in the mirror he saw his rump, a network of oozing red tributaries.

Patting himself dry, he sprayed disinfectant on the cuts, then walked into his room. It was a mess. The bedclothes lay in disarray on the floor, which was strewn with broken bottles. He picked his way carefully across the broken glass and got into his shoes. Standing in the center of the room, he tried to reconstruct what had happened. Oddly, he remembered the images he had seen. Nightmarish shapes and sounds. Then he heard Benny's pained whimper and saw him cowering in the corner, his big brown eyes laden with hurt. He looked mangy, off color. Moving closer, he appeared to be covered with a whitish sticky substance.

Grabbing him by the neck chain, Jonathan moved him into the bathroom and drew the blind, throwing the room into semidarkness. *Luminous paint*. The revelation came at him with a rush. He remembered the orange juice.

"God damn it," he shouted, feeling the rage overflow and tighten into a ball in his chest.

He dressed hurriedly, picked up the orange-juice carton, and, leashing Benny, took him downstairs. He did not even look at Barbara's closed door, deliberately trying to contain his rage. Soon, he told himself, promising that she would pay dearly. He drove Benny to the vet in Eve's Honda.

"What asshole did that?" the vet asked, looking at Benny.

"Somebody who didn't like him, I guess," Jonathan

responded.

"It'll take all day to clean him up," the vet said. "I also want to check his skin."

Jonathan nodded, then thrust the orange-juice carton in front of him.

"I also need a favor. There's something in this I want analyzed. I think he drank some."

"Orange juice?" The vet shook his head. He seemed perplexed. Taking the carton, he sniffed at it, then shrugged. "I'll call you." He looked at Benny. "You poor bastard," he said, leading him away.

Jonathan went to the office, but he couldn't concentrate. Occasionally last night's colors burst in his mind again and he broke into a cold sweat. For most of the day he lay on the couch and tried to hold himself together.

"You all right?" Miss Harlow asked, coming into his office.

"I had a rough night."

"Tomcats, the lot of you," she mumbled.

Finally the vet called. Miss Harlow put him through.

"LSD," he said. "Your dog took an acid trip. Maybe he sprayed that stuff on himself."

"Very funny." He had suspected as much. The information didn't come as a big surprise.

"He looks fine now. We got it all off. He's a tough old guy."

"So am I," Jonathan muttered as he hung up. His head felt clearer than it had all day.

He resisted calling Goldstein. Her behavior wasn't actionable because he couldn't prove anything. Remembering what he had done to her Valium, he smiled ruefully. "Ingenious bitch," he whispered. He even felt a touch of grudging admiration.

So she's getting to be a murderous little viper, he told himself. He'd show her what that really meant.

When he went upstairs to his room that night, he found a note Scotch-taped to his door. He saw Barbara's left-handed scrawl: "I'm having a dinner party Friday night. I would appreciate your not interfering in any way."

The note was unsigned, as if any identification on her part would have implied a modicum of intimacy. He crumpled the note and kicked at her door. A dinner party? Where was the money coming from? "You monster," he cried. There was no response.

He decided he needed a drink and went downstairs to the library, opening the armoire and pouring himself a tumbler of scotch. Neat. He swore off mixers, especially orange juice. And vodka. So he was now paying for her dinner parties. How much of his own victimization was he expected to tolerate? It was beyond endurance. She was flaunting him, humiliating him. Sitting down on the couch, his hurt buttocks smarted and he stood up quickly. Besides, something was nagging at him, beyond mere indignation, as if something in the room itself was awry. His eyes did a cursory inventory, like a moving TV camera, and his mind ticked off their possessions as if a page of the list had been inserted into a slot in his brain.

There was some intuitive deductive system at work, triggered by something missing. His eyes roamed, lingered, inspected. *"Little Red Riding Hood,"* his voice boomed out. Little Red Riding Hood was missing. This was different. He rushed to the phone and dialed Goldstein's number.

"Little Red Riding Hood is missing," he shouted into the phone.

"I know, the wolf ate her."

"Don't you understand, Goldstein? She stole it to pay for the dinner party. It's a Staffordshire figure."

There was a long pause.

"You should take a long vacation, Rose."

"She stole it. Don't you understand? She'll get at least two grand."

"I'm taking a long vacation. You should, too. As fast as possible. We'll worry about it when I get back."

"How can you go on vacation?"

"I go when Thurmont goes. Don't worry. It's only for six weeks."

"Six weeks?"

"We're entitled, Rose. We work hard."

"You don't understand."

"You call me late at night to tell me about Little Red Riding Hood missing. What don't I understand?"

It seemed futile to explain. The words hung in his throat.

"That's where the money is coming from, Goldstein." There was no response on the other end.

"The money . . ." Jonathan began again.

"I'm going on vacation, Rose," Goldstein said finally. "Which reminds me. You're behind on my retainer."

Jonathan hung up, staring at the phone in its cradle. So it's every man for himself, is it? he thought, feeling a charge of adrenaline stiffen his resolve. He'd show them what resolve really meant.

22

She had to polish all the silver herself. It was difficult work, particularly the rococo centerpiece, a copy of a de Lamerie. She was absolutely determined that nothing, nothing would go wrong.

She hoped, too, that he had gotten the message. She had heard the weird noises. It was not, the pusher had said, much of a dose. Just a short trip. Painting Benny was an afterthought. By now Jonathan must realize that he couldn't attack her with impunity. She was just as clever, just as resourceful. All he had to do was move out. Then it would be over.

And she was entitled to take the Little Red Riding Hood. She had never really admired the piece. And, if the truth were known, she wasn't that fond of collecting Staffordshire. They were crude figures, had no intrinsic beauty, and the expressions on their faces were insipid. All because of Cribb and Molineaux. She was sick to death of the memory. Getting two thousand for the Little Red Riding Hood was ridiculous. And the Cribb and Molineaux were now worth five thousand. She hoped he wouldn't discover the missing figure for a while. At least until Thurmont had returned from vacation. But Jonathan, too, was at a disadvantage with Goldstein away as well.

She was proud of her pluck and ingenuity. The name of the game was survival and she was determined to survive. She had debated with herself whether or not to pay the utility bills with the proceeds of the figure sale, but nothing could make her forgo the opportunity to show her wares to both her regular and potential customers. Also, they would get an opportunity to see her house. And she'd show them what style was all about. Then, perhaps, they wouldn't dare be slow to pay their bills. A little enterprise, Barbara, she told herself as she went about the elaborate preparations for a dinner for fourteen. Thirteen, actually, since she had chosen not to have an escort, as if to assert her singleness.

She picked the menu and her guests carefully, determined to prove to them she could enhance the traditional, a challenge in itself. It was the beginning of summer and the ambassadors she wanted had not yet left for their summer vacations.

She even invited the Greek ambassador, accompanying the invitation with a little note urging both him and his wife to reassess her culinary skills. Their acceptance overjoyed her. The Thai ambassador, whom she regularly supplied with *pâté* and who was considered something of a gourmet, also accepted, as well as the Fortunatos, who were fast becoming two of Washington's most prodigious hosts.

With a nod to public relations, she also invited a food editor of *The Washington Post* and his wife. His name was White and he had written a number of cookbooks, including one cataloguing famous recipes of former White House chefs. She could not come up with a Cabinet minister but settled instead for an undersecretary of the Army, whose wife she had met casually at parent meetings at Sidwell Friends. To round off the list, she invited the military attaché of the French Embassy and his wife, an attractive young couple who were present at most parties given by the French Embassy.

The plan was, she knew, a bold stroke and she was determined to make a lasting impression, to start people talking. It would be the first of many, an advertisement of herself. With the children gone, she was less harried, although the tension between her and Jonathan continued. She would just have to live with that, she decided, hoping that, once and for all, she had foreclosed on any more harassment from him. Soon, she was sure, he would come to his senses and move out of the house.

Naturally, she would do all the cooking herself. A *vichyssoise* to begin with, followed by crab imperial, beef Wellington with *pâté de foie gras,* a delicate salad of watercress, mushrooms, and endives, and for dessert, custard-filled éclairs with a warm chocolate sauce. For wines, she picked a Chablis Grand Cru for starters, followed by a 1966 Saint-Emilion. And for a dessert champagne, a good brut.

For a moment she felt tempted to break into Jonathan's wine vault, but she resisted that. At all costs she must avoid any confrontations. Also, this was her show. Hers alone. She would prove to herself that she was capable of offering a complete dinner service. She checked her china, counted out her silver and crystal glasses. So what if she was being blatantly commercial? She was in business.

She made a long list of ingredients—crabmeat, fillet of beef, potatoes, capers, endives, mushrooms, eggs, chocolate. On and on. And she haunted the markets for perfect choices. Without the children to worry about, she was able to work at her own pace, largely ignoring Jonathan's comings and goings. He seemed to be keeping out of her way, and she was thankful. She put financial problems out of her mind as well. She found she enjoyed working on projects with specific goals. It gave her life more structure, more purpose. It was delicious to savor such freedom. To be sure she got a good night's sleep, she took a strong sleeping pill. It made the nights go faster. Shut out all anxieties. She also devised a plan to thwart any malicious interference by Jonathan, just in case the matter with Benny hadn't taught him a final lesson.

On the day before the party, she moved a cot into the kitchen. Her idea was to prepare everything that day and to spend the night in the kitchen, working right up to the point when the three in help she had hired would arrive. Carefully, she inspected the food she had purchased for any signs of tampering. The wines as well. Satisfied, she began the job of preparation.

For some reason, the one arm tap in the stainless-steel sink would not run cold. She tried the other sink and the same condition prevailed. It wasn't a serious problem, but when she moved the tap arm to hot, it came out scalding and scorched her hand. She screamed in pain. It had never happened before, but after the initial shock, she countered the problem by emptying ice cubes into a large stock pot and used the resulting cold water for washing the various ingredients.

Only vaguely did she relate the mishap to Jonathan. Even if it was sabotage, she was determined that nothing would stand in her way. When one of the mixing heads came loose from the mixing bowl on the kitchen island center and flew into the ceiling, narrowly missing her face, she received her first jolt of real concern. Her fingers shook as she picked up the head, looked at its thread, then reattached it. It could have been her fault. She might not have tightened it properly.

She fitted the Cuisinart with the slicer top and fed peeled potatoes into it, watching with satisfaction as the thinly sliced pieces piled into the transparent bowl. But when she turned the bowl cover to the off position, it did not stop the blade from whirring and she quickly flicked the machine to the off position. Still it continued to whir. She then reached to pull the plug from the socket but it would not come out.

As she contemplated the problem the room seemed to be growing hotter and she noted that all the burners on the electric stove were red hot. She turned the knobs, but her action had little effect. Still she resisted any sense of panic, determined to remain calm despite the continuous whirring of the Cuisinart. Finally, in a fit of pique, she tugged at the wire and the Cuisinart fell to the floor, which loosened the slicing blade and sent it careening like a projectile into the range hood, ricocheting off a cabinet before it lost power and clanked into one of the sinks.

To avoid being hit, she had fallen to the floor; as she rose the knife box toppled, spraying knives over her body, making cuts in her thighs. Running to the sink, she inadvertently pulled the arm of the faucet, scalding her hand. As it shot away from the fiery liquid her hand brushed the disposal switch, which set the machine moving deep in the bowels of the basin. She tried to shut if off, but it did not stop. As she reeled away from it the range-hood fan inexplicably turned on, as well as the two blenders along the shelf.

Reaching for the plugs, her hand brushed the toaster, which was hot. The red light went on in the coffee maker and on the microwave oven. The dishwasher began its first whirling cycle. Joining the maddening symphony, the disposal began to rasp, offering a grating, nasty metallic counterpoint.

The sweat of fear poured down her back. Every electrical appliance in the kitchen seemed to have turned on in sequence.

The cacophony of sound stabbed at her eardrums and the blood from her knife wounds began to soak through her slacks. Her scalded hand ached as she staggered madly around the kitchen bumping into pots, pans, colanders, salad bowls, scattering canned goods and food, breaking plates. Her head banged into the copper pots hanging overhead and when she felt herself falling from dizziness, she grabbed at them, bringing them down with her and bruising herself.

She lay in the wreckage screaming and helpless. Finding the strength to crawl along the kitchen floor on her belly, she grasped at the knob to the downstairs door, lifted herself, and staggered down the wooden stairs, slipping near the landing, banging her head. The noise from the kitchen followed her. She groped for and found the fuse box, opened the metal door, and pulled the master switch, plunging everything into darkness.

She lay on the cold floor of the basement, wondering if she had died. The house was uncommonly still, the air conditioning silenced. Every part of her seemed to ache and it was the pain finally that convinced her that she was still alive. In the darkness she could not tell if it was tears or blood that rolled down her cheeks. She could not even determine which was more pervasive, her pain or her anger.

Trying to stand, she fell back. Her knees gave, but she followed a beam of daylight from the partially opened door and dragged herself up the stairs. The kitchen was a shambles. Avoiding the wreckage, she staggered to the bathroom to survey the damage to her body. There were some bruises visible on the side of her head. A crisscross of cuts ran over her thighs. The blood had caked and there were welts and bruises on her arms. Her scalded hand smarted.

But the physical pain paled beside her anger. She had no illusions about what had occurred. The bastard had booby-trapped the kitchen. As she cleaned herself and suffered the stings of antiseptic on her cuts, she felt an irresistible urge for revenge. As she had suspected when she had locked him into the sauna, she knew she had the capacity to kill. Without guilt. Without remorse. Hadn't he attempted to mortally injure her by tampering with her kitchen? By making it a weapon?

After her thirst for revenge came determination, a hardening of the will beyond anything she had ever experienced before. "You will never stop me," she told her image in the mirror.

She cleaned up the kitchen as best she could and, using tools from his workshop, pried out the plugs and disconnected all the appliances he had tampered with, including the electric stove. One sink was still operating. She did not call an electrician. There was no time. Besides, surveying the situation, she decided that she could still prepare the dinner without using any of the appliances, although she had to go to the store and buy a hand-operated meat grinder and several slicing and grating gadgets.

"Fuck technology," she whispered to the mute appliances, checking carefully to be sure that the gas stove and oven had not been tampered with. Miraculously, the gas stove had escaped. She would need that.

As she worked long into the night, she felt a grudging admiration for labor-saving devices that had been created for the benefit of the modern woman. The irony, she knew, was that these devices had been invented by men, making women obvious conspirators in their own destruction. Such thoughts kept her attitude positive and her resolve unweakened. She reveled in her independence, her creativity, her resourcefulness.

She slept in her clothes and with one hand on the handle of a cleaver, knowing that if he gave her the slightest opportunity she would use it on him. The surety of that knowledge brought odd comfort. She heard him come into the house, but he had not paused, bounding up the stairs to his room, in his wake the sound of Benny's nails clicking on the marble foyer. To further fortify herself, over each entrance to the kitchen she had stretched a taut line, on which she hung pots and pans, set to make a loud clatter at the least provocation.

She lay on the cot, eyes open, listening for the slightest sound. Let him come. She was ready. . . .

At dawn she was up again, putting the final touches on the *foie gras*, pounding the dough for the puff pastry in which she would wrap the beef fillet. By midmorning she had filled the clamshells with the makings of the crab imperial, readying it for the oven. The fillet was now being partially cooked in the oven, prior to its being coated with *foie gras*, wrapped in pastry, and decorated. The *vichyssoise* was already safely tucked away in the refrigerator.

She had kept her head. She was proud of that and when the three servants showed up—two white-gloved waiters and a maid—she felt the euphoria of victory. Nothing was impossible.

She sat at the head of the table like a presiding magistrate. She had carefully dressed in an old Galanos and had brought in a hairdresser to do her hair. Her guests, echoing her own thoughts, pronounced her beautiful and she felt high-spirited and witty, joking with the Greek ambassador on her right and the Thai ambassador on her left. She had high expectations that the after-dinner toasts would offer exaggerated compliments to her charm, her looks, and, most important, to her culinary ability. Mr. White, the *Washington Post* food editor, asked explicit questions about each dish and seemed greatly impressed by the details she provided.

She sensed how impressed they were with the house, its possessions, the lovely silver and china displayed on the table. The beef Wellington was perfect, and she was certain that some supernatural force had intervened to assist her.

"I cannot tell you all how happy I am," she told them as the waiters, skilled in the impeccable French service, served each guest a slice of beef Wellington. She could not remember ever being happier. This would be the first of many dinner parties, she decided. She would be more than the great caterer of Washington, she fantasized. She would be a great hostess. After all, she had the grand house, the charm and attractiveness, and would be, or was already, one of the great practitioners of the noble art of cookery. She would surpass Julia Child, become a great world culinary authority. International celebrities would vie with one another to be invited to her table, and her books would be published throughout the world.

"I hadn't realized," the Greek ambassador said as his fork slipped into the tender beef, "what an extraordinary woman you are." He looked at her with an expression of fawning admiration. For the first time in her life she felt a sense of power. This was her conception. Her party. It vindicated her willingness to go through the fires of hell to keep this house, this ambience.

Pleased, she looked around the table at her guests—the men in black tie, the women in expensive gowns—realizing how much this house made a statement in the pantheon of Washington. It was something she had always believed, sensed, but now she saw its real value and understood the true reason for her private war. In Washington, perhaps everywhere else, a person is known by the neighborhood he keeps, the size of his house and the possessions contained therein. For someone like herself struggling for personal fulfillment, it meant a head start.

The idea warmed her and she felt herself softening. Perhaps some compromise could be worked out with Jonathan. Now that she felt more secure, there might be more room to relax her demands. If only he would give her space. His presence crowded her. His living in the house was a constant irritant.

The Greek ambassador continued to address her. She nodded. Her mind was drifting. If only she could make Jonathan understand how important this house was to her. There was, she decided, ample room for compromise. Despite what was happening now, Jonathan was a practical man, a reasonable man. Compassionate, too. Her decision had cut too deeply. Both of them had overreacted. Besides, hadn't they once loved each other? . . .

Benny's bark intruded. Hearing it prompted an instantaneous reflex, a shiver of dread. The sound was Jonathan's clarion and, for a moment, she felt the odd panic.

Alert to her nerve ends, she listened for his impending step. The bark continued, then faded. Her eyes probed the room. All three in help were busy clearing the table in preparation for serving the dessert, working in tandem with swift, efficient, professional silence.

A sense of uneasiness gripped her and she excused herself and went into the kitchen. The éclairs were laid out on their tray, waiting to be served; the chocolate sauce was warming on a burner over low heat. To the eye, nothing seemed amiss.

"What is it, Mrs. Rose?" one of the waiters asked, startled by her presence.

"Why did you all leave the kitchen?" she murmured, knowing that the question was ambiguous. The waiter, a tall, distinguished-looking black man, looked confused.

"Never mind," she said quickly, surveying the kitchen once again. Turning, she went back to the table. The sight of her guests reassured her and she sat down, watching the waiters pour the dessert champagne.

"Everything is perfect," the wife of the Thai ambassador whispered, filling Barbara with pride, chasing her uncertainty.

A waiter served the éclairs, and another followed with the warm chocolate sauce. Mr. White of the *Post* made a round sign of approval with his fingers, which completely dispelled her anxiety and she dug into the dessert. The chocolate seemed thicker than she might have wished, but the custard filling was perfect.

A tinkling of silver on glass startled her. The Greek ambassador rose. Stripped of his title and government-provided home in Sheridan Circle, he would be a very unimposing man, but standing now, well nourished with what, she was convinced, were some of the finest and best-prepared victuals in the world, well watered with rare wines, dressed in black tie and wrapped in the patina of diplomatic finesse, he made the symbol of her elegant home tangible. What did it matter if he barely knew her? He was visibly impressed. His toast was a potpourri of accented platitudes and compliments and she loved them all. She had never heard them applied to herself.

"A hostess of rare beauty, a gourmet of the first rank, a woman of elegant taste, impeccable." The words rumbled outward in soothing waves. It was delicious. Others rose and echoed the Greek ambassador.

When they were finished and she had responded with a few modest words that she had memorized, she led them into the library for liqueurs and coffee.

"Would you mind if we made an appointment for an interview, Mrs. Rose?" White asked. "There's something special apparently at work here." She flushed and nodded, offering a touch of the obligatory humility.

"I cannot tell you how embarrassed I was over our former problem," the Greek ambassador's wife said in labored English.

"I had no idea," the wife of the undersecretary told her, kissing her on the cheek.

A waiter passed cigars, cutting each proffered end with a flourish. The men became engrossed in political conversation. The women talked of other matters. Barbara delighted in the buzz of conversation, the sure mark of a successful party.

Then, from the corner of her eye, she saw the sudden frown, a brief wrinkling of the brow of the French military attaché. She saw him whisper something to a waiter, who responded quickly, pointing to the foyer, and the man hurried off.

At that moment the wife of the Greek ambassador rose and looked curiously at Barbara, who understood instantly.

"On the first floor," Barbara said quickly. She watched the woman's gowned figure recede, but the odd, unspoken note of pleading disturbed her.

When White left the room with what seemed like uncommon speed, she began to feel the familiar tug of anxiety. With acute clarity, she heard the quick knocking on the door of the occupied hall loo. Rising, she went into the foyer and was suddenly confronted by the pale, tense face of the food editor.

"Are you all right?"

"Please." It seemed the only word he could muster.

"Upstairs. There's one in the master bedroom."

She looked after him as he raced up the stairs. As she turned, the Thai ambassador was moving toward her, a pained expression on his dark face. Reality was crowding into her consciousness.

"No. There's someone there," she cried. "On the third floor."

She was diverted suddenly by a woman's voice.

"Jacques," the voice cried, knocking on the closed door of the hall loo. She heard a muffled avalanche of French invective. The word *merde* came to her loud and clear, triggering further revelation. Turning, she saw more of her guests come toward her. They seemed to meld into one another, their voices raised in a cacophony of discordant sounds.

"I'm sorry," she cried. "You must understand . . . it wasn't me."

The house suddenly seemed to come alive. The sound of flushing toilets, doors opening and closing, hurried footsteps. She saw the front door open and people brush past her.

"Forgive me," she cried, feeling suddenly a bubbling sensation begin in her innards.

"My God," she screamed, running to the rear of the house, through the kitchen, past the startled waiters, stripped of their uniforms now, busy cleaning up.

"What is it, Mrs. Rose?" one of them called after her.

She had lost any conscious sense of direction, finding herself finally in the garden. As she squatted in a clump of azaleas near the wall of the garage, she heard an unmistakably familiar sound next to her. There he was, the Greek ambassador, his bare bottom shining in the glare of the full moon. Slowly, his face turned toward her, implacable, expressionless. It seemed disembodied, like a lighted jack-o'-lantern hanging in the air.

"Madame," the face said, nodding, offering an inexplicable smile.

"Help me," she cried, looking away, hoping she would turn to stone.

She hid behind the azaleas for a long time, inert, paralyzed with mortification, watching the house. Only when she was certain that everyone had left did she find the will to move. Standing, she felt the acid of anger fill her, inflating her with its corrosive power. If he was within reach, she was certain, she would have strangled him and enjoyed the process. As her eyes roved the deserted garden, a beam of moonlight lit up the shiny cover of his Ferrari, which she could see through the window of the garage.

As if guided by some powerful force outside herself, she entered the garage by the garden door. With slow deliberation, she removed the car's covering, then lifted off the fiberglass top, which she carefully set on its side. He had shown her how to do it. When he had first bought the Ferrari, he had let her drive it, but she took no pleasure in the process. It was a man's toy.

In a toolbox on the shelf she found a screwdriver and unscrewed the box that held the mechanism for opening and closing the garage door It was a simple matter to adjust the fail-safe mechanism. Once, the door had nearly crushed Mercedes, who had scurried away just in time,. and Jonathan had explained to her what had gone wrong with the fail-safe device. It was an extra-heavy door. The irony pleased her now, clearing her mind, enabling her to focus single-mindedly on her task.

When she had completed it, she took the remote-control gadget from its hook and tested it by opening and closing the door. Releasing the Ferrari's emergency brake, she put the gears in neutral and pushed the light car halfway through the open garage door. It moved easily. Only thirty-two hundred pounds, he had explained. Just forty-seven inches high.

She felt her lips form a smile as she pressed the down button, watching as the heavy door descended on the defenseless car. The sound of the crunching metal was satisfying, oddly musical, as she repeatedly raised and lowered the garage door like a giant hammer. When destruction seemed complete in one spot, she moved the car and began working on another. The steering column bent, the wheel broke off, the dashboard crumbled. Each stroke of the door gave her a special shiver of joy. She had never experienced such wild exhilaration, and she abandoned herself to the sheer excitement, her fingers working the remote-control gadget with relentless deliberation.

When the novelty of the pleasure subsided, she simply pushed the car back into the garage and, closing the door, replaced the remote-control gadget on its hook.

What she had done restored her courage and she felt able to go back into the house again. At least now, she thought, she could enjoy her rage in peace.

23

He sat in his office, sipping his morning coffee, eating the doughnut provided by Miss Harlow, and looked glumly out the window. He had been certain that what he had done to her kitchen would have finished, once and for all, the foolishness of her fancy dinner party. It had taken him one whole night to do the job. She'd had no right to go ahead with it, flouting him, using the proceeds from a blatant theft of his possessions. By insisting on having the party, she'd brought it all on herself.

For a while he had reveled in his cleverness, hiding in the sun-room until just the right moment; then he'd dropped Ex-Lax into the chocolate sauce, adding an extra piece to the mix for good measure. If he hadn't gone to the movies, he might have saved the Ferrari from her wrath, although he doubted it. Seeing it this morning, all he wanted to do was to cry. But the tears refused to come. He supposed he should have expected something of the sort. Fifty thousand shot to hell. And it was he who had shown her how to wield the weapon. She was one resourceful bitch. He'd give her that.

It was impossible to believe that a human being could change so much. Well, he was changing, too. He could be as unpredictable as she. The worst part for him now was to accept the idea of her strength. She was rubbing his nose in it, humiliating him.

"Some people never understand until you rub their noses in it," he had told her many times, referring to various antagonists in his practice. Goldstein would have called it *chutzpah*, which was one word for which he did not need a translation. To throw a fancy dinner party with the proceeds of what was, in purely legal terms, stolen property was unmitigated *chutzpah*. Not to pay the overdue utility bills was compounding the *chutzpah*. And this deliberate destruction of one of the great mechanical marvels of the age . . .

He felt his gorge rise and banged the coffee cup in its saucer. On his desk were dunning notices of all kinds, which he gathered up and ripped in half. The bill collectors were beginning to call him at the office and he was ducking the calls.

"They'll cut you off," Miss Harlow had warned.

"Her, too," he had responded.

"You'll be without lights, without air conditioning," Miss Harlow lectured.

"Her, too."

The children had begun to write and he was disturbed that they addressed their letters to his office, as if they had already acknowledged that the house was not to be his.

"Please write to me at home. It is my home. Our home. I paid for everything in it and continue to do so." Rereading his words to them, he thought they sounded harsh, but he did not tear the letter up. He wanted to be emphatic. He was still the master of the family ship, he told himself. He searched his mind for what else to write, but could not think of much, since he was too absorbed in his present dilemma. One obsession at a time. He sent them handsome checks and left it at that.

He carried the inventory list with him now and every night checked through the house to be sure she had not taken any more of their possessions. She had continued to write him little notes and Scotch-tape them to his door, and soon they became repetitive; one-liners about the imminent cutoff of their utilities.

"You pay them," he had scribbled, Scotch-taping the notes back on her door.

Living the way he did, from day to day, gave him a different view of time. With mental discipline, he found, he could keep his mind working, but only in the present. When an anxiety intruded that required some perspective on the future, even if only a few moments ahead, he ripped it from his consciousness. In that way he was able to cope with the impending utilities cutoff as well. No hardship, he decided, would be too much.

Ann had called him a few times at the office and he'd been deliberately cold, although he admitted to himself that he missed her. It was all part of his determination to live solely in the immediate present.

"Are you all right?" she would ask.

"Coping." Once he had hated that word. Coping implied hopelessness.

"I hear from the children regularly," she told him. "They're fine. But they worry about you."

"They shouldn't."

"So do I."

"You shouldn't."

"I miss you, Jonathan," she would whisper. At that point he would usually bid her an abrupt good-bye.

One night he returned home and found the house deathly quiet. The welcoming purr of the air conditioning had ceased and he realized that the absence of sound meant that the electricity had been shut off. The house had already taken on the clammy humidity of a Washington summer. Barbara had apparently left the windows closed to take advantage of the last lingering bit of cool air.

With the aid of some matches, he groped his way to the workshop, found two flashlights, and made his way back up the stairs. Then he remembered his wine. Without the cooling system, the temperature rise would threaten his reds, perhaps his whites as well. He had forgotten about that. He would empty the vault tomorrow, he promised himself, irritated by the oversight. So the wines, too, were innocent victims. He decided he needed a drink to calm his agitation. Led by the flashlight's beam, he made his way to the library.

The wooden doorknobs of the armoire seemed stuck, which he attributed to the moisture-swollen wood. Putting the flashlight down, he tugged on the knobs with one hand braced against one of the doors. It would not budge. He tugged again. He heard a straining, squeaking sound below him and, to his horror, the armoire tipped slowly forward, all nine feet of it, a massive wall pressing downward against him. He flattened his hands and tried to hold it up, but the tipping movement was relentless. With all his strength, he tried to become a human brace. The bottles crashed against each other as the armoire slowly moved forward. Twisting his body, he managed to turn completely and brace the weight against his shoulders, pushing upward with his legs.

For the moment he succeeded and the armoire moved back. But he was trapped under its weight. The muscles in his shoulders and thighs ached. Soon, he knew, they would weaken. His strength would ebb. When it gave out, the armoire would come crashing down on him unless he could jump out of its way, which was unlikely. Every skin pore opened and the sweat cascaded down his face, stinging his eyes.

"Help me," he screamed, remembering suddenly

his experience in the sauna. Fat chance, he thought. The ruthless bitch. His resolve hardened. He tried to shift the weight periodically and managed to redistribute it temporarily, holding that position until his shoulder was shot through with pain and each position became equally unbearable. Aside from the compelling danger, which was terribly real and ominous, he felt ridiculous. Soon he would simply have to plunge forward, accepting whatever injury the heavy object would dispense.

The muscles in his shoulders tired first, then his back, and finally he was struggling just to keep standing. His legs began to shake. Save me, he wanted to scream. Who would hear him? Who would care?

"Dirty bitch," he mumbled, hoping his hatred would fire the strength in his flagging muscles. His breath came in gasps now. He was faltering. His body was collapsing and he felt the full weight of the armoire move downward. His knees began to give. Gathering all his remaining strength, he prepared himself to take a giant leap forward. But he could not summon the strength. The weight was descending swiftly now. Finally he was on his knees. The pain in his shoulders was excruciating. The thought of injury or even his death in this manner revolted him, since it would give her the victory she wanted. Suddenly the power of hate intervened, and he felt the force of it shoot through his tired muscles. Concentrating all his energy, he lurched away from the falling armoire.

As it fell his body did not escape completely, and the armoire caught his shoe by its sole and badly twisted his ankle. The pain stabbed him. But he managed to contort his body, untie his shoelace, and painfully extract his foot from the trapped shoe.

Whiskey oozed from under the armoire, soaking through his clothes, its acrid smell permeating the room.

If she was up in her room, she surely had heard the crash. He had no illusions about her motives. This caper was no mere annoyance. It was the real thing. He crawled across the library floor, where a confused Benny had been startled to wakefulness by the noise of the crash. He felt Benny's warm tongue on his face. "Good old Benny," he whispered, embracing him, breathing in his doggy odor. It was more welcome than that of the liquor and perspiration in which he was soaked.

Raising himself on one leg, he managed to hop to the phone. It was, he was relieved to find, still functioning and he called a cab, then crawled outside to wait for it.

"You're lucky it's not broken," the black intern in the emergency room of the Washington Hospital Center told him. He shook his head. "You'd better get off the juice. This is what always happens."

"I'm not on it."

"You stink like a brewery."

Jonathan felt the futility of responding. Who would believe him? He accepted a shot of painkiller and went back to the house.

But before he went to sleep, he Scotch-taped a note to her door. The shock had weakened him and the scrawl was wispy and uncertain.

"You had better watch your ass," he had written. Like her notes, it was unsigned.

He woke up in a puddle of sweat. Every muscle ached. He felt stiff, ravaged, and his ankle throbbed. With the air conditioning not working, there was not a stir of air in the room.

He posed a question to himself: Is this me? Searching his mind, he looked for glimpses of identification.

He spelled his name, whispered his Social Security number, his date of birth, the name of his law firm, the address of his house, the names of his children. Superficial, he decided, half-amused, certain that the pained hulk lying moist and terrified in the two-hundred-year-old canopied bed was not himself at all.

Himself, he declared, was a forty-year-old man named Jonathan Rose, with two beautiful children, Eve and Josh, and a lovely, loyal, beautiful, wonderful wife named Barbara.

The name set off a musical lilt in his mind. Barbara. Dear Barbara. Whatever had happened to her? Where was everybody?

He had lived with and loved someone for nearly two decades and all she was, was an object of his imagination, something without substance or reality. He wished he could blot her from his mind, all the years, all the false roles.

He got out of bed and opened the drapes to the rising sun. Opening the windows, he was disappointed to discover that the outside air was as hot as it was inside. He had forgotten how hot a Washington summer could be.

Something was missing in the room. Benny wasn't there. Somehow he had got lost in the shuffle of last night's events. Sticking his head out the window, Jonathan shouted the dog's name, then listened for his familiar bark. Yet he wasn't worried about Benny. Benny could take care of himself.

Inadvertently, as he moved toward the bathroom he put too much weight on his ankle and crashed against the wall in agony; it took some time to gather his strength again. Peering at his worn face in the bathroom mirror, he felt the odd sensation of personal liberation. He actually felt good, and he couldn't believe it. He searched his mind for a reason. For the first time since Barbara had shocked him with her admission, he now felt the complete absence of doubt. He had no more illusions. He knew the real score. The lines were clearly drawn. The bitch would not be satisfied until she had his balls in her hand. Never, never, he vowed. It was the moment of truth. Basic hate. Basic war.

He winked at his image in the mirror and, making a fist, shook it in front of his face. There was no undue heat to his anger now. The cutting edge was cool. He knew what he had to do. He picked up the phone.

"I'll be away for a few days," he told Miss Harlow.

"You need a vacation, Mr. Rose."

He paused, deliberately giving weight to her suggestion.

"I know what I need," he whispered, hanging up.

24

She had always hated the armoire in the library. Big, bulky, and overpowering, it was, as she saw it, typical of some compensating masculine desire for bigness. Sawing the front legs where they joined the cabinet and cementing the front doors had been practically a labor of love.

But she had expected, and hoped for, a larger crash. Perhaps she hadn't quite thought it through and applied the energy and zeal that he had expended to booby-trap her kitchen or ruin her food. What she had done to his Ferrari she dismissed as "compulsive inspiration." Of course, he was more adept mechanically than she. It was time, she decided, to get tough, really tough. She was prepared to devote herself totally to the task. Like everything else, this chore, too, she would have to take on herself. Thurmont, she decided, was only out to line his pockets.

With her children safely tucked away at camp, the house empty, she was free to maneuver. She'd drive him out of the house or die trying, she vowed.

The armoire tactic, although disappointing, could be considered a warning of things to come. From her window she had seen him hobble off to a waiting taxi with what seemed like a comparatively minor injury. Then she had heard him return and limp up the stairs.

The night was unbearably hot and she had opened the windows. The sounds of the city were unfamiliar and that and the heat and listening for Jonathan inhibited her sleep. As daylight emerged she got up, showered, and, surprisingly, felt refreshed.

As she quietly closed her door she saw the note he had written. Removing it, she scrawled a line in lipstick and reattached it to his door.

"Hell is coming," the note read.

Holding her shoes in her hand, she moved downstairs stealthily to the kitchen. She removed the containers of still-frozen *pâté* and chicken *galantine* from the freezer and loaded them into her car. She had decided that rather than let them spoil, she would give them as gifts to her various customers, those that she could still count on. She had written off her recent dinner guests. Her mortification lingered. She hoped she would never have to face any of them again. As for the others, she hoped they would remember her generosity. Adversity, she had found, spawned resourcefulness.

The next few weeks would be slow, businesswise, anyway. Most people fled Washington in the summer, at least from mid-July to the end of August. She had more immediate and pressing problems on her mind.

Although she wasn't used to anticipating events, she moved some cartons of canned goods and perishables from the refrigerator up to her room. Just in case, she told herself, proud of her newfound wiliness. In case of what? she wondered. But that thought did not diminish her new feelings of pride and self-reliance.

"I'll be away for a while," she told the proprietor of the French Market, who accepted her *pâté* with a flourish and a kiss on both cheeks. It took her three hours to make her rounds.

Returning, she let herself in through the back door. Cautiously, she ascended the back stairs as if she were walking through a minefield. She must learn to be alert, she told herself, wondering if he was still in his room.

A note was Scotch-taped to her door, scribbled on a piece of jagged cardboard ripped from a piece used as backing for laundered shirts. He had torn away the note she had pasted on his door.

"It has come your way." The words were written in his sloppy, doctorlike scrawl. Her bedroom door was open a crack and an odd odor emanated from within. It confirmed what she had intuitively known. He had made another key to her room, which explained how he had tampered with her Valium.

Inside the room, she discovered that he had outdone even her most exaggerated expectations, despite her determination not to be surprised at anything he did.

He had methodically opened all the canned goods she had brought to her room and emptied their contents in the sink, the bathtub, and the toilet. The food had already begun to give off a foul, rotting odor and the sight was equally offensive. She was annoyed that she hadn't been able to predict such an action. But she fought down anger. Anger was one emotion that she would resist. Stay calm, she cautioned herself, noting that the windows were now closed. She moved to open them but couldn't get the casement knobs to move. Inspecting them, she realized that he had cemented them closed.

Without giving the act another thought, she picked out one of her high-heeled shoes and, using it as a hammer, knocked out all sixteen lights of each window, carefully removing the glass with a handkerchief and dropping the slivers into the bushes below. He had, by some strange quirk of fastidiousness, placed the empty cans in their cartons, as if he were determined to limit the damage to their rugs and furnishings. She smiled at that, since it told her that the damage she had inflicted on the armoire had meant more to him than this incredibly ridiculous act of revenge.

She felt almost exhilarated as she went into the bathroom determined to clean up the mess as quickly as possible. Again she had not anticipated his actions. He apparently had shut off the water. Very clever, she told herself. She knew, of course, where the main water valve was located and, moving downstairs, discovered that it was not shut off, which meant that he had blocked the water pipes to her bathroom.

The kitchen taps worked fine. She filled as many stock pots as she could find and laboriously carried the water upstairs, dumping it into the bathtub. Again he had foiled her. He had, of course, blocked up the drain.

Her sense of calm purpose was ruffled. Despite the air coming into the room, the odor was still offensive, and it was obvious she could not stay there for long. The effort of bringing up the pots of water had left her with sweat-soaked clothes. She changed into jeans and a T-shirt. No underwear. No shoes. Her battle dress. She saluted herself in the mirror.

Throwing a canvas shopping bag over one shoulder, she went downstairs and proceeded to fill it up with what she considered useful items, a flashlight, candles, matches, bread, cheese, cookies. Then she chose the sharpest, heaviest cleaver she could find among her cutting tools. Thus armed, she went into his workroom, surprised to find it unlocked. She put a hammer and screwdriver into her canvas bag, then slowly, methodically, emptied all the containers on his neatly lined shelves in the workroom, all the screws, bolts, nails, nuts, every small item that he had carefully catalogued and put in its proper place.

In her heart, she knew she had always wanted to

make this place a jumble. Its perfect organization had always offended her. His oasis, he had called it. The thought merely intensified her passion for destruction. She cut all the wires off the power tools and drowned most of the other tools in a tub of lubricating oil.

There was a certain logical progression to everything she did, she assured herself, like the relentless course of true justice. She was even able to maintain a superior moral position about what she was doing, remembering Jonathan's often quoting a line attributed to Hemingway: "Moral is anything that makes you feel good." And she felt good, deliciously buoyant.

It was growing dark and she made her way by flashlight up the stairs, sprinkling bottles of remaining screws and bolts on the steps. Any obstacle was a weapon, she told herself, feeling shrewd.

Passing his room on the way to the third floor, she noted, through her flashlight beam, that the cardboard was no longer on the door. So he had ventured outside his domain.

Silently, she padded up to Ann's old room. The sleigh bed moved easily against the door and she lay down on its bare mattress, alert to any sound. Her hand tightened around the cleaver handle, its blade cool against her cheek. She hoped he would try to attack her. She was ready.

25

In the flickering candlelight he could see the long row of wine bottles that he had rescued from the now-useless vault. He had finished one already, the Grand Vin de Château Latour '66, nibbling simultaneously on some Camembert he had found in the fast-warming refrigerator. Now he uncorked a '64 of the same wine. Definitely inferior, he told himself, letting the liquid slowly roll on his palate. That done, he upended the bottle and swallowed deep, greedy drafts.

Stripped down to his jockey shorts, he was sticky with perspiration. Through the open windows he could hear the night sounds of the city, a honking horn, a screeching tire, a child's scream. He thought of what he had done earlier, opening all those cans. What an unsightly mishmash. He erupted into peals of hysterical laughter.

Surely there were other delights ahead, he told himself, finishing the bottle and rolling it under the bed. Earlier, he had whistled to Benny. He missed Benny. He needed him to talk to. Benny truly understood. He stuck his head out the open window and shouted, "Benny, Benny, you horny old bastard." He would have to call the pound in the morning. Once or twice Benny had strayed too far from home and the dogcatcher had caught up with him. "I'll whip your ass, you desert me now," he vowed. "In my hour of greatest need." He knew he was drunk. There was no point in being sober. Not now. Not ever.

Taking another wine bottle, and with flashlight in hand, he limped out of his room, listening at her door. Through the cracks where the door fitted into the jamb he could still smell the repugnant mess he had created. He was sure he had driven her from her room. Their room. It was a first step. He toasted the victory with a long pull on the wine bottle. He went into Eve's room, fiddled with the dial on her large portable radio, and, finding the most raucous rock station, turned the music on full blast. The exploding sound filled the silent house. He opened the door to Josh's room, looked inside to be sure it was empty, then put the radio in the corridor outside, first pulling off the volume and selection knobs. Barbara, he knew, hated loud rock music even more than he did. "Enjoy, bitch," he muttered.

Holding on to the brass banister for support, he found it difficult to carry both the flashlight and the wine bottle. Emptying the latter in a long draft and then discarding it, he moved cautiously downstairs. In the library, concentrating the beams of the flashlight, he saw the armoire lying on its belly like some dead monster. The room stank of liquor. He shrugged and turned away. No sense mourning any dead soldiers now. There surely would be many more. Leaving the library, he limped along the hallway, past the kitchen, to the door that led to his workroom.

Although there was a fuzzy edge to his mind, it had not, he assured himself, affected his motivation, his single-minded purpose of driving her from the house. *His* house. Holding the flashlight high to light the stairs, he stepped onto the first step. He had struck out with his good leg, but his foot hit something unsteady. His leg buckled in pain. He could not get a firm grip. His balance gone, he dropped the flashlight and slid down the wooden steps, grasping along the wall. Stabs of pain speared his skin as he lurched into metal objects strewn along the staircase.

The impact had broken the flashlight, plunging the area into darkness. The loss of balance and the pain sobered him instantly. He sensed he was lying at the entrance to his workroom. Feeling about his torso, he picked off metal objects, some of which had embedded themselves into his flesh. He knew he was bleeding. As his eyes became accustomed to the darkness he was able to make out objects in the workroom and to comprehend the devastation. Crawling carefully, he moved toward the sauna, lifting himself by the wooden handle, opening the door, and feeling his way inside.

He felt as if he had crawled inside a black hole. Unable to see anything now, he stretched out on the built-in redwood bench, knowing he was trapped here until the natural light filtered through the ground-floor windows. With the tips of his fingers he assessed his injuries, picking out more bits of metal from his flesh.

Vaguely, he imagined he could hear the discordant strains of the rock music. The idea that she, too, was tossing in the agony of wakefulness comforted him somewhat, although he felt a keen sense of his own inadequacy. The elation he had felt earlier had disappeared. He cursed his stupidity, his failure in not predicting the extent of her next act of retaliation. He was, apparently, still thinking of her as the old Barbara, not as the cagey viper she had become.

The shock of his fall had jogged his mind into alertness. He laid out the house in his mind, every nook and cranny, every pipe and wire. He was certain he knew it better than she. If it was to be a weapon, then so be it. He could devise a thousand more horrors. The house was his and, therefore, a trusted ally. They would fight her together. Nothing in life was worth anything if you didn't fight for it, he told himself, stimulating his courage. And his patience.

Sweat rolled down his body. Periodically, he would open the door to see if the light had come yet. The night seemed interminable.

When dawn did come at last, he moved out of the sauna and picked his way among the wreckage of his workroom. His resolve had become specific now and he knew exactly what he was looking for. He was surprised that the silicone spray cans and the large square can of lubricating oil were intact and where he had originally stored them.

Picking them up, along with a crowbar for which he had no other specific purpose in mind than its use as a weapon, he picked his way among the rubble and carefully ascended the steps, brushing aside the tacks and screws and bolts with the flat of his hand. As he limped through the corridor nothing intruded on his sense of purpose, although he gave himself a passing glance in the hall mirror, quickly turning away from the ravaged, unshaven visage.

The smashed radio lay in ruins at the foot of the second-floor stairs. She had apparently attacked it, beaten it to death unmercifully. With the aid of the banister, he pulled himself up the flight of stairs to the third floor, concluding that Barbara was holed up in Ann's room.

With the crowbar, he pulled out the tacks that held the carpet runner on the stairs, rolled it downward step by step, uncovering the bare wood. Then he calmly sprayed each step with silicone. When that ran out, he poured a thin film of oil on the remaining boards.

Despite the incongruity of doing the work in jockey shorts, he felt methodical and businesslike, as if he were writing a brief or dictating to Miss Harlow. What he was doing was necessary, a tangible countermeasure to soften her blind and corrosive stubbornness. This could all have been avoided, he thought, if only she hadn't been obdurate and grossly unreasonable. There was simply no other alternative.

When he had completed his self-assigned task, he walked up the back stairs. When he reached the top landing, he jammed a wooden wedge into the door to prevent its opening and, like a man who had completed the day's work, retired to his own room. He felt he deserved a drink and opened a bottle of Lafite-Rothschild '59. It was, after all, a special occasion. Finishing it quickly, he lay down exhausted on his bed. He imagined he could hear Benny's familiar bark in the distance. It reminded him to pick up the phone and call the pound. But the phone was dead. In disgust, he pulled it out of the wall and flung it across the room, where it crashed and split. He opened another bottle of wine and finished it.

He awoke, his mind on the outer edge of a bad dream, but could not remember where the dream ended and reality began. The room was dark, the heat unbearable. He lay in a pool of fetid moisture. Struggling out of bed, he moved in fits and starts toward the bathroom, feeling waves of nausea. His throat burned and he put his head under the faucet and turned the tap. Nothing came out. Groping back through the room, he uncorked a bottle of wine and poured some of it over his head, gargled some and spat it out. Then he took a long drink.

The drink steadied him and he lit a candle, carrying it to the mirror to view himself. Surveying his face, he shook his head with despair. His beard was growing out, his eyes were encased in deep circles, and his bare torso seemed pocked and scarred.

Opening the door of his room, he half expected to see her unconscious body on the stairs and he was already feeling his disappointment at not having heard her screams of pain. He had wanted, more than anything, to hear her scream.

Standing in the hallway, he felt a strange sense of *déjà vu*, and for a moment was disoriented, lost in time. Strange odors seemed to permeate the air, but now, suddenly, he could pick out the familiar smell of her cooking again. The idea of it seemed bizarre, considering what was happening.

Turning suddenly as if she were prodding him, he saw a note Scotch-taped to his door, written carefully in what seemed now a much surer hand.

"This can't go on, Jonathan," the note said. "We must talk. Meet me in the dining room at nine."

The note was oddly tranquilizing. He felt a brief wave of shame, which changed quickly to hopefulness. Perhaps he was emerging finally from the nightmare. Was she coming to her senses at last? He read the note again. Of course. This could not indeed continue to go on. As if to buttress his optimism, the clock in the foyer offered nine chimes. Aware of his nakedness, he went back to his room and put on a print robe. The least he could do was dress for a possible reconciliation.

26

Ann had registered for summer school more as a ploy to keep her in town than to acquire additional credits toward her master's. Only a sense of guilt and regard for her dwindling finances kept her going to classes. What she had on her mind was the Rose family, particularly Jonathan.

Other than making brief phone calls to his office, a subterfuge to hear his voice and check his attitude, she had resisted any further contact. In the first place, she told herself, she had had more than her fair share of unrequited love. It was foolish, adolescent. Worse, it was one-sided. She was not a fool, she assured herself. Besides, it was time to find out whether he missed her. It annoyed her to be at the mercy of such a treacherously time-consuming and obsessive emotion. Yet, no amount of self-imposed discipline could chase it away. It was a curse. Its most insidious damage was to give her a sense of hope, hope that once the divorce was finally settled, he would choose devotion over indifference. She could make him a truly happy man. Besides, she loved the children. Every day she expected a call. None came. She wrote to the children. Periodically, she telephoned Eve.

"Do you see Mom and Dad?" Eve had asked.

"Oh, occasionally," Ann lied.

"I got a letter from Dad and one from Mom," Eve volunteered vaguely. Ann detected her unhappiness. "The principal problem for Josh and me is how we're going to handle Parents' Day."

Ann caught the tone of rising anxiety. Deliberately, she did not react, offering placating humor instead.

"I should be home," Eve said. "It was wrong for them to send me here."

"It's their problem, Eve. They have to work it out."

"I know." But nothing could move her. "I should be home with them. They need me."

"They'll be fine."

The words were uttered without conviction.

When she didn't hear from Jonathan for a couple of weeks, Ann called Jonathan's office, only to be told that he had left for vacation. She wondered vaguely why the children hadn't mentioned that in their letters, which were becoming increasingly anxious.

After much debate with herself she called the house. A recording informed her that the phone had been disconnected. Armed with innocuous questions, she called Goldstein and Thurmont. They, too, were on vacation.

Nevertheless, her curiosity was aroused. Why hadn't they told the children? The mystery irritated her, giving rise to all sorts of black prognostications. Unable to remain passive, she walked up Connecticut Avenue one afternoon to Kalorama Circle. From the outside, the house seemed its old gleaming, imperious self. She went around the back to the garden and looked through the glass panel of the garage door. The Ferrari was a battered hulk, a fact that both startled and confused her, but Barbara's station wagon and Eve's Honda were in their accustomed places. They offered no clues.

Perhaps the couple had somehow reconciled and were now vacationing. And how had Jonathan's prized Ferrari been wrecked? She allowed her mind to dismiss everything but the central question: Where were they? And why hadn't they contacted the children?

Walking around to the front again, she met the *Washington Star* paper boy, whom she knew casually.

"They canceled," he said with a shrug.

"You mean stopped delivery for some stated period?" she inquired.

"No. Canceled," the boy answered, throwing a paper on a neighbor's stoop.

Despite his assertion, she went up the steps and clapped the knocker, which automatically set off a carol of pleasant chimes. Waiting for a response, she stepped back and looked at the upper windows. The draperies were drawn. They were drawn at the lower windows as well. She clapped the knocker again, waited awhile, then went away. Later, she debated calling the police, then rejected the idea. It was too soon to declare them missing.

In the morning she called Miss Harlow.

"I'm sorry. He's on vacation," the woman reiterated.

"The kids are worried," Ann responded. "So am I."

"They called here as well," Miss Harlow confessed. "And I'm worried, too."

"And Barbara?"

"I called the French Market. They think she's on vacation as well." There was a long pause. "Do you suppose they've reconciled and just gone off together?"

"Maybe," Ann responded without conviction, acutely troubled now. She wondered if she should mention the Ferrari. It's not my business, she decided, and said good-bye.

Early the next morning, after a sleepless night, she

went back to the house. She noted that *The Washington Post* was not being delivered, either, certain evidence that no one was at home. Few Washingtonians ever started the day without the *Post*.

As she prepared to leave, something rooted her to the spot. She inspected the facade and noted, for the first time, that the panes in the master-bedroom windows were not reflecting the morning sunlight. After a closer inspection she realized they were gone.

Perhaps the panes had been broken by accident, she reasoned. It was not uncommon for empty homes to be vandalized in this manner. But all sixteen panes of each of the two windows?

She could not concentrate on anything that day and went back to the house in the late afternoon. For a long time she stood in the shade of a tree across the street, watching the house until dark. The street lights went on. But no lights appeared inside the house. Still not convinced, she knocked again, waited, then went back to the YWCA.

A few days later, she called Eve.

"I haven't heard from them for two weeks," Eve said. There was more than a passing note of anxiety in her tone. "No letters. Or phone calls. We can't understand it."

"Things are fine," Ann lied. "I saw them only yesterday. They both looked great."

"Then why don't they write? Or call?"

"Your dad's been traveling. And your mom is extremely busy with her catering business."

"It's not at all like them. Don't they care?" Eve began to cry. "Parents' Day is next week. I'm frightened, Ann."

"They're under a great deal of strain," Ann said, hating having lied. "Be patient," she cautioned Eve, who hung up still crying.

It was not like them to neglect their children. But anything was possible in their present state.

Still, she wasn't satisfied and returned once again to the house. She felt exceedingly foolish as she banged on the clapper. As before, no one answered. She put her ear to the thick wooden double door but could hear only the ticking of the big clock. It was impossible to contain her anxiety now. She dreaded having to tell Eve the truth. Either her parents were being deliberately neglectful or they were missing. *Missing*. Ann shuddered at the thought.

The question didn't occur to her until late that night. She awoke with a stifled scream on her lips. Who was winding the clock? For a long time she lay shivering in bed, groping for logic. Perhaps a maid was coming in. Or they had a house-sitter or someone who made periodic visits. But why wind the clock? She was determined to get to the bottom of this mystery.

Early the next morning, she went back to the house. Spreading some papers under a tree across the street, she sat down and did not budge from the spot all day long. Nothing changed. Cars passed. Their occupants looked at her with curiosity. But she remained, undaunted, determined. But this role of sentry made her uncomfortable. She had no idea what she was waiting for. Godot, she told herself, ridiculing her foolishness. She was, she supposed, acting out her own theater of the absurd. Inexplicably, the role, despite her passivity, was exhausting and she closed her eyes as she slipped into drowsiness. But when she opened her eyes again, she knew instantly that something had changed. Suddenly shocked into alertness, she surveyed the facade. The upstairs shutters of the master bedroom were closed. Her heart lurched. She stood up and stared at the closed black shutters. Then she ran across the street and banged the knocker again. The chimes began to reverberate through the house. Soon they faded.

"Jonathan, Barbara," she cried. "Please. It's Ann."

Listening with her ear against the door, she heard only the relentless clicking of the big clock. A neighbor came out and stared at her.

"I think they've gone on vacation," she told Ann politely but with an air of rebuke. "Not that it's my business." She went back into her own house.

Paranoia about privacy was endemic to the neighborhood. Everyone lived his own life. But she knew she was not mistaken. Someone had closed the shutters. Someone, she was certain now, was in the house. She had to get in somehow. But she didn't want to be seen and, perhaps, be taken for a burglar. She patiently waited until it was nearly dark.

Iron bars made it impossible to break in through the ground-floor windows. She went around to the rear of the house and tried the door that led to the basement and Jonathan's workshop. It was shut tight, locked from the inside.

Remembering that Jonathan kept a ladder under the eaves of the garage, she opened the garage door and moved the ladder to the rear of the house. Leaning it against an outer wall, she climbed up and peered into the sun-room. A three-quarter moon gave her some light and her eyes quickly grew accustomed to the semi-darkness. The familiar room seemed perfectly normal. Empty flowerpots lined the inner wall just below her. With her shoe she broke the window and carefully picked away the shards of glass. As she crossed, a piece of glass scraped her knee. In her effort to avoid it further, she inadvertently kicked the ladder, which fell to the ground.

The cut stung but wasn't deep. Disregarding it, she moved cautiously into the kitchen. It was too dark to make out anything but shapes and she had to rely on memory to get around. She moved with extreme caution.

Something, she sensed immediately, was radically wrong with the configurations of the kitchen. Nothing seemed in its rightful place except the work island. She groped around with her hands, taking short, cautious steps. Suddenly something loomed in front of her, a rope. She tugged at it and a rain of pots came down, making an explosive, ear-splitting, clanging noise. She screamed, tried to run, then fell. Nothing was placed as she remembered it. She rose and moved into the corridor that led to the foyer, but as soon as she reached the marbled surface there was no friction. Her feet gave way and she hit the floor, sliding along the surface. She could not rise. Every surface she touched was too slippery to hold.

Under other circumstances, she might have been reminded of a fun house in an amusement park. But this was no fun. It was frightening. Beyond her understanding. The law of gravity seemed suspended, but with a superhuman effort she groped her way backward to the kitchen. Her shoulder touched something and she felt the pressure of a heavy object bearing down on her. It was the refrigerator. Panicked, she managed to jump aside just before it hit the floor. She screamed again, wondering if she was losing her mind.

Feeling for the knob to the basement door, she pushed it open and, reaching for the banister, took a step forward. There were no steps and she felt her legs swinging free. But she did not fall. By some miracle she had locked her arms around the wooden banister. Instinctively, to save herself, she kicked upward and, with her legs against the walls, wedged herself in the narrow space of the stairwell. By careful maneuvering, she managed to lower herself, finally letting go as she touched the basement floor. Just in time. Her back and leg muscles had just about given out.

Bruised and hysterical, she crawled along the cement floor until she found the door. But it was wedged shut. Her groping fingers found the wedge, but it wouldn't budge.

She was, she was sure, experiencing some bizarre dysfunction of reality. The house and everything in it were conspiring to terrorize her. It was an idea that made no sense; perhaps she had wandered into a madhouse or into someone else's bad dream. She lay panting on the floor, weakened by fear.

She heard sounds above her. *Footsteps.* Her impulse for survival forced her now to ascertain the landscape of her surroundings. Some of the dark shapes around her took on meaning. She was in what remained of his workshop. It was a shambles, but she groped around for some tool that might remove the wedge. In a nearby corner she found a sledgehammer. Standing up, she tried to lift it. Fear goaded her strength. Help me, she screamed to herself, miraculously finding the energy to wind the hammer over her head. Swinging it, she crashed it into the door. The blow unloosened the wedge and the door flew open. She ran into the garden. But as she swung open the gate she could not, even in her terror, resist the impulse to turn back.

She saw him through the shattered window of the sun-room. He was gaunt, bearded, his eyes staring out through shadowed sockets. For a moment she hesitated in mid-flight, unable to choose between compassion or fear. Was it the Jonathan of her fantasies, of her other life? The Jonathan to whom she had given her love?

She did not stay long enough to find out.

27

Barbara had filled all ten sockets of the silver rococo candelabrum with candles. She had never done that before and the glow cast on the dining-room table was beautiful. Flames danced and flickered like fireflies over the polished mahogany surface of the table. She had also put out her silver goblets and plates at either end of the table. On his silver plate she put a large slice of her freshly made *pâté* and a little pile of melba toast.

It was, she had decided, poetically just for her to arrange this meeting in the dining room, her domain. She had cleaned herself up as best she could, and now waited for him, seated at the head of the table. She reached out to the shopping bag beside her right foot, feeling the cool blade of the cleaver. It reassured her about her resolve, her bravery. We are down to basics, she told herself.

At first she had been concerned that he would not come. Perhaps her invitation had sounded too much like a summons. But she had prepared just the same, listening for signs of movement now that the big clock had chimed nine.

She heard him almost at the same moment that she

saw him. He was wearing the print robe she had bought him for their fifteenth anniversary. Or was it their sixteenth? It pleased her that she was unsure. Her history with him was becoming vague. The past was disappearing. He was carrying an armful of wine bottles, as well as a crowbar. Lining the bottles up in front of him, he opened two and slid one of the opened bottles in her direction. They poured each bottle simultaneously, filling the silver goblets. He lifted his.

"To your health, my darling," he said with a Noel Coward-like inflection. She obliged by sipping cautiously while he emptied his goblet and refilled it quickly. She did not take her hand off the handle of the cleaver.

"The last of the '59's," he said. "Quickly approaching imperfection."

"Still very good, Jonathan. Good body, neither sweet nor dry."

Putting down his goblet, he bent over and smelled the *pâté*. Daintily, he spread some on a cracker and ate it slowly.

"Marvelous, Barbara. Nobody can make a *pâté* quite like yours."

"You've always had an appreciative palate." She smiled, pleased that he liked the dish.

He lifted his goblet again, drank, and ate more of the *pâté*. She watched his bearded face in the flickering light. It had an eerie cast, waxy, like the candles. The shadows stripped him of his age and she saw him as he had looked in his younger days, an image she detested, especially now.

"I hope you're now convinced, Jonathan, that I do not intend to retreat. Not one inch."

As he lifted the goblet again his hand shook.

"You invited me here to tell me that?" he said, frowning. This was not what he had expected.

"I can take anything you can dish out. All your creative punishments."

"Is that why we're having this little tête-à-tête?"

"No," she said emphatically. "I have a proposition."

"I'm listening." He poured another gobletful and drank.

"I'll let you have your pick of half the things in the house. Except in this room. Or the kitchen. And the furniture in the kids' rooms. Take the books, the paintings, the Staffordshires."

"You're very generous," he said sarcastically.

"You can take it now. Only get out with it." She had thought about her offer long and hard. "It's a damned good deal."

He seemed to ponder the idea, rubbing his chin in contemplation.

"It's as far as I go," she said. "I keep the house."

He looked around the room, waving his hand. "And this as well."

"And this as well," she repeated. "I think I'm being exceptionally reasonable. No lawyers needed. Just you and me, kid."

"Yeah, just you and me," he said bitterly. She watched him coolly. She was pleased that her words were crisp and forceful, her courage unfaltering.

"I am not afraid," she said. "I'm capable of resisting forever if necessary."

She watched him wash down the *pâté* with more wine and then look at the ceiling. Perspiration shone on his cheeks. The candles had raised the temperature unbearably. He stood up, took off his robe, and, barechested, sat down again.

"And I'm capable of resisting your resistance," he said. "Forever if necessary. This is my house. I paid for it. No matter what. Even if the courts decide otherwise. I'll find a way to get it."

"Over my dead body."

"Hopefully. If I can get away with that."

She reached down and touched the cool blade of her cleaver.

"You're not going to intimidate me," she said calmly. She finished her goblet of wine and poured herself another.

"We've passed that stage a long time ago, Barbara."

"What I can't understand . . ." She hesitated, sipping her wine. "What I can't understand is why you are having so much difficulty understanding my position. Other people get divorced. You didn't have to stay here. You could have avoided all this . . . this unpleasantness."

"It's not unpleasant." He giggled. "Rather interesting, I'd say."

She looked at him and shook her head.

"You are a bastard."

"I'm just not going to reward you for being a bitch, for destroying our family. People shouldn't be rewarded for destruction."

"Always the family. The *family*. Why should I have to live in an institution I hate, that has tried to do me in?" She banged the table with the flat of her hand. The plates jumped and the candelabrum bounced. "I want out and I want to be compensated for my sacrifices."

His face glistened with sweat. He smiled but transmitted no warmth.

"You were a dumb little shit when I married you. My brains put you in this house. My money bought all these things. My support and indulgence pushed you to become a gourmet cook. If it wasn't for me, you'd still be living in some clapboard house in New England, boiling potatoes for some half-assed clerk."

"My undying gratitude." She had spat out the words.

"I'm not getting out," he cried, his speech thickening. She tightened her grip on the handle of the cleaver. "Nothing gets split up. Only us."

"Well, then, my conscience is clear."

"You haven't got a conscience."

She watched him, suddenly feeling a great well of pity bubble up inside her. He was as much a victim as she. Some vague, unexplainable concept that the world called love had cheated them both.

"You don't matter to me anymore, Jonathan," she said sadly. "You just don't matter. I loathe you."

"A good loathe is hard to find. I'm still working on hate."

"I'm beyond hate, Jonathan. Far beyond it. I've lived with it for too long. It's not really your fault, either. You were just there at the wrong time and the wrong place."

"Please, Barbara. Don't declare me innocent. I need my hatred just as much as you do. How else can I sustain the battle?" She caught the sarcasm but couldn't find the humor.

"Well, look at it this way," she said. "At least we got the kids out of it."

"The kids? I hadn't thought of them for a while."

"Neither have I."

"They're fine, I suppose."

"No news is good news. I'm glad they're out of the line of fire."

"See how civilized we can be, Barbara." Silently he raised his goblet, then she did.

"People don't matter," he said gloomily. "Only things. Things are loyal. Always there. Always true. Some things increase in value. Never people. People diminish." He looked at her and smiled drunkenly.

"Maybe you're right," she snapped. "I'll just take back my offer."

"And all you have to do is take half the value. Cold cash. Lots of it. Then get out. *Fini.*"

"Not till hell freezes over," she said.

"It won't in this heat."

"Then we'll just have to tough it out, won't we?"

"I'll drink to that." He upended his goblet, then opened another bottle. He held it up and looked at her. "Château Beycheville." He squinted at the label. "A '64. I think we had a good year in '64."

"Only in your mind, Jonathan. Never in mine."

Upending the bottle, he drank from it. Then he held it up again, pointing it for emphasis.

"I want you out of my house," he said. "This is my place."

"Exactly my sentiments, Jonathan," she said coolly.

He raised his voice. "I have more rights to it than you."

"Don't talk to me about rights."

"I love it more than you do. I deserve it. You don't love it."

"I don't have to listen to this crap."

"You can't take everything away. You've got to leave me something."

"Don't get maudlin."

She felt the tension building in him.

"You're selfish and grasping, Barbara. Loathsome. A loathsome bitch."

"I worked for it. I'm going to fight for it."

He drained the bottle and let it fall to the floor. It rolled, unbroken, under the table. He staggered toward the door.

"Thanks for the *pâté*," he croaked.

"Don't thank me." She paused until she was sure she had his attention. "Thank Benny."

"Benny."

He staggered against the wall, putting out an arm for support. He sagged but with effort straightened up and looked toward her, his eyes spitting rage. She sensed the reflex even before he moved, his raised hand suddenly materializing, holding the crowbar. Reaching for her shopping bag, she lifted it, clutched it to her chest, and got up, overturning her chair.

She saw the crowbar fall in a long, sweeping motion that pushed the candelabrum from the table. Methodically, he stepped on each candle, putting out the flames.

The darkness was total. She reached for the cleaver handle, then held it above her head, fully prepared to use it in self-defense. She was determined to show him the full extent of her stubbornness and her courage.

She had expected him to come at her and was surprised when he didn't. He is afraid, she thought.

A deafening sound roared through the room. She heard the nerve-tingling scrape of metal on wood and the sound of his crowbar biting into the Duncan Phyfe table. The pain of the injured wood seemed to transfer itself to her own flesh. Under cover of the darkness, she backed out of the room and moved silently through the hall corridor, up the stairs, and into Josh's room.

She curled up in Josh's closet, her shopping bag in her lap, her fist clenching the handle of the cleaver. The beating of her heart partially obscured the sounds of his destructive tantrum.

28

For a long while he lay on the floor of his room trying to reenter time. He was procrastinating, since finding time again meant he would also find pain. Without time he could lie here through eternity. He would be able to avoid existence. Existence was the enemy.

The room had grown dark, then light, then dark again. He was not certain of the chronology. That would mean he had reentered time. He lay in a pool of his own fetid moisture. Discovering this condition irritated him because it meant that he had also reentered space. When it became apparent that such consciousness was unavoidable, he opened his eyes.

It was daylight, of some day. He was determined to avoid the concept of time as long as possible. The room was strewn with empty wine bottles. The movement of his legs jostled some and they rolled against one another. The sound reminded him of his thirst, and he began to crawl on his hands and knees in search of filled bottles.

Finding one, he lifted himself up to a squat and, unable to find a corkscrew, smashed the neck against the floor and poured the wine into his mouth. It splashed over his chin and onto his bare chest. It did not even occur to him to try to identify the wine. It could have been white or red. His palate was numb, his sense of taste gone.

When he felt vaguely restored, he lifted himself to a standing position by grabbing the bedpost. Dizzy and nauseated, he dry-heaved, then swallowed. Time was crowding in on him now. There was no escaping it.

His ear picked up vague sounds, and he was sure his ally, the house, was trying to communicate with him. Something croaked in the distance, a chopping sound. It was trying to tell him something. He was sure of that. It wanted to communicate its pain, its outrage.

The idea of its helplessness steadied him. It also brought him fully back to time and he realized suddenly that the clock in the hall was not chiming, that he had forgotten to keep it alive by winding it. A renewable life, he assured himself.

Although the present now existed, the immediate past was unclear. History unreeled backward from now. He had searched for her. He had looked in the kitchen, the sun-room, the garden, the garage. He had ripped out the back stairs to prevent her from leaving if she was still in the house. Then he had combed the sides of the house, letting himself in again by the front door. He had got it into his head that she was in the attic, and he had dashed up the stairs, then foolishly tried to ascend the upper flight, forgetting what he had done to make it impassable. He had slipped and fallen before he had gone two steps up. Apparently he, himself, had made the attic invulnerable.

Although the obstacle was of his own making, it had sparked his caution. If she had done that to Benny, she was capable of anything. Anything. And if he were eliminated, who would guard the house?

Once, he had heard sounds and had followed them, hearing screams of pain, and he had arrived in the sunroom to see a vaguely familiar form running in the garden. Ann. He had not set these traps for Ann, and he was thankful that she had escaped. It was not her war. The traps were for Barbara.

It was that idea, he remembered, that had brought him back to his room, where he had let time disappear. He was certain that she was somewhere in the house. Probably living like a rat, burrowing in every nook and cranny. What he had to do was to flush her out. Cautiously. Cleverly. Nothing must be safe.

He lay down, letting his mind grope for a plan. It started to grow dark again. On the night table beside him he found a half-spent candle and lit it with a match. The flickering yellow light calmed him. He felt safe again and his mind became fully alert.

He ate some stale bread and washed it down with wine. Carrying his crowbar and the candle, he carefully opened the door. His foot hit some object and he heard a crunching sound. Bending, he saw a broken Staffordshire figure, one of the most valuable, Garibaldi. Eschewing mourning, he lifted the candle. In its glow he saw her familiar scrawl in lipstick. She no longer used paper or cardboard, but wrote directly on the door.

"I'll break some every day," he read.

He did not allow himself the slightest emotion, concentrating only on what he had to do. Gathering his tools, first he removed all the bolts from the hinges of every door but his own—closets, room doors, everywhere there was a hinge. No door but his own and those leading to the outside world could be opened without barking out a signal. He set each door carefully so that the slightest motion would make it fall. Then he went to work on the furniture, loosening bolts, removing legs and supports, tipping every piece so that it would fall on touch.

He avoided the dining room, which was a shambles, although he could not resist looking at what he had carved into the tabletop: BITCH. He loosened every screw and bolt in the kitchen he could find, especially those that held up still-intact overhead pots, leaving them just at the point of weakest tension. He did the same with shelves and cabinet doors. Working methodically, concentrating only on his actions, he was able to shut out extraneous thoughts.

The candle went out. By then it had started to grow light again. Thankful for the natural light, he moved the heaviest cast-iron pots and put them at the top of the first-floor landing. Others he wedged into the corners of the risers.

Working now with accelerating speed, he loosened the winding brass banister, then partially removed the tacks that held the stair carpet to the risers. Just brushing against the banister would send the carpet flipping over into the chandelier well.

The clock offered another challenge. He fiddled with the pendulum to make a longer stroke so that it would hit the wooden sides. Working with the mechanism, he changed the calibration so that the chimes would be noisier and make more of a clanging sound. Then he loosened all the fasteners that held the pictures on the walls of the library and the parlor.

He reveled in his creativity, rejoicing in the imaginative scenario of destruction that would be set off by the slightest vibration. Everything would go off at once, like an explosion in a fireworks factory. The thought made him giddy. With extreme caution, he made his way up the stairs to his room and quietly locked the door.

Searching among the existing bottles, he found two, both 1969 Dom Perignon. Despite its warmth, he opened one. The cork made a noisy, popping sound and the champagne foamed out. Drinking some, he poured the rest over his head, as athletes do when they win a championship game.

But he hadn't won yet, he admonished himself.

Not yet. He'd save the other bottle for that victory.

29

From her makeshift bed, composed of insulation pads piled one on top of the other in a corner of the attic, she heard him puttering around beneath her. The attic air was stagnant, blazing hot, and she had removed everything but her panties. Beside her was the canvas shopping bag, containing all her movable possessions.

For the past days and nights she had shifted from place to place, moving stealthily, using all her senses.

The movement below was something new. For some time he had been snoring, with froglike regularity, and she had slipped out of her hiding place to make a sortie into other parts of the house. She had gone into the library and put some Staffordshire figures in her shopping bag, crushing the Garibaldi and sprinkling its contents outside his locked door. Then she had calmly written her warning on his door in lipstick.

She let herself into her old room, looking for some change of clothing, but the room stank from the rotting food and she had to hold her nose. Every object in the room, including her clothes, was permeated with the stench.

Because her inner antenna was so alert, she sensed

that someone was watching the house. Peeking through a crack in the drapes, she saw Ann dozing against a tree across the street. It took a while to identify the figure, since she had closed the door on the past. Who was Ann?

She remembered Ann as an enemy, hostile, and she quickly removed the girl from reality by closing the shutters, sealing off the room.

She made her way upstairs, defying his trap by sitting on one step at a time and bracing herself against the wall. It pleased her to have conquered this obstacle. She had already withstood all his assaults. Indeed, she had come up with a few of her own. Her weapon, she decided, would be tenacity. She would outlast him.

He was making no effort to be quiet, and she was able to slip from the attic through the square hole in the ceiling of a storage closet at the rear of the house. Crawling toward the edge of the stairs, she listened to the sounds he was making, trying to recognize them to identify his actions. He was fiddling with doors and furniture. She heard him go into the kitchen, come out to the foyer, then move up the stairs.

Her instincts were sharp, and by the sounds he made she was able to map his progress. Finally, she came back to the storage closet and hoisted herself back into the attic, pleased with her catlike agility. Lying horizontally across the square opening, she continued to listen. He was setting traps, constructing obstacles, creating new dangers. The idea amused her. Didn't he know that the house was her ally? Nothing he devised could really hurt her. How foolish of him not to realize that.

In her mind each isolated sound outlined his little ploys, his booby traps. She was certain she knew exactly what he was doing. Well, she had a few tricks of her own up her sleeve.

She groped on hands and knees through the blazing-hot attic, half lit by daylight filtering through slatted vents. Over one shoulder she carried her shopping bag. She had made a sling for the cleaver and carried it stretched across her chest like a bow.

Once before, she had crawled into this attic space. Years ago, when the men had come to attach the chandelier. An engineer had determined that the main beam had to be reinforced if the chandelier was to be safely attached, and additional wooden beams were superimposed over the original one.

She found the exact spot where the chandelier's chain was embedded by spikes in the beams. She remembered that the men who had attached it were proud of their handiwork. And, indeed, they should have been. The chandelier was perfectly balanced and safe, considering that it was hanging from a chain three stories high.

She hacked away at the wooden beam with her cleaver. It was hard work. The cleaver was not as effective as an ax. Sweat poured out of her, and she had to rest periodically. Her objective was to weaken the beam and, therefore, the stability of the chandelier. Just in case she needed an ultimate weapon. He, too, she knew, was sparing no energy, concocting ingenious traps.

After hacking away for nearly an hour, she lay exhausted on the insulation pads until her energy returned.

It was dark when she let herself down from the attic hole. She heard him close the door of his room, as always the signal that she could leave the safety of the attic. Her fingers moved ahead of her, like fluttering antennas. The closet door, she noted, was not quite true and she quickly realized that he had removed the hinges. Opening it slowly, with minuscule movement, she slipped through the crack. Did he really believe that the house would hurt her? Not now. Not ever.

Moving on her hands and knees, she reached out her arms, touching everything in front of her, like a mine detector. The floor was slick, with little friction. He had separated and loosened the carpet on the landing. Stretching herself on her back lengthwise, she slid slowly down the steps, landing gently. By now her eyes were accustomed to the darkness and she saw at once the odd shapes on the stairs to the first floor. Her mind had created a map of everything in the house and the slightest thing awry was enough to trigger a reaction. The lightest touch of her fingers, for example, showed her the banister was loose.

Proud of both her deductive ability and her stealth, she moved toward the back stairs. He had removed the wedge he had placed at the door to make the missing bolts more hazardous, a problem now easy for her to deal with. Using what she thought of as the sled method, she slid down the stairs on her back. The obstacles he had placed on the flat surfaces were easily avoided and she was able to crawl along the corridor to the library and carefully gather up armfuls of the Staffordshire figures both on the library mantel and in the parlor. She put them in her shopping bag and carefully retraced her steps, avoiding all his crude booby traps.

She got up the back stairs by applying a type of rappeling, using her cleaver periodically to dig into the wall, then hoisting herself up by its handle. For every measure there was a countermeasure, she told herself, proud of her resourcefulness, crowing over how badly he had underestimated her ingenuity.

Squatting in front of his room, she selected two Napoleons from her shopping bag and with her cleaver beheaded them and stood the figures on the floor in front of his door.

With her lipstick she wrote on the door: "Off with

their heads." Unable to stifle her giggles, she moved away and, again using the rappeling method, shimmied up the stairs and back to her attic hideaway.

She lay on her makeshift bed of insulation, ignoring the heat, the sweat of her body, and whatever physical discomfort she was supposed to feel. Only one emotion seized her. The joy of having bested him. Her body, too, seemed suffused with a sexual response, an exquisite sensation of unspecific ecstasy, a postorgasmic afterthrill. Her nipples were erect, her inner parts moist.

She was Barbara, her identity clear, unmistakable. Mistress of herself. Surviving in the jungle.

30

Ann's fear immobilized her. She lay on the bed in her room, listening to the sporadic rhythm of the faulty air conditioner. It seemed to be running in tandem to the beating of her heart. Did she have, she asked herself, some obligation to report what was occurring in that house? But what could she report? She could not put any order to her explanation. What was really going on in there? She imagined conversations with detectives in urine-smelling rooms.

"I think they're trying to kill each other."

"How do you know?"

"I was inside. The entire inside is unsafe."

"What were you doing inside?"

She was not afraid of being charged with anything. Or was she? Perhaps if she had talked to Jonathan. Touched him. Was that really Jonathan she had seen, that ravaged, zombielike figure? Surely not the man she had loved. Loved? The word repelled her now.

Yet even the mute, worn figure of Jonathan conveyed less terror than the house itself. It had become alive, a chilling, bloodless monster. The memory of its brutality recalled her body's punishment. Their mutual hate had breathed life into it. A house? She detested it now. Her revulsion gave her the strength to rise from the bed.

She could not stay another minute in her room. She dressed and went downstairs. At the desk she found a message. It was from Eve. "Please call me ASAP."

It was early in the morning, but she called anyway, reaching the disgruntled camp director, who was uncooperative until Ann insisted it was a matter of the utmost urgency.

"I haven't heard from either Mom or Dad in three weeks. I'm scared, Ann." There was an unmistakable note of hysteria in her voice. "Josh is a nervous wreck. We're worried sick."

"They're probably still on vacation."

"I don't believe that. Why was the telephone disconnected? I even sent them a telegram. It came back stamped 'undeliverable.' But my mail doesn't come back."

"There," Ann said bravely. "They didn't leave a forwarding address. That means they're not planning to be away long."

"I called both grandmas. They haven't heard from them, either. They're worried also."

"I really don't think there's anything to worry about. They just needed to get away and took separate vacations."

"I don't believe that, Ann. I'm sorry."

Ann's words hadn't carried much conviction and she knew it.

"I intend to come home and see for myself," Eve continued.

"Now, that is really absurd." Ann's lips could barely form the response.

"Well, then, why don't they call? Why haven't they written? Whatever the differences between them, we're

still their children." She began to cry as her voice tee-
tered on the edge of panic. Ann felt her own sob begin
in her chest. They mustn't, she begged.

"I'll make a deal," she said hurriedly. "I'll find out
where they are and tell them that they have got to call
because you're worried. I'll call at the end of the day. I
promise." She needed time to think. And she had to
keep them away from that monstrous house.

There was a long pause. She heard Eve's sniffling.
The agony was real, compelling. She wanted to hold the
girl in her arms, comfort her.

"All right," Eve replied, the words carrying an implied ultimatum.

"Just don't do anything foolish," Ann warned, instantly sorry for what she had said, knowing it would
put Eve on alert. "Please," she added.

"I'll wait for your call," Eve said, colder now. Ann
lingered for some time in the phone booth, her hands
shaking. She dreaded going back to that house.

She walked, moving counter to the rush-hour foot
traffic, careless in the way she crossed the streets, ignoring the honking horns.

She had no plan. Again she debated calling the police. Had she the right to meddle? Her thoughts were
confused. One thing was certain. She would not, ever
again, enter that house.

It looked as innocent as ever, its white facade and
black shutters glittering in the sunlight. Stepping up to
the door, she banged the clapper. Her hands shook. Her
heart pounded. As before, there was a long silence. This
time she vowed not to be deterred. She persisted, banging at a rhythmic pace, shrilly urgent, a persistent stac-
cato. Sooner or later, they would answer.

When no one answered after twenty minutes, she
began to bang on the door with her fists.

"Please," she cried. "It's about the children. Please."

She raised her voice to a scream. Nothing stirred in the neighborhood, which was as quiet and serene as ever. No one ever became involved. Everyone was protected by a big house, walled in. Besides, many of the residents had gone away for the summer, and the buzz of the air conditioners of the occupied houses nearby assured auditory privacy. Everybody was living his own life, unaware of the pain or outrage of others. How little relationship rich people really have to each other, she thought. Every house was a private armored ship in which its occupants steered their own course.

She determined to be relentless. Not to falter. The palm of her hand became numb with pain.

"I know you're in there," she cried.

Something flashed into her peripheral vision and she looked up suddenly. She saw his face in an upper window through an opening in the drapes. Shielding her eyes from the sun, she stepped backward.

"Jonathan," she yelled through cupped hands. She saw him lingering in the shadows.

"Jonathan."

He moved closer to the window. His face startled her. It was gaunt, bearded, disheveled. His eyes were vague and glazed.

"The children," she shouted. "You must call the children."

Jonathan continued to look down at her, uncomprehending. He seemed confused. Indifferent. "Your children," she cried. His face was chalk-white, expressionless.

"I'm Ann," she cried, feeling foolish.

He nodded slowly, his response unclear. What is happening? An image of ghosts in a haunted house popped into her mind. A scream choked in her throat as she saw Barbara's face at one of the windows of the third floor. She was smiling benignly, contentedly. Her appearance had altered. Her hair was unkempt, her face gaunt and gray.

"You must call the children," Ann cried, hoping that both of them might hear. She was surprised to see Barbara nod as if she had comprehended. Why did she have to plead for this? Eve and Josh were their children. Their indifference revolted her. Jonathan continued to look at her without expression. She saw him lift a wine bottle and take a long drink. Who were these people really? she wondered.

"Do you understand?" she called.

Barbara continued to nod, like one of these perpetually nodding little toys. Jonathan, watching her impassively, took another swig from the bottle. She felt helpless and inert. Remembering the condition of the house's interior, she shuddered with anxiety.

The exterior seemed to mock her now. The happy house. She wished it would fall to the ground like the walls of Jericho. It was offensive, unclean, masking ugly secrets. She was disgusted by its clean white facade, its arrogant, aristocratic air. Finally, she turned away, depressed, and began to move off. When she turned again for one last look, they were gone. She had, she assured herself, done her duty. She never wanted to see either them or the house again as long as she lived.

She walked for a long time, trying to comprehend what she had seen. The man in the window was not the man she had loved. Remembering his vague expression, she nevertheless dismissed the idea that he was merely in a drunken stupor. What she had seen went beyond that. And Barbara. So ridiculously contented. She seemed drugged, divorced from reality.

She walked down Twenty-second Street, across Washington Circle, down to the Lincoln Memorial, then onto the bridge and along the bicycle path past the Pentagon. Possessions—what good were they? It was better to own nothing. Possessions carried their own seeds of destruction. Compared to human values, they were worthless gewgaws. Having no possessions made her feel pristine, virtuous. She would own nothing, she decided. As for love, perhaps Barbara was right after all. Love lied, she had said. But to whom?

She was so absorbed in her thoughts she did not notice the sun had set. The impending darkness jogged her memory. She had promised to call Eve and now began to search for a phone. Someone told her there was one along the path, but it was farther than she had expected and she did not reach it until it was dark. She didn't have the proper change and finally she had to cross the highway on foot to reach the Marriott Motel. A clerk changed a dollar.

Finding a phone, she waited impatiently as Eve was summoned. Then a voice came on the phone that Ann did not recognize.

"Eve's gone," the voice said in a whisper.

"Gone?"

"With Josh." There was a long moment of hesitation. "Is this Ann?"

"Yes."

"I'm Kathy, Eve's friend. They haven't noticed that she's gone yet. She said she'd call you when she got home."

"What?" Ann fought to catch her breath.

"She was worried about her parents. She took Josh home. They took a one-o'clock bus."

"When will that get them to Washington?"

"About eight."

"Why didn't she wait for my call?"

"She couldn't stand it anymore. She had to go see for herself. Every night she cried herself to sleep."

"The fools," Ann cried into the phone. Kathy gasped. "Not you," Ann assured her, thanking her and hanging up. She looked at her watch. It was nearly eight-thirty.

Running to the front lobby, she hailed a cab.

"You've got to make this the fastest run ever," she told the driver. "Please."

31

On his hands and knees, Jonathan groped in the forest of empty bottles. His candles had burned out. His matches were gone. Occasionally he would find a bottle with a few dregs of wine still in it, but never enough for a gulpful.

His frustration gave way to rage and sometimes he would pick up a bottle and smash it against a wall. Occasionally a shard of broken glass would open a cut in his flesh. By now even physical pain was irrelevant. Finally he found a full bottle, uncorked it, and drank. It was tasteless. But that hardly mattered anymore.

What mattered was that his mind continued to focus narrowly on the vision of his mission. He must drive her from his house. Everything else was extraneous and unimportant. As if the image were a distant memory, he recalled seeing a young woman on the street below. An image of warmth, of a soft, yielding, loving body, had flickered briefly in his mind, had forced his recognition of a vague longing, some forgotten need. But his mind was already programmed to reject such thoughts. The only thing to be resolved was Barbara's whereabouts.

In his mind—was it reality or imagination . . . or both?—he had heard her moving almost soundlessly in his manmade jungle. At first he thought the soft, padding step was that of Mercedes. It was the same catlike tread. The memory of her crushed and lifeless body floated into his consciousness. Mercedes was gone. Benny was gone. The thought of Benny stimulated a sour, chalky taste in his mouth and he gulped.

He listened. Every tiny movement displayed itself on the kaleidoscopic screen in his mind. So far she had cleverly avoided the matrix he had created. Sooner or later, she would falter and start a chain reaction of destruction. It was only a matter of time.

Taking a deep pull on the bottle, he knew he was trying to drown out reason. Reason was his enemy. Like love. Like devotion. Reason weakened the will. He opened the drapes and looked down into the street again. It was dark now, but he vaguely recalled the woman's cries. Something about the children, he recalled. The children? This was not their affair. What was happening had nothing to do with them. It was not fair to invoke the children. Hadn't Goldstein told him that? "Go away," he shouted to the empty street. He screamed again. "Go away." But that was meant for Barbara.

Out of the vapor of his thoughts, a girl child emerged in memory. A wave of old anxieties washed over him. Her baby cries tormented him with their helplessness. He had not the courage to let her cry. He, the father. He had explained that to Barbara once. They owed this child their protection, their shelter, their warmth. She had protested his spoiling Eve but had moved in their bed to make room for the baby. They held her between them, loving, warm. Now she is safe, he told her.

Then Josh had come. A boy in his image. In their

image. Now we have a complete family, he had said, or surely must have said. Barbara had agreed or seemed to agree. They were pictures in his mind, the four of them against the world. Husband. Wife. Son. Daughter. *Family*.

He had created a fort to protect them. This house.

"You just don't matter anymore," she had told him, as if she were throwing the first handful of dirt on his coffin. "Not to me."

"You could have told me that years ago, before you let me build this life." Perhaps he had responded that way. He was no longer sure. A jumbled conversation surfaced in his mind.

"I didn't know."

"Didn't know?"

"I was blinded by love."

"Blinded? Does love blind?"

"Yes."

Well, then, it blinded me as well, he shouted within himself. How dare she take away my life? My whole life. My family. But the house was his. His. She would never get that. Never, never, never, never.

It was a pustule. He could not keep his fingers from it. It itched. He scratched. He wanted to tear it open and let the pus run out and free himself at last.

Sounds intruded—the squeal of tires, the throb of a car's motor. He looked through the drapes and saw the outlines of the cab in the muted light of the street lamp. Familiar, shadowy figures emerged. A girl and a boy. They stood looking at the house as the taxi pulled away. His mouth opened, but he could not find words. Instead he stepped away from the window. The closed drapes plunged the room into darkness again. He moved backward, losing his balance as his feet hit the bottles. Reaching out, a wall supported his weight. He cowered in a corner, hoping that they would go away.

On his knees he prayed, looking upward. To whom was he praying? he wondered.

"God help me," he whispered, trying to get up. His body wanted to hang back, stay in that safe corner. He heard the beating of the knocker, rhythmical, persistent. The chimes had died. Still he hung back. Perhaps they would go away. Rising now, he listened.

The knocking sound disappeared. Silence. Then a new chorus began, a persistent clarion in a stormy night.

"Mom. Dad. It's us."

Who are they? he thought.

The knocking began again, drowning out their voices. He heard faint whispers, then a metallic sound and the thing that he had vaguely dreaded became a reality. The door was opening.

He sprang out of the room, but his footing was unsure, made more so by the broken figures in his path. He lost his balance and fell. Through the brass slats in the banister, he saw the door open and heard the children's screams as they fell on the slick surface, struggled upward, then fell again, groping toward the stairs.

"Go back." The words formed, then burst through the din. They stumbled forward.

"Go back. Please."

It was not his voice. *Barbara's.* He saw her on the landing above him, looking down, her face frightened, terror-stricken.

"Mom."

Their voices rose in tandem. Seeing her, they stumbled forward, their hands tearing at the stair carpet for balance. The untacked carpet gave way and the cast-iron pots began their avalanche with a clanging roar as they rolled forward. The clock chimes, too, began suddenly, booming out in an abrasive rhythm, vibrating in the air. Pictures fell off the walls. Eve and Josh pressed themselves against each other, just managing to escape the falling pots.

"Go back," Barbara screamed, her voice shrill, panicked. She lowered her eyes to his, imploring.

"Save them, Jonathan. Our children."

Her sobs stirred him and, for the first time since the nightmare began, he saw the old softness, the other Barbara.

"Our children," he repeated, swallowing deeply, desperately trying to clear his mind. Time compressed itself. They looked at each other for what seemed like an endless moment. He sensed what had passed between them at Chatham years before. Perhaps it was still there, after all. Were her eyes begging for what he yearned for—another chance?

Eve and Josh started to move. The clock continued its interminable clanging. More objects fell. Then Barbara's scream echoed and reechoed through the house, above all other sounds. She had inadvertently moved too close to the banister, which had fallen into the chandelier well to the floor below. Barbara had lost her balance and now was hanging precariously over the unprotected ledge, dangling two stories above the floor.

"Hold on," Jonathan shouted. "I'm coming."

He called to the children, "Get out. Please. I'll save her. Just get out of the house." They scrambled forward, slipping amid the litter, and made their way out the open door. They stood outside, peering in, their frightened faces taut with fear.

"Hang on, Barbara. Just for a moment. Hang on, baby."

His heart pounded. He moved to the balcony's edge, calculated the distance to the chandelier, flexed his knees, and jumped. Reaching out, he grasped the heavy chain, and with his feet on the metal rungs of the chandelier, he shimmied up to a point parallel to where

Barbara hung. Forcing the chandelier to swing like a pendulum, he made a wide arc. Then, after a number of too-short passes, he finally reached the ledge and gripped it.

"Steady, baby," he cried, reaching out with his free hand to brace her faltering grip.

"I can't . . ." she mumbled.

"Yes, you can," he said firmly. He heard a creaking sound above him. The chandelier seemed to bounce.

"Hold out one hand and grab my forearm."

She shook her head.

"No, Jonathan." She was sobbing, hysterical.

"You must listen to me," he pleaded.

Again she shook her head, but it was obvious her strength was giving out, and he had to pry loose her grip. In a reflex action, she reached out with the other hand and held him in a tight embrace as her weight was transferred to the chandelier. The creaking sound above them increased and the chandelier bounced again.

He had barely time to look up. Then he felt the chandelier slip beneath him. He was falling, Barbara with him, and above, in slower motion, he saw the ceiling open up like an earthquake fissure in reverse. There was no time to scream. He gripped Barbara tighter. Everything was coming down at once. As he fell, looking upward, he wondered if he would soon see the sky.

32

Ann heard the crashing sound just as the cab had pulled away from the curb. She stood rooted to the sidewalk, watching a cloud of dust float out from the open entrance door. Her legs would not propel her forward.

She saw the children standing in the dust cloud, looking at the house. Dust had begun to settle on their faces and their hair. They looked like apparitions. She called their names. They turned toward her, their eyes glazed with terror. Tears were running in rivulets down their dusty cheeks. Then they turned away and suddenly started to move toward the open door.

"Don't," Ann shouted, finding strength. She ran toward them.

"They're in there," Josh shouted, moving forward with Eve. She reached them quickly and, flinging herself in their path, held them firmly. From inside the house emanated the continuing clatter of falling objects.

She held the children in a tight embrace, hearing their sobs of hysteria. Finally the sounds from the house abated. Turning, Ann looked through the doorway. It was cluttered with debris.

"Let me," she said gently, moving forward. But the children followed and she hadn't the will to stop them. Standing in the doorway, she observed the destruction. It was ghastly. The roof had collapsed and the interior walls had buckled. Near the door, the long clock lay on its side, its face of Roman time smashed. Shards of crystal from the chandelier covered every surface. More clouds of dust had risen.

She moved into the interior, her eyes smarting as she searched in the debris. Behind her, she could hear the hesitant footsteps of the children and their sobs.

"Mommy, Daddy," Eve cried. "Why did they do this?"

Ann shook her head. Then, suddenly, she saw them. Jonathan and Barbara, encased in a shroud of white dust, their faces paralyzed in a mask of death. Under the rubble, they appeared to be embracing, their lifeless eyes locked together in an eternal stare. She gasped and turned away. It was a long moment before she became conscious again of the children moving behind her.

They were poking around in the rubble, Josh on his knees, Eve moving the debris with the toe of her shoe. Clutched in her left hand was an object, a familiar statue, its black head remarkably shiny and clean. The buffed figure of Molineaux was, miraculously, intact, poised as always in its eternal pugilistic pose.

Josh stood up, looking oddly victorious. He rubbed the companion figure against his shirt and blew the dust away. Ann's eyes focused on the perfectly intact figure. She saw Eve's hand reach out, her fingers wrapping themselves around Cribb's torso.

For a frozen moment the children held the figure with equal strength, then Josh grasped the Molineaux at its base.

"It's mine," Josh cried.

"Mine," Eve screamed.

With a snapping sound, like the crack of a pistol shot, the two figures seemed to explode. Ann watched as the children, with a glazed, stunned look, studied the shattered bits of plaster in their palms.

Ann turned away, heading toward the entrance. The speed of her steps agitated the dust around her ankles.